ROSSETER'S MEMORY

Canadian Cataloguing in Publication Data

Levesque, John, 1953 -
Rosseter's memory

ISBN 0-88962-486-0 (bound) ISBN 0-88962-485-2 (pbk.)

I. Title.

PS8573.E8R6 1991 C813'.54 C91-094044-4
PR9199.3.L48R6 1991

Published by MOSAIC PRESS, P.O. Box 1032, Oakville, Ontario, L6J 5E9, Canada. Offices and warehouse at 1252 Speers Road, Units # 1 & 2, Oakville, Ontario, L6L 5N9, Canada.

Mosaic Press acknowledges the assistance of the Canada Council and the Ontario Arts Council in support of its publishing programme.

Design by Marion Black
Cover Illustration by Katherine Porter entitled "No Weeds In This Garden, 1990."
Typeset by Aztext

Printed and bound in Canada.

ISBN 0-88962-485-2 PAPER ISBN 0-88962-486-0 CLOTH

MOSAIC PRESS:
In Canada:
MOSAIC PRESS, 1252 Speers Road, Units 1 & 2, Oakville, Ontario L6L 5N9, Canada. P.O. Box 1032, Oakville, Ontario L6J 5E9

In the United States:
Distributed to the trade in the United States by: National Book Network, Inc., 4720-A Boston Way, Lanham, M.D., 20706 USA

In the U.K.:
John Calder (Publishers) Ltd., 9-15 Neal Street, London, WCZH 9TU, England.

ROSSETER'S MEMORY

a novel

By John Levesque

MOSAIC PRESS
Oakville · New York · London

For Renee and Christina

I

(1963-1977)

1

> Forget about the milestones of life. If you want to know what really happened, roll the boulder over and study all the insects underneath.
>
> —Theodore Ng

The train rejoined Lake Superior at Marathon, but Steven Rosseter dozed through the stop. When he awoke, the African rhythm of the train had resumed and an old woman was sitting next to him. He gazed blearily at pine and spruce trees flickering by in the late afternoon sun.

The tracks skirted the lake from here to Thunder Bay, but Steven wasn't going that far. Every now and then the bush gave way to open views of Mother Superior. He could have taken some nice photographs of the greygreen lake if he wanted, but he preferred the anonymity of muskeg.

Before dozing off, Steven had been reading about the city of Presley in a folder his new boss sent him. The cover of the folder showed a fish, one of the famous fighting muskellunge, leaping out of the placid violet waters of Lake Mead. You couldn't see the hook and line in its mouth that doubtless led back to a local angler or

American tourist who had no urgent desire to eat muskellunge but thoroughly enjoyed the spectacle of such a fish fighting for its life. Local tourism officials thought so highly of the photo of this desperate fish that they put it on the cover of their folder. Something was wrong with that, Steven decided.

Presley, the folder said, was named after Isaac Rosario Presley, a turn-of-the century lumberjack who parlayed a land purchase from the Canadian Pacific Railway into a thriving pulp and paper concern. In the early 1950s, the remnants of the founding family settled in Duluth, Minnesota, a couple of hundred miles to the south. Isaac Rosario was believed to be buried in Florida, where he wintered. A wood and wrought-iron totem pole still stands in the heart of the town he founded as mute testament to his colourful personal legacy. So the folder said.

Steven yawned and looked out. A sheet of desaturated snow persisted in the denser bush. The floor of the sunny train coach, past where his left hand clutched the photo of the jumping muskellunge, was caked in mud. His shoes were caked in mud. The entire north country had turned to mud this particular March.

His eyes settled back on the folder. Presley, pop. 37,400, was no longer a town. As of July 9, 1949, it became an officially incorporated city. The shallow Kekagami that wound through the heart of Presley on its way to the Lakehead was upgraded from a creek to a river. Lake Mead, a few short miles to the north, was always close at hand. The folder said the area was a four-season recreational paradise. The future belonged to Superior North. . . the land of Map-O-Spread. . . O how it tasted good on toast when he was a runt. . .

The folder slippled soundlessly out of his dangling hand and landed on a clod of mud. The African rhythm of the train lulled him, yet a question continued to play in the back of his mind as he was carried to the far side of the great lake: Was he escaping, or had he been banished?

"The motive doesn't matter as much as the motion," he mumbled in concert with the beat of the train. The old woman next to him asked if he was talking to her. He said no.

. . .

As atonement for their lack of civic-mindedness the rest of the year, residents of Presley gathered every Easter weekend for a gala function at the Isaac R. Presley Sportsmen's Show & Community Trade & Recreation Complex. Prior to the dance, the Presley & District Catholic Women's League threw a turkey and bean banquet for citizens of all denominations. No one questioned the compatibility of turkey and beans, nor why this peculiar custom had arisen. Steven Rosseter's future mother-in-law had a city-wide reputation for the creamy cole slaw and chocolate marshmallow rolls she annually donated to the feast.

The year Steven Rosseter met Kathleen O'Hagan was the last chance Presleyites got to sample Pauline O'Hagan's specialties. Her weak heart prevented her from attending the Easter banquet of 1963, so Kathleen escorted her father to the feast. Steven was introduced to them by a fellow accountant at the 4P, Presley Pulp and Paper Products. Steven had the lean, sallow features of a French-Canadian martyr though his blood was mainly Anglo-Scottish. He addressed Kathleen's father as "sir" and wore a navy blue string bowtie that was conspicuous even by the fashion standards of that period.

"Tell me," said Preston Wilhelm O'Hagan as, plates of turkey and beans in hand, they took seats at one of the long tables deployed in military formation on the drafty community centre floor, "is there a special significance to that tie of yours?"

"Beg your pardon, sir?"

"Your tie. Is there something we should know about it? Perhaps it's a talisman of some sort?"

Steven glanced at Kathleen, at his tie. "No, sir. I guess I just—"

"I thought maybe you were a Pearson supporter. He's been known to wear absurd bowties on important occasions."

"I don't know, sir. I guess I just. . . Is this an important occasion?"

No," said Preston Wilhelm, "but that undoubtedly is an absurd bowtie."

"I kind of like it, Daddy," Kathleen said.

P.W. didn't acknowledge the remark. He worked his beans over with knife and fork.

"Steven got a job at the 4P, Daddy. He's in the accounting office.

He says there's talk of more timber rights being granted. A bit of a boom. Isn't that right, Steven?"

"Well, I don't know if I'd—"

"Ha," said P.W.

"I don't think I'd go so far as to say it's a—"

"This riding has gone to the Liberals since before the war. Diefenbaker doesn't do a thing for this riding because we have some kind of Liberal fixation. Don't ask me why. 'The party of the future,' they say, as though the future was automatic. Does anybody believe the Russians took all their missiles out of Cuba? Do you believe it?" P.W. said, pointing his knife at Steven.

"I can't say I've given it—"

"I certainly don't believe it. Otherwise the Americans wouldn't be so anxious to install missiles of their own up here. The missiles won't fly across the Atlantic, as most people think. They'll loop over the Arctic and across the Pole. That's the quickest route. If we elected Conservatives in this riding they'd probably have built that defence base, the whole NORAD shooting match, right here in Presley. Instead they chose North Bay, of all places. Imagine all the Yankee tourists flooding into North Bay— bumpkins from Lima, Ohio wanting to have a gander at their defence base, their thermonuclear war. Don't talk to me about timber rights. We've got to rely on our totem pole for our prosperity. The only boom that's going to happen here in the foreseeable future is the kind that vaporises you before you even hear it. Pass the salt, please."

Vincent Atwater, past-president of the Presley & District Chamber of Commerce, was making a brief and inaudible address to the banqueters over the P.A. system. P.W. intently sprinkled salt on his beans.

"That's an interesting point you make," Steven said.

"You think it's a 'point', do you? When the facts stare us equally in the face."

"I mean about the totem pole downtown. It's one of the first things that struck me when I got here. I asked people at the 4P about it and they all started apologizing. They said some local crook put it up years ago, that it was designed by a construction subcontractor, which is why it looks more Italian than Indian. A wood and wrought-iron totem pole strikes me as having an awful lot of tourism potential."

"Isaac Presley's the name of the guy who put it up," Kathleen said. "He was one of those frontier-type woodsmen. The city is named after him."

"I read something about him," Steven nodded.

"He was a cretin," P.W. muttered into his beans.

"I used to think the town was named after Elvis," Steven said with a laugh.

"There's another cretin for you," the old man said. "People have been talking about putting up a statue of him gyrating his hips somewhere downtown, maybe near the totem pole— two cretins for the price of one. That was a joke I made about the tourism value of the totem pole. Apart from that piece of Indo-Italian scrap, all the Presley family ever was interested in was dogfighting. They put on dogfights for mobsters from Toronto, Hamilton and Buffalo in the old days. Family pets were always disappearing, then turning up wrapped in brown paper in the back alley of Chow's Chow."

"The city has some reservations about Isaac Presley," Kathleen said. "That's why the push is on to officially adopt Elvis. I think it would be deeky."

"It's all academic, of course," said P.W., "since we're on the brink of nuclear war."

"I don't think we're on the brink of nuclear war," Steven said. "My dad got a job at the NORAD base in North Bay a few months ago. My mother's not allowed to visit him and he's not supposed to talk about his work even though he's only on the excavation crew. If the Americans are building such a complex and secret place, they must be confident they'll be able to use it for some time. I agree with you that it's their war, not ours. But I think you're being a bit naive about the future— with all due respect."

P.W. peered at Steven. "I liked it better when you called me 'sir'."

Kathleen smiled nervously. "Do you want me to go get you some more beans, Daddy?"

"Thanks but no thanks."

"How about you, Steven? Would you like more beans?"

"I have plenty here, thank you."

"I don't really want any more beans either," Kathleen chuckled. "I guess none of us want any more beans."

"Wants," P.W. corrected.

"Pardon, Daddy?"

"None of us *wants* any more beans. None takes a singular

verb."

"He's right," Steven said. "We all want to have none of the beans, even if they do taste singularly good." He smiled at Kathleen, who smiled back.

"Timber rights. . ." P.W. grumbled.

The conversation went downhill from there. Kathleen understood that her father felt no particular compulsion to enjoy himself, what with his wife sick at home. But there was more to it than that.

"Was it something I said?" Steven inquired after a long, uneasy silence.

"Will you look at this turkey meat, Kathy. It's so stringy you could knit a sweater with it. Am I supposed to eat it or strum it? Ask one of the women, will you?"

"Always eat white meat in the key of C," Steven said.

"How's that?"

"The turkey: Eat it in the key of C."

Volunteers from the Catholic Women's League had already begun washing dishes. The clink of utensils punctuated the silence at the table.

"You quite colourfully compared the turkey to guitar strings," Steven explained. "I'm saying that the key of C would be appropriate. I'm making a joke based on your comment about the stringy turkey. I'm trying to hold up my end of this conversation."

"Don't exert yourself on my account," said P.W., wiping the corner of his mouth with a napkin.

"Oh, you mean like playing the guitar," Kathleen chimed in, laughing too hard. "That's a good one."

An executive of the Catholic Women's League, her apron stained with bean juice, tapped the microphone at the podium and proceeded to say something no one could hear. Kathleen soldiered on: "Tell us, Steven, is the work your father does very dangerous?"

"Do you mean the work he used to do in the Soo or the work he does now?"

"Any of it," she said with a nervous wave of her arm. "Is any of it dangerous."

"Well, he did routine construction work in the Soo. As for his work in North Bay, I really couldn't tell you, because he—"

"—isn't supposed to talk about his work," P.W. interjected.

"Exactly."

"That much of what you're saying I can follow."

The simple fact was that Preston Wilhelm O'Hagan could not recall, in the course of his 35-year legal career, ever having been called naive. Steven Rosseter, on the other hand, fancied himself used to derision and contempt. Each new hostile encounter reinforced his general world view, which was that it's muskellunge eat muskellunge. But he saw that Kathleen liked him, so he resolved that evening to balance the ledger somewhat by stealing her heart. It was uncommonly easy.

As The Mellotones ravaged Nat King Cole and the crowd began to thin, P.W. grew drowsy. Steven and Kathleen chatted quietly, then took to more or less staring at each other. By the time the band had deconstructed "Ebb Tide", P.W. was ready to go home to his ailing Pauline. Steven volunteered to drive them; Kathleen talked her father into it. Everyone had especially loved Pauline's cole slaw and told him so on the way out. He promised to pass the compliments along.

. . .

"Is there a word for the opposite of charisma? I must look that up," P.W. O'Hagan said to his wife three weeks after the banquet. "What does Kathleen see in him, and why is she inflicting him on us? Is it something I did? I don't remember doing anything. Surely she wouldn't consider ruining her whole life just to spite me for something I'm not even aware I did. What do we know about him? We don't know anything about him."

Pale in the verandah sun, Pauline took her husband's hand. "Kathleen has a good head on her shoulders."

"It's not *Kathleen's* head and shoulders I'm worried about."

That evening, while Kathleen was upstairs finishing her face and Steven was being swallowed by one of the living room chairs, P.W. gulped a mouthful of air and said, "Just what are your intentions."

"Sir?"

"I would like to know your intentions vis-a-vis my daughter," P.W. repeated, rocking steadily in his chair. "Her mother and I value Kathleen a great deal. She intends— and we intend for her— to begin her university studies in Toronto this fall. We are not about to leave anything to chance in this important respect. Your intentions."

Steven shifted in his chair. "We were thinking of going to a movie for starters."

The old man nodded and continued to rock. Finally he said, "Mr. Rosseter, I don't know whether you are impertinent, plain stupid or some newfangled combination of the two. I pride myself on being a man of faith. I trust gut impressions. Right now, my gut is telling me to watch you closely. Why do you suppose my gut is telling me this?"

"Something you ate?" Steven suggested.

"My gut is telling me this because there's something not quite right about you. I've known it from the very start. I can't put my finger on what it is, but when I do, so help me, you'll be the first to hear about it. I just want you to know I'm watching you very closely, Mr. Rosseter. I didn't spend 35 years around confidence artists and not learn a little bit about human nature. Nor does my Jesuit education hinder me in this regard. I'm a student of human weakness, Mr. Rosseter. My father came to this country from Cork City to toil in Isaac Presley's wretched bogs so that I might have a better life. I married a fine woman of French-Canadian extraction and practised law in this town so that our daughter would in her own time rise above my circumstances. My right eye is made of glass, Mr. Rosseter, the better to spot a three-dollar bill from a mile away. I'm sixty-two years old and I stay informed. Believe you me."

"I believe you," Steven said.

"What movie were you planning to see?"

"*The Great Escape.*"

"My daughter abhors war movies."

"It's the only movie in town."

"Fair enough."

Nothing the old man said could change destiny. He realized it as soon as Kathleen descended the stairs. Her shining face, framed by long red curls, seemed to ignite at the sight of Steven, barely discernable amid the upholstery.

With his haunted eyes, his humble background, his bursts of passion and angular sincerity, Steven was a revelation to Kathleen.

He was the tormented, romantic hero of some 19th-century novel—Raskolnikov minus the fever and the police on his back. She fell in love with the idea of falling in love with someone like him. Therefore, she fell in love with him.

To her, the summer of '63 was so much more heady than the placid, aimless seasons that had preceded it. Steven spoke, without ever coming right out and saying it, of the infinite possibilities that arise with coming of age. In moments of weakness he morbidly listed the missed opportunities in his life up to that point. To her they were merely promises unfulfilled. At his happiest he interpreted clouds and invented absurd aphorisms. She took to ironing her hair and reading Jack Kerouac, who also seemed to be pointing her in the direction of some unimaginably distant horizon. All the water in the world was upstream in the summer of '63.

P.W. was crestfallen when Kathleen announced that university and the formal pursuit of English literature could wait one year, while she sorted things out.

"Sort what out?" the old man mournfully asked his wife. "What could there possibly be to sort out at the age of nineteen?"

On the last weekend in August, Steven and Kathleen drove to Nipigon Bay with some friends. Steely cold Lake Superior, the pristine air and an overabundance of sweet wine made magic of the afternoon. Steven said he preferred to speak of the future than of the past, so together they dreamed of adventure and abandon, feeling twice-blessed to be young and know everything. At dusk, numb to the cold and the outside world, they professed their love in the manner of young people at that time— easily, almost casually, as though love were everywhere for the making. They lay together on a sleeping bag spread on a patch of scrub grass near the water. It was Kathleen's first time. Steven said it was his first time too, but she doubted it.

"Do you promise you love me?" she asked him afterward.

"I love you."

"Do you *promise* you love me?"

"What do you mean?"

She curled up closer to him and said, "I don't know, but promise anyway."

"I promise I love you," Steven said, "cross my heart and hope to die," which made Kathleen feel sadder than she had ever thought possible. Wrapped in a sleeping bag to ward off sand and a cold west wind, she thought about her mother as Giles Robert Rosseter was about to be conceived.

Kathleen tearfully broke the news to her father the afternoon President Kennedy was murdered in Dallas. Wet snow was falling. "It can't be true," a woman cried on a rainy downtown Chicago street. P.W. switched off the television.

He set his law practice aside for a few weeks to sulk and to care for his rapidly deteriorating wife, who seemed to make peace with the news from the moment she was told.

"There's going to be a family, Preston," she whispered, "and there is absolutely nothing wrong with that."

P.W. wasn't sure which broke his heart more: his own family fated to dwindle by two-thirds, or the other family slowly taking shape inside his only daughter.

Next to no one in the sleepy city of Presley bothered to raise an eyebrow when, seven months after her secret wedding to Steven and less than five months after Pauline O'Hagan died in her sleep, Kathleen gave birth to a boy. Perhaps everyone was too busy worrying about World War III.

. . .

During his first year on earth, while father and mother grew weary of lurching from delight with their child to horror at the sudden compulsory sameness of their days, baby Giles Robert vegetated on any number of clean, downy surfaces. Sometimes he vegetated on the living room floor of the small semi-detached house the Rosseters rented, flourishes of stucco swirling in his eyes. Sometimes he vegetated in his crib, vaguely aware of birdsong, an occasional passing car and the musical voice of his mother. Sometimes it was on his grandfather's verandah, in a makeshift playpen, as fluttering poplar leaves counted time. Sometimes it was in the stroller, the turn-of-the-century facades of downtown Presley drifting by, or on a path by the river, where the smell of moist earth and rotten wood was permanent.

Baby Giles Robert's senses absorbed even less than his diapers.

Most impressions faded before they were stored. Absence of memory gave his face the glow of a sublime idiot's. In time he grew to identify his immediate family, but in the primitive way instinct grasps the necessity of routine: Mama nurse Baba; Mama carry Baba; Dada lift Baba in the air; Mama change Baba; Dada lift Baba in the air; Dada go away; Baba cry; Mama hold Baba; Mama nurse Baba; Baba spit up on Mama.

When he wasn't hungry, feeding, chafing or sleeping, Baby Giles Robert liked to lapse into a mild catatonic state in honour of those nine idyllic months in the womb. His pale blue eyes slid from animate to inanimate object without the slightest change of mood or demeanour.

Late the third morning, after he and his mother had come home from Riverside Hospital, Baby Giles Robert lapsed into one such stupour. His depressed mother had just finished breast-feeding him and was half-heartedly rocking him to sleep when she noticed the baby's gaze seemingly boring into her. At first it cheered her up. She craned her neck away from him, tilted her head from side to side. "Baba look at Mama?" Silent eyes of a smart cat followed her every move. She grew uneasy. "Why does Baba look at Mama that way? Baba still hungwy? What Baba want?" For much longer than seemed wholesome, Baby Giles Robert scrutinized his mother.

"I wish Baba would stop peering at Mama now," Kathleen said, strangely perturbed by the awareness that this was the first official request she had made of her infant son. Yet he stared. His eyes betrayed not a hint of love, dependence, devotion, awe, joy or enthusiasm; just the condescending detachment of a voyeur. If only he would smile, she thought. Or gurgle, better yet. "Go to sleep sweetie-kins," she implored the baby.

J'accuse, said those oversize pale blue eyes.

"Mama's a good person and you're a healthy, happy baby. A June baby. The Beatles have a song about you. `Little Giles, little Giles, little Giles won't you dance with me. I'm so sad and lonely, baby take a chance with me.' That's about you. I love you, Daddy loves you, Grampa loves you and your Grandma would have just adored you. You're the sweetest baby in the world. Please, darling."

J'accuse.

She shuddered when the baby started to wet himself without taking his eyes off her. She began to suspect her son was a little android sent by a righteous superintelligence from a distant planet to pass along a message. The message was designed to make the android's earthling mother confront the enormity of her sin. She stood up, as did the hair on the back of her neck. Holding the baby away from her, she rushed to the kitchen table and deposited him there. "You're not ordinary," she whispered, backing slowly toward the telephone.

She apologized to Steven for disturbing him at work, and was about to pass on the horrifying news that their baby knew everything that had gone on when, with a cough, little Giles Robert brought up a rivulet of yellowmattercustard and started to cry.

"Gotta go," Kathleen said and hung up. Now the baby was on her shoulder, having his little blue terrycloth backside patted. "There, there," she whispered. "Poor sweetie-kins. You were naughty to fwighten Mama like that. Pwomise you won't fwighten Mama ever again. Okay? Pwomise you won't look at Mama funny anymore. . ."

Giles Robert was oblivious to his mother's second official request. He was examining the bowl of overripe apples on the counter near the telephone, taking it all in and forgetting it.

That evening, P.W. diagnosed the episode as a mild case of infantile possession. "It's not all that unusual," he told Kathleen. "For example, when you were seven months old you spent several days speaking fluent Ojibwa."

"Come on, Daddy," Kathleen said with a laugh.

"At first your mother and I thought it was just a form of gibberish. But a fellow I was representing who was from the reserve came by the house one day and turned palefaced when he heard you talking. 'Your baby is telling a story about the bird-spirit.' That's all he said. 'Your baby is telling a story about the bird-spirit.' Then he excused himself. I imagine he hired another lawyer, because I never saw him again. A week later you quit speaking Ojibwa, just like that."

Steven gaped at P.W., then guffawed.

"Laugh if you want, Cedrick," said P.W.

"My name's Steven and I don't think I've ever heard anything as ridiculous."

"Haven't you now? I'm flattered."

"'Bird-spirit'. I mean, really."

"Daddy, how come you never told—"

"If it weren't God's own truth," P.W. said, stuffing tobacco into his pipe, "what possible motive would I have for telling such a story?"

"You like to argue," said Steven, cheerfully.

"I like to argue. I'm a liar and I like to argue."

"I never said you were a liar. All I said was—"

"Kathleen, you tell us what Cedrick said."

Kathleen worried about it being an uncommonly warm June evening. She worried about crib death. She worried about pipe smoke poisoning the baby's lungs. "Daddy, you have to admit it's a little strange to be speaking Ojibwa when you're just a—"

"It's more than a little strange," agreed P.W., taking the pipe out of his mouth. "But Cedrick, here, seems to think I—"

"What I said, Mr. O'Hagan, if you'll allow me, is that it was a ridiculous story. I never said you lied."

"But you implied it."

"I didn't imply anything. You yourself admit it's a—"

"You implied that I lied to start an argument."

"I never said—"

"I'm not interested in what you said. It's what you implied—"

"You two are going to wake up the baby."

"It's the implication behind what you said that concerns me," P.W. continued, *sotto voce.* "I'll tell you something, Cedrick: I don't say anthing for nothing."

"You just did," Steven murmured.

"Say again?" said P.W., hand cupped behind his ear.

"You're trying to get on my back but I'm not taking the bait tonight, Mr. O'Hagan. It's a nice night for fishing but I'm not in the mood for bait. There's too many fish and not enough water to go around as far as I'm concerned."

The old man turned to his daughter. "What in heaven's name is he talking about?"

"What are either of you talking about?"

"What bait?"

"*Bait* bait," said Steven. "You serve up this little cock-and-bull story out of the blue because you like to throw people off. I'm sure there's no such thing as infantile possession, Ojibwa or otherwise. Why don't you stop trying to spook your own daughter?"

"You're calling me a liar."

"Jesus God, Daddy. Cedrick is not calling you a liar. Why can't we just drop it? Who cares if I spoke Ojibwa, pig Latin or any other language? Can't we spend one evening together without a fight?"

The small living room of the semi-detached house was suddenly silent. Upstairs, Baby Giles Robert slept on. The old man flipped open his Zippo with a flourish and relit his pipe. Steven massaged the bridge of his nose in the flickering light of the television. Kathleen looked at him, at her father:

"What gives?"

Steven rubbed his face with both hands, took a deep breath and gazed wearily at Kathleen. "My name is not Cedrick," he sighed.

. . .

Sometimes P.W. and Steven dueled for Kathleen's loyalty. Other times they dueled for the sheer sport of it. The elder basted his grief in the outrage of the suddenly dispossesed, while the younger blamed his predicament on the man who supposedly had lost everything.

For his part, P.W. abandoned forever the comforting myth that the journey into old age would consist of equal parts serenity and senility. In actual fact, life didn't let go of you until the moment you expired. It went right on happening.

"You were born naked," he informed Giles Robert two summers later, while babysitting him on the verandah of his once-stately home. "The Church said you were tainted with original sin and the doctor gave you a cuff on the bum on behalf of the state. As you slipped into the bright light of this world, you worked up to that first scream that would serve you so well throughout your life. 'Waaaaaaaaa,' you said to all the frightening creatures in this cold, blinding world. 'Waaaaaaaaaa.' You spend the rest of your life trying to forget that moment."

Robert watched the lilacs.

"On the day you were born," the old man said, "you were handed a lot of what's called emotional luggage. One of these days you're going to fall in love, get married and have children— all in the belief that these people will help you with your luggage. What you've got to remember is that these people have luggage of their own to worry about. In fact, what they probably have in mind is for you to help them with their luggage. Remember that."

But the boy was destined, or had already learned, to forget.

* * *

2

> What is mankind if not an accident of biology happening over and over? What is history if not a diagnosis of the injuries up to this point?
>
> —Theodore Ng

The O'Hagan-Rosseter debates became legendary in the neighbourhood. Kathleen grew to be revered as a kind of saint— Our Lady Of Perpetual Aggravation. Her son was pitied. *Now that Pauline's dead the whole family's going to pot.* That's what the neighbours said.

As a toddler, Giles Robert spent unrecorded hours by himself in the basement with his box of crayons. Kathleen, meanwhile, threw herself ever more fiercely into her housework. As the months of married life— and married life itself— unravelled, the list of things that needed cleaning grew at an exponential rate. Jesus God, the wall nearest to the oven was a phlegmy dull yellow; the shower tiles had lost their sheen; the chrome of the kitchen sink had turned battleship grey; the arms of the chesterfield were blackening with ink from Steven's hands; the living room windows were opaque with applesauce fingerprints and littleboy's breath.

The transition from youth to adulthood— from homework to housework— had been a painfully seamless one. Still, her surrender to the humdrum had a certain nobility about it. She wasn't an ideal mother— there is no such thing as an ideal mother, she told herself again and again— but she embraced housewivery with the determination to measure up in her appointed role. As she grew more adept at battling household entropy, Steven and P.W. discovered ingenious new ways of disputing the most meagre point. "They're the ones who make the dust come back on top of the television," she boldly thought to herself one evening while scouring the toilet bowl. "They're the ones who knit hairballs under the bed." A serene house would need no dusting. Flies would not dare die at the foot of lamps in homes where peace reigned.

Kathleen didn't bother with the unfinished basement of their semi-detached home. The basement was limbo, or Bobby's Space, as Steven put it. There, in the company of shiny black poly-legged bugs that revolted his mother, young Robert painstakingly created a fresco on concrete walls stained dirtybrown and white by summer dampness and winter frost. Crayolas didn't travel well over the coarse surface, but he was patient and the mood brought on by drawing was very like the stupour he loved so much when he was even smaller. He drew orange shapes and red shapes and blue shapes and yellow shapes. In the spaces between the shapes he drew black asterisks. He saved the green crayons for shapes with big sharp teeth or pointy arms. Days, weeks, months were recorded on those walls. The fresco was everything Robert knew and thought about the world up to that point. It reminded P.W. of *Guernica.*

"Just look at the way the whole thing seems to come together. And all those green fish. You'd swear—"

"Fish?" said Steven.

"Sure. You can see the pointed fins and the eyes. The boy has a gift."

"They don't look at all like fish to me," Steven said. "Do they look like fish to you, Kath? They look like crocodiles or alligators. Wouldn't you say so, Kath?"

"They're just shapes," said Kathleen, sorting socks from underwear.

"They can't be 'just shapes'," Steven said. "They have to be something."

"Why?" Kathleen said, looking for a matching sock.

"Germane question," said P.W.

"Because little kids don't think in abstract ways. When they draw something, it represents a thing that's real to them. As if a little kid would bother drawing just patterns. Those are alligators."

"They look like shapes to me," Kathleen said.

"Then explain Picasso, Cedrick," said P.W., running the palm of his hand over the rough concrete. "He says it took him most of his life to learn how to paint like a child. Wouldn't you say the work he does these days is abstract?"

"Not really. It's just that in his paintings you can mistake one thing for something else. Different people interpret different shapes differently."

"So that a horse might look like a dog?" P.W. said.

"Right."

"Or a fish might look like an alligator?"

". . ."

"Or everything is just a shape that can look like anything?"

"Just a minute now," said Steven. "What I mean is—"

"We're both right, Kath." P.W. picked up the child, who was trying to peel paper from the end of a black crayon; time for asterisks. "Good grief," he said with a grimace, "the boy is ripe."

"That's not what I meant and you know it," said Steven. "The shapes themselves—"

"Here!" said Kathleen, taking the child from his grandfather, dropping the socks and underwear in the process. Together they fled up the stairs and into the deepest darkest room of the house. She changed him, made him fresh all over again. He laughed and she sang a song. Away; away from those two and their strange bond of oneupmanship, provocation, apology and resentment. What Kathleen feared the most, what she foresaw the most, was the day when she too would be sucked into their game, like a lost hairpin up the nozzle of her Hoover, protesting all the way, then beyond retrieval or redemption, the victim of her own fierce housework.

"They can rot forever down there," she told her son.

. . .

Slowly, dimly, Robert became aware of the passage of time. He noticed that his bright crayon masterpieces faded. He noticed that his mother and father didn't wrestle as often in bed at night on the far side of the thin skyblue wall of his room. Maybe they were getting along better. Maybe his grandfather didn't visit as often because he was on safari in Africa, hunting for wild animals and new friends. His grandfather liked to talk about Africa, where tigers with teeth like spikes ate dead animals, where elephants rolled in the mud, using their trunk like a big hose, and man-lions slept in the shade while woman-lions went hunting for dead animals to bring back to their sleepy husbands. The tigers, elephants and lions ate, time passed, then they got hungry again. (He didn't know if elephants ate dead animals, too.) He imagined them all sleeping peacefully together in the bush at night. He wondered if the bush there was like the bush here, with lakes and chipmunks and tents and trailers.

Every year in late May, people here fled back into the wilderness from which they came. Children pedalled their bicycles down muddy roads and set up mildewed tents in a bog; others drove to Kekagami Provincial Park and hunkered near pre-cut wood and other amenities; others polished their Coldstreams and established a makeshift suburb on a cleared hilltop overlooking Presley, the Kekagami River and the bush. Every day an enterprising youngster navigated her ice-cream tricycle to the top of the hill. The ethereal tinkling of her vehicle mesmerized children within a radius of two hundred metres. In the evenings a dense cloud of Pic draped the campground, driving all the insects down into the city, where less fortunate citizens examined their lawns then retired to their living rooms to watch *The Tommy Hunter Show.*

By mid-June, forest fires customarily began to char thousands of acres of timberland in the surrounding area. Robust adolescents found lucrative work battling the blazes alongside the trained men. The pay was so good that the youths could afford to spend the rest of the summer lolling in a booth at D'Agostino's Confectionery, feeding quarters into the jukebox, swilling Pepsi and devouring plate after plate of french fries and gravy. They liked to trade anecdotes about particularly troublesome fires, their voices animated yet oddly clipped, in unconscious imitation of the men from the nearby reserve who made excellent firefighters.

When Giles Robert was old enough to be sent to D'Agostino's for bread or milk, he liked to linger near the booths as Creedence Clearwater Revival blared on the jukebox. What he listened to was not "Proud Mary" or "Green River". What he listened to was the banter of his elders. He wondered what it felt like to go into the woods with a hose and put out burning trees. Was it spooky? It never failed to chill him when, on a Sunday drive down bushroads with his mother and father, they came upon a tract of forest turned to ash, husks of trees like giant matchsticks spanning a narrow hopeless spectrum of grey to black.

"That was real somebitch last week," Robert heard the boys in D'Agostino's say, their words muffled by mouthfuls of french fries. "Real dicey for a time."

That was real somebitch last week, Robert repeated to himself on the way home, searching for the exact intonation.

"Please don't slam the screen door," Kathleen said as he dropped the loaf of bread on the kitchen table.

"That was real somebitch last week," he replied, "real dicey for a time," forgetting not to slam the screen door on his way out to the backyard. Perhaps one day he too would battle blazes in the bush, get his face good and sooty on a fifteen-hour shift, be fed and washed in time to make an evening of it at D'Agostino's, everyone caught up in the kind of brute chivalry that meant something to a young man in that part of the world. As an adolescent, Robert rarely dredged up memories of those early years in the wild silence of Presley and environs. Better to have fought metaphorical forest fires than to have surrendered to the ticking of clocks in airtight rooms. Better to have lived heedlessly for the moment than to have submitted to the sentimental tyranny of time.

O to be an infant forever, with no compulsion to remember at all, let alone in detail. To live without the intermediary of consciousness forever spreading ugly rumours about the world.

But it can't be so.

Sharp as a test-pattern against the blur of those first years of Robert's life was Thanksgiving Day 1970, with its heady procession of Niagara white wine, turkey, canned cranberry, shame and regret. In his mind's archives, this day had a file of its own, all the more engrossing for its incompleteness.

It began with the high pastel skies that signal a change of season. In the evening, Robert liked to stretch out on the front steps of the house and watch layers of cirrus clouds lazily intersect. P.W. had told him the earth was forever spinning around. His face to the sky, Robert imagined he could feel the planet's movement under him. It made him happy and sad at the same time. Come winter he would draw those clouds and colour them.

"Mom! Dad! Come see the earth spin!" he wanted to cry out, but they were busy indoors. Sometimes P.W. indulged the boy, but he preferred to watch the more dramatic cumulo-nimbus and hammerhead of mid-summer. High cirrus were an acquired taste.

He could hear his mother doing the dishes. His father was in the kitchen with her. Their faint voices consoled him as the sky slid by.

"You haven't gone hunting since before we were married."

"I know that."

"When did you want to go?"

"Tomorrow. The weather's been so nice I thought we could—"

"Tomorrow is Thanksgiving."

"I know that, Kath."

"What about dinner?"

"We'd be back in plenty of time for dinner. I'll make sure of that."

"'We'?"

"Bobby and me."

"You want to take *Bobby?*"

"He's old enough, Kath. It would be a great experience for him. I remember when I was a kid my father and uncle took me on some of their hunting trips. It made me feel like a man."

"Come off it, Steven. You've told me a hundred times how much you hated those hunting trips, how your father and your Uncle Edgar would get drunk and ignore you for hours, then they'd pass out and you'd be all by yourself in that cold little shack in the middle of nowhere, imagining grizzly bears were figuring out how to work the doorknob. You said you used to cry yourself to sleep. Did that make you feel like a man?"

"You don't have to mock me."

"I just don't understand why you'd even think of taking Bobby hunting."

"This would be different, Kath. It's not as if we'd catch anything. It's just something about being out in the wilds. There's no way I can make you understand. It's strictly a male thing."

"A *what?*"

By now, twilight had drained most of the brighter colour from the clouds. Robert wondered if the clouds moved the same way at night, or if the moon just now rising made them change direction or move in a strange way. Grampa would know. A chill having descended with the darkness, he was grateful when his father summoned him into the house.

Thanksgiving Day morning was bright and unusually warm. Steven's Camaro left the neighbour's dog in its wake after a couple of blocks. They encountered little traffic on their drive through town to the northern city limits. The peak of autumn colours had come and gone early this season. The bush, in the longer October shadows, was an unprepossessing blend of greys and browns. By the time they parked the car at the side of the dirt road and set out on foot, the sky had grown opaque but the day was no less fair. Steven carried his rifle aimed skyward. Robert was enchanted by the shape and apparent heft of the weapon.

"Can you smell those leaves," Steven said. "We should do this more often. It gets the pulp scum out of our lungs. Makes us wild animals again." When they stopped to survey an area of bush, the silence was complete. A crow soared in the metallic sky.

"This is what it sounds like in space," Steven told his son. "In space there's no sound at all. You wouldn't even be able to hear my voice."

"Grampa says space goes on forever."

"Nobody knows for sure, in spite of what your Grampa says."

"But space is big, right?"

"Right."

Robert picked up a stick and waved it experimentally in the air. "Grampa says there are people like us that live in space."

Steven turned to his son. "We're on a hunting trip. Put that stick down. You're scaring off game."

Robert obeyed. They walked on in silence. The boy grew intrigued by the sound of his father's breathing, wanted to ask him about it but decided it wouldn't be wise.

"Not many hunters out this way today," Steven said after a few minutes. "That's a good sign."

"It is?"

"It means the animals think they have the bush to themselves.

It makes them less cautious. But try to walk more softly."

Robert walked with his head down, to avoid cracking branches. "Grampa says the Indians can tiptoe through the forest without making any noise."

"'Grampa says, Grampa says'. For God's sake, will you concentrate. How do you expect to become a hunter this way? I really don't care what Grampa says."

They passed a stand of charred evergreens. Robert imagined he was an Indian firefighter, tiptoeing through *real somebitch*. "Stay close," his father called out from a few feet ahead of him.

Toward noon, they rested in a small clearing and lunched on devilled ham sandwiches Kathleen had prepared the night before.

"How do you like it so far?" Steven said, biting into his sandwich.

"It's deeky," Robert said.

"Not bad, eh? We should do this more often."

The hike back to the car was not as deeky. A damp breeze had come up and the boy's boots were soaked. He tried not to whine about it; he knew his father didn't appreciate whining.

Just as Robert was beginning to think the walk back to the car would never end, they were startled by the cracking of a nearby branch. Steven turned to his son, his finger to his lips, cocked the rifle and aimed it ahead of him.

"What is it?" the boy whispered. Steven shook his head.

As if someone had tripped a switch, Robert's heart started to race. He was convinced this wasn't fun anymore. But there was nowhere to run. Another branch snapped to his right. Amid the brittle undergrowth in a stand of bare trees he spotted a lumbering mass of solid brown.

"Daddy!"

Steven pivoted and fired. The explosion rang on in Robert's ears, then left him deaf. Thus was he spared the cracking of branches and the thud of an adult bull moose collapsing in a bog of leaves and rotting wood.

"Jesus Christ," Steven said, his rifle barrel still trained on the animal. "Jesus Christ."

The silence of the bush, so full of so little, flowed back into Robert's ears. "Is it. . . dead?" He was answered by the animal's thrashing.

"What the hell do I do now," Steven murmured to himself. "I don't even know if I'm in season. What the hell do I do now."

"Daddy, I feel sick. . ."

"Shh."

Steven finally began moving toward the wounded animal. Robert trailed him. From a safe distance Steven could see that he had hit it in the right foreleg. Satisfied that the animal was incapable of rising yet cowed by its continued thrashing, he moved in closer.

"Daddy. . . "

"Shut up, Bobby!"

Once Steven was close enough to the moose to touch it with the barrel of his rifle, it ceased all movement and stared glassily up at him. Steven recalled his uncle Edgar's boast that he always named his animals before finishing them off and dragging the carcass back to camp. All Steven could think of, the only name he could think of, was Bullwinkle. He turned to his son. "Give it a name," he said.

"Daddy, I want to go home. . . "

"Give the thing a name. Now!"

Robert saw tears welling in his father's eyes. That scared him more than anything.

". . .Ed," the boy said meekly.

Steven aimed his rifle at the animal's head, closed his eyes and fired.

Ringing. The sound of space. Then earthly silence.

. . .

"I don't have to explain anything to you or anybody or their brother-in-law," Steven told P.W. as Kathleen took the overdone turkey out of the oven. "I goddamn don't. Especially in my own goddamn house."

Robert had been ordered upstairs by his mother to make himself squeaky-clean for dinner. Upon returning to the kitchen he saw that she was pale and tired. His father sat at the table, a bottle of Niagara white wine before him. He was filling the silence with his voice and the glass with his wine. P.W. sat opposite him, his back to the window, his face obscure against the late afternoon sun that had returned to highlight the grit on the glass and the stubborn leaves that clung to the bastard maple at the side of the house. His father's face, though bathed in the light, was like a face in a dream: still, grey and only half there.

"Grampa says I traumatized you, Bobby. Isn't that a nice word? I think I'll try to use that word more often in regular conversation."

"You're making an even bigger ass of yourself," P.W. said. "Why don't you quiet down."

"Why don't *you* quiet down," said Steven, setting his glass abruptly on the table. The old man flinched. A wine stain spread on Kathleen's pretty linen tablecloth.

"Bobby, go find something to do," said his mother. "Dinner won't be ready for another fifteen minutes."

Robert went outside to the back steps, stretched out and looked up at the high clouds. It was turning colder. He heard the clink of bottle against glass, the cutting edge of his father's voice. Poor Ed. He wanted to tell his mother and his grandfather something nice about his dad, but the voice he heard was that of someone going far away, waving goodbye over his shoulder, putting as much Niagara white wine as possible between himself and the rest of the world. So Robert perused the clouds, purplish streaks sliding against a uniform baby blue.

". . .Don't tell me what I am, Mr. O'Hagan. I know what I am. I'm Cedrick of Sault Ste. Marie, last of the great white hunters. You don't know me any better than anybody else knows me. My background may not be as picturesque as yours, but don't tell me what I am. . ."

And if you waited long enough, and if you didn't blink, you could actually see the wisps of cloud change colour as the evening sun moved through the sky. Purple draining pale.

"You failed your son today," P.W. said.

"I failed my son a long time ago," said another voice, "before you entered into it. We almost did the right thing, Kathleen and I. But now he's the son of a son of a failure. It might please you to know the first Thanksgiving I remember was the year my father threatened my mother with a breadknife. Uncle Edgar came over and kicked the shit out of him. He left my father lying on the living room floor and took my mother and me over to his place. 'An asshole drunk,' was how he explained my father to me. I got an air-rifle for Christmas that year, it seems to me."

"You never told me this," Kathleen said.

"So?"

"How come you never told me?"

Steven laughed. "You people," he said, filling his glass.

"What I think you ought to do," P.W. calmly interrupted, "is put away the wine and go out and have a talk with the boy instead of sitting here feeling sorry for yourself."

"I didn't ask your opinion."

A flash of late orange sun bathed the Camaro and the driveway. Robert wondered: Did the sun get cooler at the end of every day?

"I didn't ask your opinion before Bobby was born, either. We just sort of knew it, didn't we, Kath? We were all by ourselves then. We thought we had finally made up our minds. We really thought we had finally made up our—"

"That's enough, Steven."

His mother. Sound of the utensil drawer crashing to the floor, handful of knives, forks, spoons, corkscrew, can opener, nutcracker.

"We thought it was the thing to do, and we almost did it. We almost did it."

Chair legs sliding on tile floor, a struggle, someone falling.

"What are you— I'm not done yet. I have to tell your father the whole story so he'll understand. I'm not through yet. I'm... not... through."

Here Giles Robert's memory dissolved into a fog of words and impressions: His father telling a long, sad story. He going into the house, standing in the kitchen doorway. His mother, hair ignited by sunlight through the window, pointing at him in alarm. His grandfather leading him out of the house by the hand. His father sprawled on the kitchen floor, his back against the curpboard, telling a long, sad story.

. . .

They strolled down sidewalks made more interesting by leaves ripe for kicking into the gutter. He trotted ahead, kicked the leaves hard, then stopped and waited.

"Look at Mr. Cutler's yard over there," his winded grandfather said in the fading light. "If he doesn't soon get raking he's going to have a real time of it in the spring. Being Mr. Cutler, he'll probably put it off another day, just as he did yesterday. Then the first snow will come and he'll wait for it to melt, but it won't melt, and it'll snow again, heavier this time, and he won't have a chance to do any raking at all."

"Maybe he'd like me to rake the yard for him," Robert said. They turned the corner.

"How long were you listening in the house?" P.W. asked. "What did you hear?"

"I didn't hear anything," the boy lied. He kicked a heap of leaves. "What's wrong with my dad?"

"He's okay," said P.W. "Are you okay?"

Robert nodded. He noticed now the sky was violet and clear. Just one crayon to colour this whole simple sky.

* * *

3

> The only way to counteract illusions is
> to accept that everything is an illusion,
> which is not an especially realistic idea.
>
> —Theodore Ng

Had Thanksgiving Day 1970 not been a statutory holiday, Steven Rosseter would have staggered out of the house that evening, fallen into his Camaro and woven his way to the Riverview Hotel to cap off the evening. Or, had it not been so late, he might have called a few friends together to drag the dead moose, Ed, out of the bush. But the thought of moose meat nauseated him. So he retired to the small upstairs den for the night.

The next day, after work, he repaired straightaway to the Riverview. From his table in the corner of the beverage room he watched the regulars file in. Most of them were 4Pers who, years before, had quaffed Pepsis at D'Agostino's. Now they drank draught, played shuffleboard and smoked Export Plain. Steven was perplexed by the continuous flow of conversation at the millworkers' tables. These gruff men in their lumberjackets never seemed at a loss for words. Tempers occasionally flared at the shuffleboard table as small bills changed hands and some of the players pushed and shoved. This made the men sitting at the tables laugh. "Hey Danny," one of the them said, "why don't you quit while you're behind?" and everyone laughed. The oldest of the group, whom they called Pisser, laughed and laughed and coughed and coughed until he looked like he might need oxygen. "Up yours," said Danny and everyone laughed anew, including Pisser.

Steven, feeling ample with self-pity, wondered what they talked about when they didn't talk about their shuffleboard acumen. Maybe they told war stories. People like Pisser were old enough to have been in the war, though he more likely had been toiling at the 4P since his early teens. The only war Steven could talk about with any degree of passion or sincerity was Vietnam. He watched from the comfortable remove of his television as scenes of young American Marines slogging through the jungle, loading the dead and maimed into helicopters, flashed on the little screen. He knew no personal stories of good buddies blown apart or MIA, villages napalmed off the face of the earth, or sultry evenings with professional sluts in the backstreets of Saigon. All over America, and in some Canadian cities, people his age had been marching for years in a vain attempt to put an end to that war. It was Steven's impression— this day, at any rate— that most of those who took part in the protest marches didn't know where they were going any more than the wretched young soldiers in the trackless boobytrapped jungles of Southeast Asia. Some people got caught up in movements, marches and merriment. Others got caught up in Claymore mines, punji stakes and sniper fire. He, Steven, sat alone and sipped draught in the Riverview Hotel, marooned in the limitless muskeg desert atop Lake Superior.

While elsewhere cities burned and soldiers died, Presley City Council hotly debated whether to dismantle Isaac Presley's totem pole. The only hippies around were the ones thumbing through town along the Trans-Canada Highway. More of them might have settled along the banks of the Kekagami, near the boat launches and barbecue parks, but Nirvana was said to be west of the Rockies. Some Presleyites found these soft-spoken wanderers with the glassy eyes and dirty long hair strangely endearing. Older residents were reminded of the hoboes of the Depression, who had drifted across the land in search of work. But the hippies weren't looking for work. Most of them were refugees from affluence, looking to escape work. They fancied they were surfing on a tidal wave of enlightenment. They could feel it in their music, in the clothes they wore and the generous, non-denominational love they made.

The wave, for a time, seemed to engulf the continent. But Presley was far from any shore where the wave broke hard and clear like a windowpane. Here it was a ripple from the wake of a passing Evinrude lapping against the almighty remorseless Precambrian Shield. Steven knew he was missing a lot, knew he was lonely. He wondered if Pisser or any of the other 4P boys would care to hear a story about a dead moose named Ed.

Still, a ripple is a ripple. The clientele in the beverage room had changed gradually over the years. Lean, urgent-looking young man arrived to sip draught and discuss abstract matters. The 4P regulars reluctantly gravitated closer to the shuffleboard game and nearby tables. That corner of the room, opposite the picture windows looking out on the brown Kekagami and the bright sky, became their pasture. The millworkers felt supplanted by a new generation of regulars, less prone to laugh at fistfights or undress waitresses with their eyes; outcasts, misfits, rebels, liberators, "faggots," Pisser grumbled. But the millworkers mainly let the new customers be, and sometimes sat quietly bemused while a couple of them discussed free will or good dope, or both.

Steven, pinned down between the beverage room's two camps, was fascinated by the new arrivals. These young men asked Adrienne, the waitress, why there was no music by the Grateful Dead or the Band in the jukebox. Anything but a warped old 45 of "These Boots Are Made For Walkin'". The machine should have "Tears Of Rage" or something by Neil Young, not some Mafiosa's daughter in vinyl go-go boots. Is there any way of getting a few chairs outside so they can watch the river flow? They're on their way to Nanaimo or Portland or Juarez and they'd like to score some smoke to tide them over 'til they hit the Andes. What about something by Cat Stevens? Nancy Sinatra is such a bringdown... You have free will if you can tap into the cosmic energy source with enough conviction to liberate some of it for yourself. Otherwise you're spinning your wheels fulfilling someone else's nine-to-five prophecy. Jung was heavy, Nietzsche was heavy, a lot of cats were very very heavy. Castaneda went off so he could write another book about that Hopi sorcerer, Don Quixote? The Hopi taught Castaneda how to vanish. Someone's ghostwriting his next book for him... We're interested in hash primarily because the buzz is so much smoother. Have you ever smoked Thai stick? Vietnam: what a colossal bringdown. . .

Steven made the acquaintance of Ansel Bedrosian, who had emigrated north from Etobicoke in search of Canada. "What the fuck is Canada?" Ansel wanted to know, sweeping the hair out of his face and pushing his draught glass away from him. "The fever-dream of a few fatcats? I say it's the Indians, man. They got here first. They own the place because they gave themselves to it. The place owns them. We're nothing but squatters here until we connect with the harmonies of the land the way they did. Drugs help. You've got to take everything the Man says with a grain of acid, ha ha."

Steven laughed along. Ansel's anger seemed so soft, his resentment so cheerfully serene, that it almost didn't add up to anything negative. Steven, by comparison, churned inside like a badly balanced washing machine in the "spin" cycle. His frustration and loathing often made him dizzy, so he drank draught to settle himself down, listened to what Ansel Bedrosian had to say and prayed to an unseen god for inspiration.

By the summer of 1971, Steven felt estranged from all but the lean, urgent clientele of the Riverview Hotel beverage room. Through the windows he watched stray logs drift downriver and fancied himself a slab of wood, powerless against the eddies of life on a random journey into a vast, oblivious sea.

But there was a magic vibration in the air and in those currents. It may have been somewhat stale magic by then (you couldn't read about it in any of the popular magazines), but it was magic nonetheless. To grab hold of some of it involved reappraising his value system, reupholstering his psyche, redefining his goals. What he had to do was to strip himself of all artifice.

"Come into focus," advised Ansel, who by then was driving for Union Taxi at night. "You can't do a thing until you focus your energies. Do you think I can't see it in your face and your eyes?"

"What do you see?" Steven said.

"I don't know, man. A lot of things. Confusion. I knew a chick in Toronto who could read people by the shape of their mouth and the way they formed words with their lips. She was so good at reading people's mouths that she knew what they were going to say before the words came out. I look at the shape of your mouth and I see. . . well, I don't see a hell of a lot because I don't have that chick's particular gift, but you know what I mean. You've got to focus yourself. Meditation helps. I'd meditate more myself, but I always seem to fall asleep. It's like I'm already so focused I lose consciousness altogether."

"At one with Rip van Winkle," Steven murmured, watching a waterskier slalom up the Kekagami on his bare feet.

"I guess so. I never thought of that. He's the dude who fell asleep and grew a long beard, right?"

"Right. Him and Rasputin."

"Did Rasputin sleep too?"

"No. He just grew a long beard."

"Right. Far out," said Ansel. "Another thing about when you meditate is that you hook up with all that Eastern shit: Buddhists practising anti-gravity in olden times when nobody was supposed to know anything, and blimps floating over Atlantis thousands of years before Jesus. There's hints of it all through the Bible if you know where to look. Cosmic consciousness puts you in touch with so many amazing possibilities."

"Like the cover of *Abbey Road*," Steven said.

"Oh yeah, definitely. Paul McCartney's death pointing to a conspiracy involving the Kennedys and the number 64, which is 23 plus 39, and 39 is 3 times 13, which is close to the number of letters in Lee Harvey Oswald's name."

"64 is 23 plus 41," Steven corrected.

"Right, right," said Ansel. "So maybe Oswald's ancestors had one of those long ethnic names with 41 letters in it. It's been a while since I read about it. Opening yourself up to the infinite possibilities of the cosmos can be scary, but it's always informative as hell. It makes you paranoid sometimes, but sometimes you have reason to be paranoid. The point is you come clean and that's what counts. You get relevant."

But what if there's nothing beneath the artifice, Steven wondered as Adrienne cleared the empty draught glasses from the table and he tried not to look down her blouse for the umpteenth time. What if you strip everything away and zilch remains?

"Think of life as one long movie," Ansel said, his head bobbing to an inaudible beat. "Forget the artificial soundstage and go on location, man. Just go with it. Pure person."

Stoic and contemplative as trading-post Indians, Steven and Ansel stared out at the window, to where the brown water slid slowly by.

. . .

The first thing he needed to change was his home. As a result of all those epiphanies in the yeasty cloister of the Riverview beverage room, his home was found wanting in many respects. He sensed something profoundly bourgeois about the cleanliness, the modest furniture and Kathleen's tasteful decor. Whom were they trying to kid with all this orderliness? Ansel arranged his sofa diagonally in the tiny living room of his apartment precisely to disturb the vibes that were now stifling the Rosseter's own semi-detached home. Arranging a sofa diagonally was an exciting idea even if it ate up a lot of floor space. Where was Kathleen's sense of adventure now? What had become of the wide-eyed woman of 1963? She even wanted a ruffle for their bed, at a time when he was inclined to do away with the box-spring altogether and just plop the mattress on the floor— diagonally, if need be.

And Bobby: Something had to be done about Bobby and the television before it sucked all the imagination out of his head. Ansel didn't condescend to have a television in his apartment. He listened to Erik Satie on a portable hi-fi in the evenings. He made exotic salads of fruits and kidney beans and rapped with his friends into the night. He sat cross-legged on the floor and smoked giant marijuana cigarettes whenever he pleased. Steven didn't imagine marijuana was the appropriate TV-substitute for his son, but something had to be done.

On those increasingly rare evenings when he was home, Steven decided to take a supervisory role in the television-watching. Kathleen had her father over every Sunday for roast beef and potatoes, Yorkshire pudding and mashed turnip just the way her mother used to make it, after which they all settled down to watch *Bonanza*. One such evening in the fall of 1971, Ansel Bedrosian paid his first official visit to the Rosseter home. Just off an enervating 15-hour shift at Union Taxi, he wasn't anxious to be alone.

"We were just starting to watch the Cartwrights," Steven said, guiding Ansel into the family room.

"Oh. Far out," said Ansel.

"I don't personslly care for it," Steven explained, "but it's my son's favourite show and occasionaly it makes some worthwhile points."

The introductions went reasonably well. Kathleen offered to take Ansel's faded U.S. Army jacket and asked if he would like a glass of ginger ale or something. P.W. nodded at Ansel while clanging his empty pipe in a heavy glass ashtray. Robert, lying on his stomach on the blue shag rug, was already too engrossed in the vicissitudes of life on the Ponderosa to acknowledge the visitor.

The evening's episode was the one in which Hop Sing, the Cartwrights' loyal cook, has his pigtail lopped off by desperadoes. The atrocity stunned Robert. Hop Sing, somehow, had come to be his favorite character. As if cued by the string crescendo that always preceded the Chevrolet commercial, he began to sob.

Ansel, wedged between Steven and Kathleen on the small couch, swept hair out of his face and leaned forward. "Heavy," he opined as a Chevrolet smoothly negotiated a curve on the edge of what appeared to be the Grand Canyon.

"Why did they do that to him?" Robert asked between sobs. "He didn't do anything to those guys."

"Are you in the armed forces?" P.W. inquired of Ansel.

"Me? Ho no," said Ansel, laughing.

"You're wearing the uniform of a sergeant in the U.S. Army. Were you aware of that?"

"He loves his hair," Robert said. "He's not the same without it. And he'll never be able to grow it back. It'll take years."

Kathleen leaned forward and touched her son's leg. "It's okay, sweetheart."

"No it isn't," Robert said. "He'll never have his ponytail again."

"It's Army surplus," Ansel said. "I wear it out of solidarity for all the Americans who've come up to here to avoid the draft. It's the people's uniform now, not the army's."

"What people?" said P.W.

"It's only a TV show, honey," Kathleen said. "Hop Sing didn't really lose his hair. It's just for the program."

"Oh God," Steven moaned.

"The people of this planet," Ansel replied.

"You mean it didn't really happen?" said Robert, brightening a little.

"Not to the man who's playing Hop Sing. He's not really Hop Sing."

"He isn't?"

"Oh God," said Steven.

"It occurs to me the last thing those Americans would like to see is the uniform of the army they deserted," P.W. said.

"Then who is he?" Robert asked, fresh tears welling.

Steven leaned forward. "Kath, why don't you let Bobby—"

"He's an actor playing Hop Sing," Kathleen said. "It's probably not even his real hair."

"Now just a minute," said Steven. "You should let Bobby come to terms with his feelings. If the fact that Hop Sing lost some of his hair upsets him, he should be free to express it."

"Not if we all work together to appropriate the army from the Pentagon and give it back to its rightful owners," Ansel rejoined.

"He's already expressed it, Steven."

"And how do you go about doing that, Edsel?" P.W. wanted to know.

"What's the use of a story if you can't get emotionally involved in it? What's the use of any kind of fiction if someone is going to control the way others respond to it?"

"Step by step," Ansel said. "Rome wasn't torn down in a day."

"Jesus God, Steven, can't you see he's over-reacting?

"Forgive me if I don't hold my breath," said P.W.

"Mommy?"

"Who are you," said Steven, "to decide what's a valid emotion in another person? What makes you the supreme judge of Bobby's feelings?"

"It's just a matter of time," Ansel predicted.

"Mommy?" said Robert, tugging at Kathleen's pant cuff.

"As far as I'm concerned," Kathleen said, rising, "you can take your 'valid emotion' and shove it sideways up your ga-ga."

"...Just a matter of time..." Ansel repeated, this time to fill dead air.

"Mommy?"

"What is it, Bobby?"

"You haven't told me who Hop Sing really is."

"There is no Hop Sing," Kathleen roared. "It'a just a fictional character played by some Oriental actor. There's no such thing as

Hop Sing. Forget about him."

Robert stared numbly at the television. Ansel swept hair out of his face and gazed in awe at Kathleen. "What an absolutely mind-blowing concept."

"'Ga-ga'?" said P.W.

"This is truly sickening," Steven announced. "You won't allow Bobby to feel any empathy for Hop Sing, so you just snuff out even the idea of a Hop Sing. I'm astounded."

"Spare me, Steven. Bobby doesn't need any more upheaval right now, but you wouldn't know about that, would you?"

"Wouldn't know about what?"

"Shhh," said Robert.

The program had come back on and Hop Sing was emptying his heart to Ben Cartwright. The room fell silent except for an occasional sniff from Robert.

"It's like he's a phantom of our imagination now," Ansel whispered, staring awestruck at Hop Sing and his silver-haired employer. "I never thought of it that way before. It's sort of creepy, all these characters just figments of our imagination, like in books. They don't really exist and yet we watch them and identify with them as if they were actually alive. Spacey."

Ben Cartwright was relatively successful at consoling his cook, but the scene was lost on Robert, who was busy mourning the outright extinction of Hop Sing. "I loved Hop Sing," he said.

"That's okay," Kathleen replied. "You can love someone that doesn't exist in the normal way. Think of Santa Claus."

"Oh God," Steven said.

"We all love Hop Sing," P.W. said. "Don't we, Amstel?"

"I don't know him that well," Ansel said, "but he seems a together enough cat."

Robert found it hard to accept that here was a mere facsimile of Hop Sing, who didn't exist to begin with— an actor playing an imaginary person. Later in life, he may have tried to devise an ontological proof of the existence of Hop Sing. But at seven years of age he had to content himself with adjusting to the new reality. In time he would adjust quite nicely. He would grow accustomed to watching thousands of imaginary persons get wasted, offed, blown away on the TV screen. The trick, he later discovered, was to care enough about the characters to keep the show interesting, but to know when to draw the line. After Hop Sing's predicament had been more or less resolved, after Ben and Hoss and Little Joe and Candy had reined their horses in the direction of the soundstage sunset and the last Chevrolet commercial had faded from the screen, Robert nevetheless felt a lingering sense of loss that somehow pertained to more than just an imaginary hank of hair.

. . .

As a reaction to Steven's long, involved journey to the centre of his psyche (and goddamnit she resented forever reacting to things Steven did or thought) Kathleen felt herself grow harder and more self-sufficient. If he was so intent on inflicting change on their lives, she would do everything in her power to live by the rules of stability and practicality.

During one quarrel, Steven told her she was so down to earth she was choking on humus. This became the focus of their general conflict. Since change is the unifying force of the physical world, Kathleen was at a clear disadvantage.

Steven's search for deeper meaning in the everyday was, to her, no more productive a use of time than her father's hours spent with the *Presley Gleaner* folded on his lap, solving yet another exasperating crossword puzzle with its exasperating five-letter rivers in Zambia. The crossword puzzles at least relaxed her father, whereas Steven's odyssey to self-realization seemed no more than a walk down a long lit fuse to inevitable dynamite. Sometimes the fuse dashed a great distance in the blink of an eye or the turn of a phrase; sometimes it settled into the slowest of burns. But the fire never went out.

Kathleen tried to fill the gap left by her husband's flights of fancy with her maternal duties— loving, feeding, clothing, sheltering, comforting and scolding Robert when necessary. Most things that seemed to have come naturally to her mother's generation felt like a conscious chore to her.

Now that Robert was in school, her days felt pointless and more tiring than ever. One evening, Steven volunteered to babysit Robert so Kathleen could have a night out with her old friend Helen

Munsinger. Kathleen tried to work up the energy to explain to Steven that the time fathers spent with their sons didn't qualify as babysitting. Instead, she thanked him and went to Chow's Chow with Helen Munsinger for take-out *subgum guy ding* and sympathy.

Helen Munsinger lived in a two-bedroom apartment near the Rosseters' semi-detached home. The apartment struck Kathleen as an uncanny representation of her own domestic ideal, even if the furniture was nothing special and the old plaster walls were warped and cracked. It always seemed warm and cosy in Helen's place, as though it were full of invisible, inaudible loved ones she never had to pick up after.

"You always keep your place so nice," Kathleen said.

"My mother says it's too stark. She wants to know why I haven't started collecting Waterford crystal. I told her I got a set of perfectly nice tumblers from the Texaco. Expectations cause ulcers, Kath. She wants me married. She never imagined I'd waste my whole hope chest on myself."

Helen set down two cups of Spanish coffee. Kathleen took her cup and blew into it.

"Sometimes I wish I was single."

"Promiscuous, you mean," Helen said.

"I'm serious."

It wasn't sex she craved, or even love. Just an even keel for a while. Calm seas, like Helen's apartment. Doldrums, even. She tried to explain it.

"Steven wants more of everything, but he's prepared to do less and less. I'm willing to do more and take less, because I find the more I do, the less concerned I am about how much I'm taking. Do you know what I mean?"

"More or less," said Helen.

"I just don't know if I want to do more of anything with him anymore."

"*For* him, you mean," Helen said, lighting a Benson & Hedges. "That's always what it boils down to in a relationship. Look at the thing biologically and tell me the body-language of love isn't a bunch of ingrown male fascism. Look at who does the invading and who does the accommodating. We live longer than men but they win all the battles. Multiply this by a thousand generations and what you have is a world run by penis-mongers."

"Penis-mongers?"

"Absolutely," said Helen, exhaling a cloud of smoke. "They act and think and run the world with their weenies. Swords, guns, rockets, bombs— you name it. It all boils down to biology. Men exploit biology to exploit the world and the women in it. We still haven't learned to identify ourselves as something more than a warm place men visit from time to time after they get tired of maiming and killing each other."

"I'm not interested in identifying myself, Helen. That's Steven's hobby, not mine. All I want is to feel I have some control over my life, without having to tell myself every few minutes how wonderful it is to have control."

"If you want some control you have to step out into the world. Get a job, Kath. Show those penis-mongering sons of dogs a thing or two."

"Jesus God, I can't just drop everything," Kathleen said, wondering exactly what everything consisted of.

"Get a part-time job. Your dad could sit with Bobby now and then. He's at your place a lot of the time as it is. You said yourself he spends more time with Bobby than Steven does. Bobby's at school all day. There's nothing to stop you."

Kathleen looked around Helen's orderly living room with its thriving houseplants. Maybe some people and houseplants were instrinsically more alive than others. Maybe she, Kathleen, was meant to spend her life in a *demi-monde* of nagging doubts and drooping philodendrons. Helen struck her as a slimmer, brighter, more voluptuous variation on herself (not that she wanted to use those criteria for determining intrinsic worth, and not that Helen saw herself that way at all). In short, she felt like a 25-watt bulb.

"What would I work at?" she sighed. "And how do I know that getting a job would suddenly make everything all right? I'd like Bobby to be happier, to come out of himself more. I'd like to feel I have some say in where my life is going. Other than that. . ."

"And Steven?" said Helen, butting her cigarette. "What do you want for him?"

Kathleen tapped her nails against the arm of the couch. "I guess I want him to find whatever he's looking for, but to do it in a hurry. I want him to get it over with, whatever it is."

"Everybody has to give up their illusions. That's what you're saying."

"Is it? I don't even know what the illusions are."

"If you did," said Helen, reaching for another cigarette, "they wouldn't be illusions."

When the time came, it didn't seem to matter what the work was. What counted most was to get out from under Steven, to play at life rather than have it played on her. Through a friend of Helen's she found a part-time job in the record and tape department of Presley TV & Audio. Never mind that her only co-worker, Charmaine, was nineteen, a Who fanatic and her boss. Never mind that Steven said the job was beneath her dignity and intelligence. What did he know of her dignity and intelligence, he of the Friday afternoons and evenings at the Riverview, consorting with philosopher-transients? Since he seemed to be spending so much time interrogating everything, Kathleen vowed to restore the balance by questioning her own instincts as little as possible. This helped her tolerate all the Who records on the store stereo. Eventually she took one home and actually played it, as a symbol of her resolve. She even grew fond of one of the songs. It was called "Won't Get Fooled Again". It became her anthem.

. . .

On Fridays, when Kathleen had to work late at the record store and Steven was agonizing at the Riverview, P.W. joined his grandson for supper. Kathleen put the meal on in the early afternoon, during her lunch break, and left precise instructions for her son to eat his vegetables. More often than not the vegetables were frozen green beans that seemed to glow on Robert's plate. He hated them and told P.W. so.

"Mom says if I don't eat them I'm wasting food and that's a sin because so many people are starving in Bang. . . Banga. . ."

"Bangladesh," P.W. prompted.

"Mom says thousands of kids are starving there. We saw pictures on TV of babies with great big bellies and flies all over their face. She says it's a sin for us to throw food away when those babies are so hungry. We wouldn't have to throw the green beans away if she didn't buy them. The babies in Bangadesk probably wouldn't even know it was food."

"Bangla*desh.*"

"Mom could buy cream corn, or even beets. I don't mind those. Or we could mail the green beans to Bangadesk, if she wants."

"As charity, you mean."

"Yeah. To help them out."

"That's not charity," P.W. said. "That wouldn't count for anything."

"Yes it would."

"No it wouldn't, because you wouldn't be giving up anything you wouldn't rather do without. What's your favourite food?"

Robert stared at the swiss steak on his plate for a moment. "Shreddies," he said.

"Then send Shreddies to the babies in Bangladesh. Give every bowl of Shreddies you were going to eat over the next six months and mail them off. Even if the Shreddies go bad before they reach Bangladesh, at least you'll be sacrificing something to honour those babies."

"That's *stu*-pid," Robert said.

"Define your terms," P.W. demanded, adding salt he wasn't supposed to add to his steak.

"I like Shreddies. It's the green beans I want to get rid of."

"That's the whole point," said P.W. "Just because you're finishing your plate doesn't mean you're not wasting food. We have so much to eat in this part of the world that it doesn't really matter whether we eat the green beans, or the Cutlers' dog does, or it goes straight into the garbage and out of the house to be turned into landfill. The food goes back into the earth whether you eat it or not. If you put it in the mail, it'll go bad, get thrown into the garbage. No matter what you personally do today, some babies in Bangladesh will die and go back into the earth. Everything and everyone does eventually. You, as one little boy in Ontario, can't really help the people you saw on television. But you can honour them and give them a bit of extra dignity, Bob, by eating all those green beans and giving up Shreddies for a while."

P.W. took a long sip of tea while Robert rolled a greenbean around the plate with his fork. "That's *stu*-pid," he reiterated.

P.W. abhorred the word "stupid". He wondered where his grandson had picked it up. Probably at school, among his little peers. He let it pass.

"What your ma probably has never told you," he said, "is that we're just as poor as all those babies in Bangladesh, only in a different way. We're poor because we haven't any idea what real poverty is. No one has ever seen God on a full stomach, Bob. Check the Bible. Your ma's generation wants for nothing, but they feel very far away from God. They want to want. They go around looking for something to want. The TV points them in the direction of electric toothbrushes and emotional luggage. Everything points them far, far away from God. Those babies in Bangladesh, believe it or not, have great big bellies because they're full of the grace of God. I'm old and my bones ache because God is creeping into them. God is in the earth, waiting for all the food that gets thrown away and for all those babies in Bangladesh to come back home. God is in those green beans," he said, pointing at the boy's plate.

"These?" said Robert, incredulously.

"Every last one of them."

Robert gaped at his vegetables.

"Eat 'em up and send 'em home to earth."

Robert didn't fully grasp the lesson, but he ate his green beans anyway.

In an effort to take his grandfather's words to heart, he began to look for God in the nooks and crannies of his house and the world. He did it discreetly, because he sensed his mother and father didn't care about God and wouldn't have approved. It wasn't that his mother and father were against God, but they weren't exactly cheering for him, either. He remembered the time his father told him about the myth of Jesus, God's only begotten Son who was born to suffer for the sins of the world. Steven said a lot of people still believe Jesus was God's only begotten Son, but we should think of him instead as a very great man who still inspires millions of people two thousand years later, just like the great prophets in the myths of other races. Robert wanted to know what "begotten" meant, and Steven said that he, Robert, was his, Steven's, only begotten son, which didn't clarify the matter in the least and in fact left Robert with the impression that he and Jesus were a lot alike.

Privately, Robert wondered what was the use of a myth if it wasn't meant to be believed. He enjoyed the stories about Jesus and thought of him as a kind of ancient superhero who was capable of interceding on earth in the name of truth, justice and so on. But it wasn't until he met Eddie Laverty that he learned there was potentially more of Jesus and God in some places than others.

Eddie Laverty had assumed the artifacts and implements of faith in his home were as common to all households as toasters and toilets. He began to discover otherwise only after his father, an editorial writer with the *Gleaner*, pulled him out of the separate school system. It was Mr. Laverty's considered opinion— though he was not at liberty to editorialize on it— that the Catholic Church was pushing ecumenism too hard. "Better no religious instruction at school than watered-down religious instruction," he informed Mrs. Laverty, who informed the principal of Mother St. Bride Separate School, who informed one of the trustees of the separate school board, who informed his good friend Tony Gerbasi, Mr. Laverty's boss at the *Gleaner*, who informed Mr. Laverty that an editorial on the subject would not now or ever be welcome.

Steven and Kathleen decided early on not to send their son to a Catholic school. Kathleen had heard too many horror stories about the nearby College of St. Vitus from her father, who had been deported there for several formative years by his father to master Greek, Latin and the art of eating bad food without complaining, and emerged with a *summa cum laude* diploma and profound misgivings about the Catholic system. He passed these misgivings on to Kathleen, who agreed there was something altogether too militaristic about the Jesuits. Steven's lack of piety was similarly handed down from his elders, though more out of neglect than philosophical doubt.

Robert Rosseter and Eddie Laverty were fish out of water at Sir Charles Tupper Public School. The two boys didn't properly make one another's acquaintance until the second grade when, in accordance with a regional directive, the local public school board ordered a trial moratorium on the recital of The Lord's Prayer in class. Their teacher, Miss Hornung, spent the better part of a cold November morning alternately explaining the new directive and railing against it.

"The school board has to follow the rules and that's all there is to it," Miss Hornung said, slapping one dry red hand onto the palm of the other to emphasize key words. "Whether you (slap) like it or not, whether I (slap) like it or not—which I don't (slap)—even whether Mr. Brunk (slap) likes it or not doesn't change the fact that we have to obey (slap) the new rule. These are times full of permissive (slap) ideas, but we still (slap) have to abide by the rules (slap). Do you all un(slap)der(slap)stand(slap)?"

"Yes, Miss Hornung," came the desultory reply.

Most of the children didn't have a strong opinion one way or the other on The Lord's Prayer. But Eddie Laverty seemed genuinely distressed by the news. At recess, he and Robert gravitated to the fence at the far end of the schoolyard, where they took to kicking the gravel around.

"My dad won't like it," Eddie said. "He makes us say the rosary every night at home."

"What's the rosary?" Robert said.

"It's a string of beads you say prayers on. You keep track of where you are with the beads. One time my cousin was sleeping over and we were watching *Star Trek.* My dad turned off the TV and told me to lead the rosary with my little sister. I felt about this high."

Robert tried to picture the scene. In recent weeks his father occasionally insisted on quoting a passage of Kahlil Gibran. Steven expected Robert to sit attentively.

"And then I get teased about it," Eddie said, "because only fairies are pious."

"What's pious?"

"I don't know. People who say the rosary every day. My dad says Pope Pius was pious."

"Who's Pope Pius?"

"We have a picture of him at our house. He was the leader of the Catholics."

Robert dug into the gravel with the heel of his shoe. "I wouldn't tease you about the rosary," he said.

"Do you have the same thing at your house?"

"No, nothing like that. My parents never pray. I don't think they believe in God. My dad's an accountant."

Eddie kicked gravel through the chain-link fence and said, "Do you believe in God?"

"I guess so. Sure." No one had ever asked him that before. "My grampa says God is in green beans."

"Green beans? Yuck."

"He says God is in everything."

"Even the Seymour tree?" Eddie said skeptically.

The two boys glanced in the direction of the atrophied elm,

alone and terminally diseased near the asphalt play court. The tree was named after Rita Seymour, a grade seven student who, according to legend, had languished in the same class since the Second World War. Rita Seymour had long dirty hair, a wart on the end of her nose and yellow-brown teeth. Most of the younger students didn't doubt for a moment she was a witch. The diseased elm was called the Seymour tree because one day Rita Seymour decided to climb it during recess, and the tree began to die soon afterward. The students didn't dare touch the Seymour tree, for fear of catching the disease.

"God's not in the Seymour tree," Eddie said.

"I don't know. I'd have to ask my Grampa."

"Sometimes I don't think God actually hears the Hail Marys and Our Fathers. He must be tired of them by now. My mother says God hears everything and people saying their prayers together makes him happy."

"Like before class in the morning."

"Yeah, or in church."

Robert nodded and kicked the gravel. He wondered what church was like. He and his dad used to play Monopoly together on Sunday morning. Now Robert watched TV alone more often than not: Italian programs with commercials about pasta and tomato sauce. Most Sundays his father slept until noon.

"Church is where God spends most of his time," Eddie said, kicking the fence itself, which produced a satisfying ring. He did it again a few times. Robert stepped forward and did the same. They were oblivious to the other children filing back to class, to the biting wind stinging their cheeks, to the gravel grown hard from the cold November nights. The low grey sky suited their mood of mysterious oppression.

Inside the classroom, Miss Hornung eventually noticed two empty seats, went to the window and spied the truants together in the far end of the yard, vandalizing the fence. Soon she was outside, pleated navy skirt fluttering in the wind as she marched across the yard.

"High mass is dull because of the long sermon," Eddie said.

"I've never been to church," Robert confessed.

"Never at all?"

"Well, for my baptism, I think, but that's the only time."

"Maybe you'd like it. It's nice when the priest gets the incense going and the. . . uh-oh, here comes Miss Hornung."

"See here (clap-clap)" their teacher said, bearing down on them.

"Is recess over, Miss Hornung?" Eddie asked.

"Is it over (clap)? Of all the permissive (clap). . ."

Just then a gust of wind sideswiped Miss Hornung. Her pleated skirt billowed up above her waist, giving Robert and Eddie, junior theologians, their first clear look at a woman's underthings— nylons, garter belt and blinding white panties. Up to that moment, they had never thought of Miss Hornung as a person of one or the other sex, let alone a female. The day was full of fundamental discoveries.

Miss Hornung didn't stay mortified for long. "We'll see what Mr. Brunk has to say about this," she said, her hands too busy subduing her wayward skirt to clap out the customary italics.

Robert's first visit to Eddie's house was an eye-opener. Prominent in the Laverty living room was an imposing portrait of Jesus. The artist had worked especially hard on the prophet's eyes, investing them with an Old Testament fury. This Jesus seemed tremendously displeased with everyone he laid eyes on.

In the dining room the Blessed Virgin Mary, in an azure robe with her heart dislodged from her body, gazed down benignly at a bowl of plastic bananas on the Laverty table.

Above an oak buffet was a framed photograph of Pope Pius XII. Robert wondered if the severe former leader of the Catholics had smiled in his lifetime.

In the upstairs hallway, over the door to the master bedroom, Christ was impaled on a large wooden cross. Bright red blood oozed from his palms and feet, with cursory wounds over the rest of the body and more blood flowing from the crown of thorns. "Deeky," Robert said.

Eddie saved the *pièce de resistance* for last. Ushering Robert into a spare bedroom, he removed a large, off-white statue of the Virgin from atop a chest of drawers, switched on a night-table lamp and held the statue close to the light.Then he turned off the light and, holding the statue behind his back, guided Rosseter into the closet. "Hurry up," he said, and closed the door behind him.

"It's pitch-black in here," Robert noted with evident lack of enthusiasm, "and it smells weird."

"Shhh," said Eddie. "Are you ready?"

Suddenly, miraculously, ascending in the suffocating darkness was Mary, Mother of God, aglow in ethereal phosphorescent green. "It's blessed by Bishop Devine," Eddie said as he caused the statue of the Virgin to soar and dive like a stunt biplane.

Later, in his bedroom, Eddie regaled Robert with tales of the Shroud of Turin, exorcism, and people in the Third World who broke out in stigmata every Good Friday. The stories, like the statues and the pictures, left Robert with an overall impression of religion as a strangely heartening brand of creepiness.

The impression lasted. For weeks afterward, most of Robert's time at home was spent hand-copying religious images from a small Bible Eddie had smuggled out of his house. Robert was particularly enchanted by a series of chiaroscuros of the Holy Family captured in moments of simple domestic bliss— Joseph making a table, young Jesus watching his father attentively, Mary cooking corned beef in the background. Here was the nuclear family idealized. Robert was at least partly drawn to these images because he saw that his own nuclear family was on the verge of meltdown. Whereas Eddie's parents seemed to have been carved from stone (Mr. Laverty reminded Robert of Moses in the little Bible with a haircut and a shave), his own parents struck him as the merest flickers of projected light. His father pondered Herman Hesse, let his hair grow over his collar and created an invisible force field around himself. His mother, apparently less committed than ever to seeing Steven through what he now called his period of transition, sensed a coating of doom over the floors, walls and ceilings of their semi-detached house. She put what little remaining trust she had in industrial-strength cleansers.

On the Saturday before Christmas 1971, after the tree was decorated and a rare atmosphere of cordial serenity had settled over the home, Giles Robert Rosseter talked his mother and father into sitting for a portrait. As snow fell softly on the front yard and carols wafted from the stereo, he sketched furiously with a pencil, studying his parents, side by side on the couch, as though he had never seen them before. He sketched the lean, urgent contours of his father's face, the sunken cheeks and eyes like coal lamps burning unevenly, dark thin hair matted and unruly. Then his mother, her hair a sea of red waves roiling around green eyes set in features as changeable as the weather in December. Robert drew and drew, wishing the minutes would last forever, wishing he had never lost an infant's knack of living outside of time.

Nothing Steven or Kathleen said convinced him to show them his rough sketch. Instead, he retired to his room to work it into shape with colouring pencils. On Christmas morning he presented his parents with a charming tableau of the Rosseter family: Steven hunched over an accounts book at his desk, Robert admiring Steven's calculations over his shoulder and Kathleen in the background, rolling dough. The title of his drawing was O Come All Ye Faithful.

The fact that Steven never brought his work home, that Robert was bored stiff by what little he'd heard about accounting and that Kathleen hadn't baked a loaf of bread in her life troubled none of them, least of all the artist.

* * *

4

> In life's equation there are no easy solutions. We are the product of our upbringing, the sum of what we feel and think, the quotient of everything we doubt, and the remainder of what we decide to do for our next number.
>
> —Theodore Ng

In the north country, seasons move like the hour-hand of a clock—ineluctably, though unseen by the naked eye. Snow and ice fade to mud and tulips; leaves mature, flare into outrageous colour, then form a slick ground carpet on rainy days. Sometimes the seasons mark outward time with such regularity that they blot out inward time. That's what was so distracting about them. Still, the greater the distraction the more sudden the reminder, whether noted or not, that time had passed and lives had changed.

The city of Presley, in 1972, was heaven for meteorologists. So closely did their various readings conform to the average that the year, for them at least, was almost impossibly perfect. Snow fell when it was supposed to and in the appropriate accumulations. The end of January was fittingly coldest and dryest. That week, a strong inversion froze the temperature at -31 Fahrenheit for two days and trapped the sicklysweet toxic emissions from the 4P over the city. Three people died of respiratory complications. (Three, naturally, was the average number of weather-related deaths in a given Presley winter.) February, right on time, was grey and dispiriting, March a hodge-podge of wind, snow and sleet, and so on and on through all the months. Not a single weather record was broken in 1972. It was an exceptionally unexceptional year; people lost track of themselves in it.

The spring of 1973, as if to make up for the previous year's lack of invention, came surprisingly early. By late March, people were wielding axes on their backyard patios, cutting away four months of snow and ice, heaping thick, grey sheets of it onto snowdrifts elsewhere in the yard to make room for lawn chairs. In the mornings, women ventured out in two-piece swimsuits, their pale dry bodies more conspicuously naked than in the summertime. They got a start on their tan as portable radios played in the background. Sometimes they even ignored the telephone. If a breeze came up, carrying remnants of Arctic air, they fled indoors and leafed through magazines until the winds subsided. Some of them were horrified to discover lost pieces of their best silverware glinting in the sun in some part of the yard where one or another of their children had played with things they weren't supposed to play with. Spring was full of surprises.

Since childhood, Kathleen's recurring fantasy had been that a body would turn up under the melting snow in her backyard—perhaps that of a hobo who had mistaken the O'Hagan house for a manse. Bums had been known to wander up to their door and ask her mother for a tomato sandwich or whatever she could manage. Kathleen's fantasy was that the bum knocked on the door in the middle of a stormy winter night but the sound was lost in the howl of the wind and the rattle of storm windows. The bum then staggered into the backyard, sought entry from there, eventually gave up and collapsed in the snow, which buried him by morning. The cold then preserved his remains until a warm sunny spring day, when a gnarled grey hand protruded from a melting drift. Invariably, Kathleen was the one who discovered the hand. Consequently she didn't believe in premature patio ice-clearing. Instead she stretched out in denim cut-offs and an old swimsuit top on the steps of the small back stoop. She wasn't due at work until two that afternoon, so she closed her eyes and snuggled in the bonus warmth of the March sun.

From one of the yards down the street came the sound of a radio. *"Daniel is travelling tonight on a plane. . . "* She drifted into a memory of when she was a girl. Her father took her to the beach at Lake Mead, where the water was as still as a window and there was a slide and monkey bars for her to hang by her legs, soaking wet, the water dripping from her hair onto the sand. *Maybe we'll just leave you there hanging out to dry,* her father teased, and she thought of bringing her wagon next time and filling it with sand to take home, with mud in the seat of her bathing suit that left a stain on the backseat of the Plymouth. *It gets on our Sunday clothes so spread out a towel over the seat, Kathy. Here's one that has your name on it: Kathy O'Hagan, princess of the monkey bars. Darwin would be proud of you, Darwin would like to meet you and put your name in his next book. . .*

"Kath?"

She opened her eyes and sat up. Steven was standing at the back door.

"What brings you home?" she said, squinting.

"How come you didn't answer the phone?"

"Answer me first."

"I told Dancey I wasn't feeling well. He bought it and gave me the afternoon off. I've got the vernal equinox blues, Kath. The reason I called was to find out what you were up to today."

"Up to? I have to work at two."

"I mean right now."

"Getting some sun," Kathleen said with a shrug.

"You look great."

"I'm as pale as a sheet."

"I like you pale."

"I want a tan."

"Pale suits you."

"Do you think so?"

"It really does. Come in and I'll show you," Steven said, taking her hand and leading her into the house.

"Steven, I have to—"

"Shh," said Steven, guiding her up the stairs and into their bedroom.

"You can't be serious. You—wait a minute." He unclasped her swimsuit top. "Jesus God, I don't have time to. . . Steven!" He tugged at the zipper of her cut-offs. "Hold on a minute, will you? You know I—" His mouth against hers successfully lit a fire under memories of past embraces.

Eventually they fell onto the bed and squirmed out of what was left of their clothes. She rolled on top of him with a conspiratorial giggle. Part of her wondered what was going on here. She thought fleetingly of the unlocked front door, the open bedroom door, of Bobby and when he was due home. Then she forgot about it and threw herself into the twisting, the breathing, the creak of bed-spring and rattle of headboard. The phone rang for a while and then it didn't ring anymore. Car doors slammed down the street. The air in the room smelled of spring. Warm skin against cold, they wrestled in a tangle of sheets.

A part of Steven was conscious of the traffic outside, of birdsong. Eventually it all faded and he was nobody, the way he liked it, just a wild animal using instinct to find the deepest, warmest part of oblivion. *Go. Go. Go. Go. Lose yourself, you nobody. Go. Go. Lose yourself. But not yet, not yet. No, not not yet wait no Jesus—*

She came, violently, and it made him come. . .

Now they were who they were again, lying on their bed. Her breathing almost a wheeze, just like always. Soon she'll want to remake the bed and put on makeup for work. She'll kiss him on some neutral spot like the shoulder, make a playful grab at his pitiful shrivelled dink.

"I didn't hear it," Kathleen said, pulling a sheet up over them.

"Hear what?"

"I'm answering your question from before. I didn't hear the telephone when you called."

"Oh. Where's Bob?"

"He and Eddie went to Daddy's house. They wanted to look at his old 78s. Did you know that our stereo doesn't play 78s? I didn't know that."

"What time did he go over?"

"You don't seem very relaxed, Stevie."

"I'm relaxed. What time."

"I don't know; around nine-thirty."

Steven sat up. "I'm supposed to be sick. Did you know that? I told Dancey there was a family crisis and he—"

"Which did you tell him?"

"Huh?"

"Did you tell him you were sick or there was a family crisis?"

"Both. Or that the family crisis was making me sick, or vice versa. A family sickness was causing a crisis. Whatever."

"You seem agitated."

"I'm fine, Kath. For Chrissake." He rolled out of bed.

"Where are you going?"

"Maybe Bob and I can go for a drive. Get a bite to eat somewhere."

"That sounds nice. When?"

"Now," Steven said.

Kathleen laughed and pulled the sheet up to her chin. Steven sorted through his clothes, put on his underwear.

"What's so funny?"

"I don't know," she said, watching her husband and luxuriating in the laughter.

"I don't see what's so goddamned funny," Steven said, pulling on his pants.

"Me neither." Yet she couldn't stop laughing.

"That's annoying, Kath," he said, looking for a stray sock. "You're going to ruin this moment if you're not careful."

"What moment?" said Kathleen, still laughing.

"There, you ruined it."

"I'm. . . s-sorry." She fought to stifle a fresh round of guffaws. "I guess it's this short but sweet romantic interlude of yours."

Steven stared at his wife. "Why do you always have to demean everything that goes on between us? Does it make you feel powerful?"

"I don't know what you're talking about," Kathleen said, her laughter stilled.

"You like to sit back and laugh at eveything. You're so busy being irreverent that your whole life is passing you by. I can't find my goddamned sock." He wrenched open a dresser drawer, dug out a fresh pair. "You have a knack for spoiling special times. It tires me out."

"What are you talking about, Steven? I didn't spoil anything. You're the one who insists on being so bloody solemn all the time."

"You're a drag, Kathleen, and you're dragging me down with you."

"Wo there, matey," said Kathleen, sitting up against the headboard. "You have no right to say that."

"I know what I know," Steven said, putting on his socks.

Kathleen felt tears welling. "What kind of son of a bitch are you to arrive unannounced and expect me to drop whatever I was doing for a roll in the sack? And in case you forgot already, I did drop what I was doing."

"How could I forget? I was the roll and you were the sack."

Kathleen's mouth formed a silent O of shock, then hardened.

"You're suck a jerk."

"And you're frigid."

"Fuck off."

"Gladly," Steven said. He walked out of the room.

From her bed, amid the debris of their love, Kathleen heard the bathroom faucet, the click of the medicine cabinet door, the flush of the toilet, footsteps down the stairs, the slam of the front door, the slam of the car door, the revving of the Camaro, and afterwards, faintly through the window, the sound of a neighbour's portable radio in an ice-jammed backyard.

. . .

Robert, Eddie and P.W. were playing gentleman's poker on P.W.'s verandah. Despite the warm sunshine, P.W. wore a woolen sweater. Steven was relieved to see them all as he pulled into the driveway; at least he wouldn't have to knock on the door.

"A full house does not beat four of a kind," P.W. told his grandson. "Somebody sold you a bill of goods."

"Hi," Steven said from the foot of the stairs.

"Dad, what's better? A full house or four of a kind?"

"Four of a kind, I think. Playing poker, are you?"

"But I thought a full house. . ."

"You should have taken my word for it," P.W. said. He gathered the pile of toothpicks from the centre of the table.

"My deal," said Eddie.

"Why are you here?" Robert asked his father, not unkindly, but Steven nevertheless winced.

"Aces and kings are wild," Eddie said. "One five-card draw, no bets before the draw."

"That's *stu*-pid," Robert said. "Why not a two-card draw with bets before and after?"

"One five-card draw," Eddie repeated. "No bets before."

"I took the afternoon off," Steven said. "Since you're not at school this week, I thought maybe you'd like to go for a drive and stop off somewhere later for a hamburger."

"Right now?" said Robert, examining his cards.

"We probably should," Steven said. "It still gets dark early."

Robert looked at his grandfather, who divided his toothpicks into little piles and said, "Go, if you want to."

"Can Eddie come, too?"

"I was hoping it could be just the two of us," Steven said.

"That's all right," said Eddie, who was trying in vain to shuffle the cards with one hand.

"Let him come, Dad. It'll be more fun."

P.W. looked up at Steven. "You look terrible," he said. "Did you just get out of bed?"

"As a matter of fact I did," Steven answered. "But I feel a lot better now."

Out on the open road the Camaro rolled smoothly, destination who knows where. Steven was at home in the car. The world looked so friendly through the windshield. All you had to do was keep to one side of the broken white line. He loved to steady his foot on the gas and turn the radio up loud, Janis Joplin wailing about her and Bobby McGee. Robert sat up front, Eddie leaned forward from the back seat. "Do you always drive this fast, Mr. Rosseter?"

Steven laughed. "Only when conditions are favourable and it feels good."

Robert leaned over and eyeballed the speedometer.

"You're doing 75, Dad." Steven eased off the gas.

Eddie watched a dumptruck recede in the rear windshield after Steven had pulled out to overtake it. "That's okay with me," he said. "My parents drive too slow. My mother doesn't let my father pass anybody."

"I've been in the car with your dad," Robert said. "He drives okay."

"No he doesn't. He drives like we're coming from a funeral."

Steven laughed.The Camaro ate up the asphalt; power lines traced sine waves out the side windows. Robert watched the power lines and bobbed his head along with them. Steven dialed another radio station and the topic shifted to poker.

"My father doesn't believe in gambling," Eddie said dolefully.

Steven glanced at him in the rearview mirror. "Is that so? Bob and me have been playing poker since he was a baby." He turned the radio up.

"We used to play Monopoly a lot," Robert said to Eddie over the din of the radio. "You should see my mom if you want to see someone who can really play Monopoly. All she ever buys are the four railroads and Baltic and Mediterranean. She says buying Boardwalk and Park Place is a waste of money. She says everybody always lands on the railroads and there are all sorts of cards that say you have to pay twice the amount for landing on Reading or B&O, and people don't mind landing on Baltic or Mediterranean even with hotels on them because they're so cheap, but the money adds up. It always works for her."

Steven glanced over at his son. "Always?"

"Just about. I don't know why you like the green and yellow properties. Houses cost too much and nobody ever lands on them."

"All kinds of people land on them," Steven protested. "I always make a lot of money off Marvin Gardens."

"My father likes the utilities best," Eddie said. "He says they're reliable and they pay their own way."

"What do you like best?" Robert asked his friend.

"Jail," Eddie said.

"That's *stu*-pid," Robert said.

"Why do you like jail, Eddie?" Steven asked, fiddling with the radio dial.

"Because it's peaceful there and you don't have to pay anybody anything."

"I guess he's got a point," Steven said. News came on. He fiddled some more with the dial. News everywhere.

"American casualties—President Nixon vowed—in major-league action in Florida—with no relief in sight—will go to arbitration—over North Vietnamese accusations in Paris— toward Mr. Hoffa—and scattered showers over most of the—free world, Nixon said."

Steven shut off the radio. Just the wind whistling through the chinks now. The road out of town reminded him of the way Sault Ste. Marie looked nowadays, all hydro wires and billboards and Dairy Queens. When he was Bob's age you could listen for the milkman's horse, clipclop clipclop, coming toward his house, then the jangle of bottles and the scraping of glass against cement at the foot of your door. In the winter the milk froze and the bottles exploded; the horseshit in the street was hard as rock and good for road hockey. But no Camaros back then. He'll gladly take a few billboards and a few Dairy Queens in exchange for the Camaro. Dad and his De Soto, now that was something. All shiny and new for years and years because he never drove it in the winter, never went anywhere in the winter. Didn't even park it. Had it stored. And he never gave the engine a proper workout on the highway to Blind River. *Why is this car a piece of junk already?* he'd say. *I've taken care of it. Steve, have you been monkeying around with it? You're the type that has to be watched all the time. You can't be trusted. What did I tell you about monkeying around in the garage? You and your damned chums. Edgar tells me the same thing. Next time it's the police, do you hear? Next time I call the police.* As if the police ever solved anything. As if the police ever made any kind of difference.

"Stop jumping from station to station like that," he said. "I'll find us a good station. What sort of music do you want to hear?"

"The Beatles," Eddie suggested.

"Not the Beatles," said Robert. "They're not together anymore. Let's find something by a group that's together now."

The later it is in the day the more stations the radio picks up—trans-border signals bouncing off clouds, people with twangy voices and strange diets of chitlins and collard greens talking up the Holy Babel and Jaysos. Something creepy about the southern States— out of control or on the verge of totally primitive. Voodoo. Sons of sons of sons of slaves with West Africa in their DNA, and the po waht folk just tranta mek they own weh, full o' the feah of Gawd and the feah o' the nigras. Mostly the nahth buhned in the '60s, 'cause they ain't many cities in the sahth, and the waht folk got they own voodoo— buhnin crosses and fran Nigras in lectic chehs.

"My father has this short-wave radio," Eddie said, "that picks up the overseas stations. He says he wishes the Vatican made some programs in English instead of just Italian and Latin. He likes the stations in Spain because of the guitar songs they play, that flamingo music."

"Y'all lak flamingo music?" Steven said, laughing, imagining long-necked birds dancing, dancing.

"Pardon?"

"It's okay. Newstime."

"Renewed tension at the peace talks in Paris when the North Vietnamese—ratified a three-year—storm that left thousands homeless—in a parade of fashions to—neighbouring Pakistan where the Indian prime minister hoped to—make the most of your shopping dollar."

Click.

"I'm hungry," Robert said. "Where are we?"

"A little bit west, following the sun," said Steven. On the road and as free as we'll ever be. (How long would it take to get to Winnipeg?) "On the road like a toad that growed."

"Let's play the rhyme game, Dad, until we find a restaurant. You start."

"Let a fart," Eddie blurted, and the two boys squealed as the sun shone a strobe light through the trees. Have a heart. Make a start. Take a part. Take apart. . .

The music is back on here in this middle of nowhere. They'll stop for a burger and fries and a Coke and banana split, eat the ice cream and nuts on the roadside as long-distance rigs barrel past, kicking up government sand left over from winter, then they'll hit the road again in the long shadows that become all shadow. The radio will play for a while, then they'll shut it off and Eddie will complain about all his father's rules and Robert will defend Mr. Laverty for no good reason, and he'll laugh and wonder what people say about him behind his back as they pass a station wagon full of sleepy Girl Guides. The Camaro will eat more asphalt while the last light of day makes a stand on the road dead ahead, and there will be no easing the pace now because this is the life, this is motion without motive, this is wild animal, this being out here.

"Bobby, I've got something I need to talk to you about. . ."

Loving every minute of it.

"Bobby?. . ."

The boys bellyful and drifting off in the backseat.

"Bob."

"Hmmf. . ."

"I've got something I need to talk to you about."

"Un-hmmf."

"Something important."

"Fleepy. . ."

"I know," said Steven, and he did know. Low beams to high beams, a wall of dark conifers on either side of him, Ursa Major floating above them all. White black white black white black white black.

"Bob?"

On off on off on off on off. . . Something cool over the radio to suit the sleepy dashboard lights. Nobody doing news anymore, just easy listening just moving and not stopping and not wanting to stop over here on this side of a broken white line. . .

. . .

"Where the hell have you been," Kathleen said by way of a greeting. Steven had carried his son from the car to the front door; the boy was swaying on his feet at the foot of the stairs, awaiting further instructions. It was a little before one in the morning.

"I was hoping you'd be in bed," Steven said. "I'm really tired and I don't want to discuss anything."

"I don't give a damn what you want, Steven." She turned to Robert, who had started on his own up the stairs, and told him she'd be up to tuck him in.

"Eddie's father already poured the boiling oil. I don't need it from you or anybody else."

"You listen to me. Stanley Laverty was on the phone more times than I could count. He got a little more angry every time he called. I didn't know what to tell him because I didn't know where his son was or when he would be home. I've spent the last seven hours being a character witness for you, for the sake of my own reputation."

"Your reputation?" Steven said, slumping into an armchair. "This doesn't have anything to do with you. If a kid can't go for an innocent drive without having to answer to every Tom, Dick and Harriet, I don't know what the meaning of freedom is."

"That's just it."

"What?"

"You don't know what the meaning of freedom is."

"And you do?"

"I know what the meaning of respons—"

"You sit here twiddling your thumbs and think you have all the answers. That's because you're a watcher and I'm a doer. There's a hell of a difference between the two."

"A doer."

"That's right. I'm not too scared to move. We're miles apart, Kathleen. We don't think the same way. We don't even think the same things."

"And what about Eddie? Maybe his parents would have liked to know where their son was come eleven o'clock. Or does that strike you doer types as too hung up?"

"Don't lay your hangups on me. Take them up with your old man or something."

"You go to hell," Kathleen said. "You can't turn it around this time."

Steven sighed. "You'd swear I kidnapped the boys and took them to a brothel. They're home, safe and sound. What is the problem?"

"Where did you go?"

"To the Manitoba border," Steven said, dangling the car keys in front of his eyes, as though trying to hypnotize himself.

"What did you do there?"

"We turned around and came home. We're a bit late. Relax."

"Don't tell me to relax," Kathleen said.

"Don't relax, then."

"You're such an asshole. You don't understand the first thing about other people's feelings."

"Oh I understand perfectly, Kath. You, your old man, Eddie's old man— my old man, for Chrissake: You're all alike. None of you can handle a little spontaneity, a little of the unforeseen. You're control freaks and you're numb because you think that's the only safe way to live. So we stayed out a little later than we planned. Who's the worse for wear? Eddie's old man made a big stink about it being Ash Wednesday, there was a Mass the whole family was supposed to go to and because of me everything was disrupted. Did Eddie at any time ask to go home to catch this Mass? All he had to do was say the word and we would have scooted back. He never mentioned it, Kath. You ask Eddie and Bob tomorrow what kind of time they had and I guarantee you they'll say they had the time of their lives."

"And that's what it's all about, eh Stevie? Having the time of your life?"

"Sister," he said, hazarding a smile, "if you don't feel free you weren't meant to be."

"You know what, brother?" she said, "I don't think I know anyone who's more full of shit and self-congratulation than you."

And so it went that balmy March night, Steven and Kathleen Rosseter plumbing new depths together. For a time Steven had the upper hand, since Kathleen was the first to enlarge the scope of the argument. But in the course of a few heated minutes he eroded what advantage he may have had by launching wild spiteful offensives calculated solely to pile up the score against his wife. Better to have negotiated a draw of sorts with a mild admission of guilt; better to have been gracious and used what openings were left him to introduce the idea he'd been leading up to these many weeks— the idea being that he and Kathleen separate for a while.

("Will you listen to the bitch-goddess," he said.)

Why did he want to separate? For the love of freedom, he told himself again and again. For an end to restlessness and dissatisfaction. For a fresh start. Too many things had changed.

("What did you ever care about this family?" she said.)

A sense of common purpose had drained out of their marriage. Then again, had there ever been common purpose? Not really. Only mistakes and consequences from the word go. When the time came that a man's marriage and home life no longer nourished him, he had to do what was necessary to correct the situation. A miserable husband and father were hardly preferable to no husband and father at all.

("You make me want to puke. Your little habits and your little ways and your Mister Clean and your Spic & Span make me want to puke," he said.)

Compassion was a two-way street. Kathleen needed support and understanding, but when had she last paid more than token attention to his problems? She couldn't even begin to understand him. She was too caught up in her own little orderly world, her kitchen chrome and her record inventory.

("Don't talk to me that way. You can't talk to me that way," she said.)

He needed to be alone for a while. She wouldn't understand that. It would hurt not to see Bob every day—

("Daddy's little princess, just doing everything Daddy tells her to.")

—but if living apart for a while could straighten their relationship out—

("I wish you weren't his father. What a mistake that was.")

—it would make them both better parents in the long run. And that's what—

("You slut.")

—was most important. That's what he and Kathleen had to keep in mind at all times, regardless of anything that might come between them.

Kathleen touched her face where he had struck her. "Get out of this house. Get out!"

After Steven had departed for who knows where, after the tears were under control, Kathleen stepped quietly into Giles Robert's room. The boy had put himself to bed. His breathing was deep and rhythmic as she adjusted the covers and brushed her lips by his forehead. "Mama," he whispered as Kathleen was about to close the door behind her, "what's happening?"

"It's very late, sweetheart. Go back to sleep."

He rolled over to face her. "You and Dad had a big fight this time."

"Everyone quarrels now and again, Bobby. Go back to sleep."

"Mama?"

"Yes."

"What's better: a full house or four of a kind?"

"You'll have to ask your Grampa. Get to sleep now. Goodnight." She closed the door.

Before long, Robert saw the light go out in the crack under his door. He turned onto his back, clasped his hands behind his head. When he closed his eyes he could see the broken white lines of the highway disappearing under the Camaro. It always amazed him, when he walked alongside the highway, how long and far apart the little lines actually were. From a moving car they seemed only a couple of inches away from each other. Cars speeding by in the opposite direction said *wow* as they passed, as though sharing in the excitement of such a compressed world. He loved to stand on the side of the highway on hot summer days and listen for a big truck coming over the hill, headed his way. *Neeeeeeeeeeowwwwwwwww*, it said as it passed. At that speed, the truck had to be out of control. But he could never see the driver; the truck came and went too quickly, hauling steel rods from a mill in Duluth to the foot of James Bay.

If he concentrated, he could make out the shape of the *Star Trek* calendar on the wall above his desk. The indirect light of a streetlamp, soaking through the curtains, exaggerated shadows. He had already peeked ahead a couple of pages to June. Spock and Kirk with their phasers drawn. For his ninth birthday he would like the following things. . .

Thanksgiving Day 1970 pays a visit. Flashes of his mother's hair, her blurry presence. A photographic negative, forever suspect. Old family photographs gone sepia with the years. Great-Uncle Joe never smoked a cigar in his life, yet there he is, standing next to a shiny Plymouth that must have belonged to somebody. The past tells lies. And yet his father, all flesh and blood, sitting at the table with his wine, is a home movie. He speaks, he gestures with his arms, he cries. What does he say? What does he say?

Later he has a dream about his grandfather. They are raking leaves together in a backyard. The old man is wearing suspenders and you can see and smell the worn leather tobacco pouch in his back pocket. The dream is in black and white. Here is the best way to pile the leaves. Now pile them high, pile them high, pile them so high that the twigs won't scratch you when you jump around in them. I'll teach you a few words in Iroquois as soon as we've raked all the leaves. When the snow comes we'll flood the yard together with the garden hose and I'll show you how to skate like Jean Beliveau. We'll have a rink here in the winter but the ice will ruin the grass. In the spring it'll be black muck. Now here come all the colours for the leaves. Orange brown green yellow red violet and black for the stars. Quick, say your prayers to all of them: Forgive us our trespasses, as we forgive those who trespass against us.

. . .

P.W. stayed with his daughter for the first few days, sat with her and helped the boy through the rest of the March break. He had to keep reminding himself this wasn't his crisis. His honour hadn't been compromised by a do-nothing from Sault Ste. Marie. His life hadn't been turned upside down. Kathleen insisted on going to work, so he sat in her living room and stewed on her behalf. Robert stayed in his room and drew and drew—drew clouds he had never seen or imagined, plus a cumulonimbus or two for his grandfather.

Why did the little semi-detached house seem so vacant now, P.W. wondered. What is it that used to fill all this empty space?

Kathleen came home for supper and said Steven had phoned her at work. He was staying at the house Ansel Bedrosian and someone else rented. He was okay. He asked her if she was okay. She said she was. He said he'd be over for clothes and other things sometime when Bob wasn't around. Was there any way she could make sure he wasn't around tomorrow afternoon? He couldn't face him just now. He was sorry he hit her. He never hit her before. It was for the best that they be apart, wasn't it? To sort things out, come to terms, work through feelings, find themselves, get real, bottom line, state of flux, personal growth, self-love, spiritual tune-up, lube job. . .

"My husband's drowning in bullshit," Kathleen said out loud at the dinner table after Robert had been excused to watch television. "He actually believes the things he says. He's more lost than I ever imagined. I think there's something wrong with him. Jesus God, what's this going to do to Bobby? How is this all going to affect him?"

"Don't worry about the boy," P.W. said, worrying about the boy. "Tomorrow he and I will go out so What'shisname can come for his things. I'll take the boy to the house to have a look around the attic. He always wants to go up to the attic."

"What about me?" Kathleen said.

"You've seen the attic."

"I mean what about me in general."

"What about you?" he said, stifling a burp. "You're an O'Hagan, aren't you?"

The next morning was a lot cooler and P.W.'s legs ached. He let the boy in the house shortly after nine. They ignored the newspapers, magazines and coffee cups strewn about the front parlour. Kathleen had been doing her best to keep her father's house the way her mother did, but she hadn't come for the past few days, and keeping two houses would be even more difficult from now on. The answer was probably to close off another room or two and use the dining room for storage, since P.W. lived in the parlour, or on the verandah in good weather, ate his lunch in the kitchen while listening to the Dominion Observatory time signal and the CBC news on the radio, and took his dinner with the boy at Kathleen's. The real answer, of course, was to move in with Kathleen and the boy, particularly now that What'shisname had decamped. But he wanted none of that. There were too many familiar corners, favourite books in their favourite places, too many comfortable smells and vivid memories of Pauline here to abandon.

The attic of the house where Kathleen Andree O'Hagan spent her childhood was full of evidence that events had occurred and time had passed before she entered the world on an autumn afternoon in 1945. She was disconcerted the first time she saw a photo album of her parents as youths. That they had been children, that they had grown up— separately, at that!— and had problems of their own, was to her the most preposterous idea in the world. Her father's face looked different before he lost his eye. More handsome but less fatherly. She grew to be jealous of that photo album and of her parents' past without her. It made her feel like a retroactive orphan.

P.W. now showed Robert the same album in the dim dusty attic. The faded photographs meant even less to him.

"This is you?" the boy said, pointing to a slim and dashing young man in knickerbockers standing next to an ancient Ford.

"None other," said P.W. "They made us play lacrosse every day at the College of St. Vitus. The priests broke our minds but built our bodies— *mens dementia in corpore sano.* The car belonged to your great-grandfather. He worked his way up at the 4P. Here." He handed Robert a photo of a stern-looking man in his Sunday suit, hat in hand, standing next to an ostentatiously-dressed lout seemingly pointing at his spats. "That's your great-grandfather," he said, indicating the man with the hat in his hands.

"Who's the other guy? He looks weird."

"Isaac Presley," the old man said. "He built the 4P and hired your great-grandfather when he arrived in Canada. He's the lunatic who had the totem pole built downtown. Your great-grandfather always made a supreme effort to be civil to him."

In another chest they found some of Kathleen's toys: a Raggedy Ann, the head and limbs of other dolls, pieces of a small china tea set, a skipping rope, a small stuffed lion, a majorette's suit, a baton, a top hat, several rubber balls and a large blue notebook.

"Your grandmother kept as many of your mother's toys as we could get our hands on."

"Mom keeps my toys, I think," Robert said. He took the notebook out of the chest.

"Someday your mother will sort through this chest and each item in it will remind her of a nice thing from a long time ago."

His mother's name was printed in large, neat letters across the cover of the notebook. The unlined pages were warped and stiff, as though they had spent time in a damp place. Robert leafed through drawings in various stages of completion: birds perched on branches, the beach at Lake Mead on a sunny day, a dog and a cat lounging together on a chair, all done in crayon with careful attention to detail. "She never told me she drew," he whispered, turning the pages with care.

"Your mother was always secretive about it, but she loved to draw, the same way you do. I wish we had more of them now. I remember one in particular she did of your Grandma and me when she was about your age, maybe ten. She did it in white and green chalk on black paper. That's when Mr. Cutler told her she was going to be a famous artist one day, and a great thinker. He said he hoped he lived long enough to see her work hanging in a gallery in New York or Paris. He made such a fuss about it every time he saw her that she got shy about showing her drawings to anyone and eventually stopped drawing altogether. I suppose she figured there was no way she could ever live up to his expectations. It took some of the joy out of it."

Robert only half-listened to his grandfather. He studied a drawing of a cat and a cardinal seemingly staring at each other. Were they friends or foes? Their eyes seemed so alike. P.W. leaned forward to look at the drawing.

"She used to draw so many pictures of cats and birds. I never did understand what they were supposed to be about."

Robert believed he understood what the drawing was about, though he wouldn't have been able to put it into words. He and his grandfather silently examined the drawing. A mouse scurried in the walls.

"I'm going to have to go down and stretch out for a little while," P.W. announced. "My legs. Do you want to stay here or to come down with me?"

"I'll stay here a bit longer."

While P.W. rested and the tea steeped, while Kathleen tried to bare her increasingly inscrutable soul to Helen at her apartment, and while Steven pulled shirts, socks and underwear pell-mell from his former dresser drawers, Robert happened upon a photo album with *January 6 1964* embossed on the cover. Opening it, the first thing he saw was a colour eight-by-ten of his mother and father on their wedding day. They looked nervous and not overly happy. His mother's face so full and flushed, as though she'd stuffed Kleenex into her cheeks. Pregnant with her son and still grieving for her mother. They looked unsure of themselves—in love to the best of their abilities. It was as though they were looking out at the present from this photo album, as though they could see over the shoulders of their son, out the little grimy attic window with the dead flies on the sill, down the street a few blocks in two separate directions, to where one of them was rubbing red puffy eyes with the back of her hand while the other filled shopping bags with bits and pieces of their shared life.

Did they know it all along? Did they take a turn they weren't meant to take and know it all along?

"Dirty stupid lies," Giles Robert Rosseter said to the attic.

When his grandfather finally made it back up the steep ladder to the attic, Robert took a long look at the one man who always told the truth, helped him over the top step and hugged him long and hard. He wanted out of the attic now. He wanted out onto the street or down by the river, where he could breathe.

* * *

5

> You have to forgive the past before you can forget it.
>
> —Theodore Ng

Steven fumbled for the telephone. An ashtray fell to the floor.
"Hullo. . ."
"Steven?"
"Uh-huh."
"It's Kathleen. Were you sleeping?"
"Uh-huh."
"Oh. Sorry. I can call back later."
"Uh?"
"I can call you back later."
". . .Maybe you better."
"Okay."
"Okay."
"Sorry for waking you up."
"That's okay."
"'Bye."
"'Bye."

The tiny voice of Kathleen in the receiver said something else, but he was already hanging up.

The phone hadn't disturbed the woman lying beside him. Her name was Carol Karayannopomos. She was lying on her side, in the foetal position. He rolled over and pressed his skin against her. From directly above, their bodies said SS under the sheets. He could see her naked body with his fingers. The cool of her hip and buttocks— white-red, probably purple under the epidermis. Then up to her breasts, always the warmest of all, near the engine of her body.

"You're waking me up," she murmured.

He didn't want to wake her up. That would be unkind (what did Kathleen—?). Instead, he pulled the sheet over his head, eased himself off the pillow and away from her. Now, in the grey light of the blinded room, undercover, he regarded Carol's supple spine, the small mole near her tailbone, the lovely curved surface of the moon and tuft of jetblack hair just above the horizon. Desire. For what? For whom? Carol turned over, moved closer to him. He closed his eyes and eventually forgot about Carol's small hand around him. He fell asleep thinking about Kathleen's mouth.

. . .

Go to your room: His mother had never said that to him. That's one of the reasons Robert spent so much time there.

With the perverse single-mindedness of a slightly demented Cezanne, he sketched the elm tree in his front yard as seen from the window of his room. As soon as he completed a sketch he crumpled it up. He wasn't interested in what he saw in the tree twenty minutes or two weeks ago. If a particular sketch seemed to capture the essence of the tree, all the more reason to destroy it. Otherwise it would distort all his future drawings or, worse yet, make the act of drawing it again a waste of time. He didn't want to waste time, he wanted to erase it. Only a dead artist would be fool enough to preserve any of his works.

Eddie Laverty didn't understand or approve.

"You could cover your wall with them," he suggested, "or at least put them on a roll and use it as toilet paper. Once I used some pages of a Canadian Tire catalogue for toilet paper. The pages wouldn't flush so I had to take them out of the toilet with my toothbrush. I think these pages would flush." He picked up one of the crumpled drawings.

"They're no good to me anymore," Robert said, smoothing a fresh leaf of his sketch pad.

"So why don't you draw something different? Aren't you tired of that tree?" Eddie threw the crumpled drawing, which hit Robert on the back of the head before joining the rest of the wastepaper on the floor.

Robert slid his chair from the desk to the window. Eddie lay back on the bed and gazed at the ceiling. "For instance," he said, "I've always had this weird picture in my mind of big pink clouds off in the distance, the way the sky looks sometimes after supper, when there's been a thunderstorm. You look at those big clouds that are miles and miles away, near the horizon, and you wonder what the world is like over there. You know the sun is shining even though it's still dark and wet where you are. Have you ever seen clouds like that?"

Robert didn't answer.

"I don't know it it's a dream I had as a baby or what, but I always picture those clouds in my head. I see buildings there, too. Everything is in pastels. Maybe it's where the world ends, or how the sky will look on the day I die."

Robert chuckled mirthlessly. "You've got this thing about the day you die. It's probably heaven you're trying to picture. Are there any angels around?"

"All I'm saying is if I could draw, that's what I'd draw. The picture is always so clear in my head that I could draw it really accurate."

"Don't ever do that," Robert said.

"Why not?"

"The day you draw it will be the day you die."

"You think so?"

"Uh-huh."

"Why?"

"Don't ask why."

"Why?"

"Don't ask."

Eddie fell silent, rolled onto his stomach.

"Maybe you're right. I've been thinking a lot about those clouds the last few days. I've got post-nasal depression and my thyroid glands are swollen. Nobody believes me. My father sees me sitting in the rec room and says 'Why are you staring at the wall? You're not doing anybody a bit of good staring at the wall.' I can't just say to him I'm thinking about big pink clouds. He says 'Why don't you pay one of your chums a visit? Why don't you drop in on the Rosseter boy?' I can't tell him the Rosseter boy is in his room drawing pictures of a tree and throwing them away. He'd think we're both sick."

"Tell him you're paying me to draw a picture of a bunch of pink clouds."

"Sure," Eddie said with a laugh. "Besides, for you to picture them the way I picture them, I'd have to draw you a picture. But then you wouldn't have to draw a picture of them for me because I'd already have a picture. Except I can't draw." He gazed back up at the ceiling. "If only someboby invented a camera that could take a picture of the things we see in our head, like in science-fiction. The things I see inside my head are so much nicer than the stuff here on Earth. Maybe I'm from another planet. That would explain why my father doesn't understand me. He wouldn't understand those clouds. You would, Bobby. You draw clouds."

"Real clouds," Robert said.

"These are real," Eddie protested. "Just because they're in my head doesn't mean they're not real. You sound like my dad. Is your drawing of the tree real?"

"The drawing isn't."

"Shut up, then. I just don't draw, that's all. If I could I would, and if I did I wouldn't be stupid and rip them up when I'm finished."

"You sound like *my* dad," Robert said.

A light rain began to fall. Robert sketched on. The silence made Eddie even more restless. He slid his legs off the bed and sat up.

"I guess we won't be throwing the football around today."

"I didn't feel like it anyway," Robert said.

"You don't feel like anything."

"I feel like you're starting to bug me," Robert said, tearing the completed drawing from his sketch pad and holding it up to the light from the window. Eddie stood up and snatched it from his hands.

"Hey."

"I'm going to save this one, if you don't mind."

"I do mind," said Robert. "Give it back."

"See you later." Eddie opened the door and left the room. He all but collided with Kathleen at the foot of the stairs.

"Hello, Mrs. Rosseter. Bobby was going to tear up this drawing but I took it from him." He opened the front door. "He draws pictures of the tree in your front yard and then he tears them up. I can't draw, so I decided to save one. 'Bye."

"What is he—" Kathleen tried to ask, but the door had closed.

Upstairs, after the rain turned heavy, Robert put away his sketch pad and sprawled on the bed. Almost everything he needed was in his room. A private telephone would be nice. He had seen on TV that in the near future all kinds of telephones would be available to the average person. Soon, people would be able to shop for groceries by telephone, select and purchase their wardrobe by telephone, earn a college degree by telephone, get married and have far-flung family reunions by telephone, vote and even pray to the god of their choice by telephone. Soon, the need to physically interact with other human beings would be eliminated. Robert imagined the world truly united for the first time in history.

Eddie had got him interested in science-fiction. One day he arrived with a cardboard box and asked Robert to store his books because his father had forbidden him to read them. Eddie now had an extensive library under Robert's bed. His favourites were stories about the end of the world and afterwards. Robert had read a few of them, including *A Canticle For Leibowitz*, which Eddie's father picked up one day, leafed through and summarily banned. Robert's favourite was *The World Inside*, about a future in which everyone lived in high-rises that rose for miles and contained everything a person might want or need. He had trouble understanding why the hero of the book rebelled by abandoning his high-rise to go live in the wilds. It wasn't that Robert was against rebellion. He, too, was a rebel, though he wasn't yet sure what he was rebelling against. Time, space: one of the dimensions.

Perhaps, Robert thought, his father was a rebel, too. Maybe that was why he seemed to enjoy living by himself downtown in a small furnished apartment he rented in the winter of 1974 after growing tired of living with Ansel Bedrosian and Ansel's friends and Ansel's friends' friends. Sometimes organisms thrive in unhealthy or disorderly ways. Sometimes they store up all their energy to swim backwards against the current of time. Maybe that's what his father was doing.

Time-travel novels intrigued him. He would have loved to travel back to Thanksgiving Day 1970, which now existed in his memory as the pivot on which the fate of his family had turned. He would have loved to piece together the missing fragments of that day as an invisible, dispassionate observer rather than the confused and frightened witness he had been. But even the hypothetical time traveller wasn't unburdened of time's emotional luggage. No one was safe. The bullets and bombs of the past were as real as the emotional luggage the traveller carried with him from one time to another.

So let it be telephones, then— the narrowest filament of human contact. The perfect illusion: escape from communication in the guise of communication.

A knock on his door.

"Who is it?"

"Who do you think?" said Kathleen.

"You can't come in. I'm changing."

"You were changing the last time I knocked."

"I'm still changing."

...

Kathleen tried Steven again in the afternoon, but there was no answer. She felt like she'd been living on the phone these past months— all those long pep talks from Helen Munsinger, who taught her how to smoke the long Benson & Hedges she'd taken up on New Year's Day 1974 as an anti-resolution, to spite fate. It was hard not to feel bitter, to feel as if Steven had got the better deal— eighteen months of flitting in and out of her life, trying to find his head-space, as he put it. She hadn't misplaced *her* head-space. "Do you remember where you last put your head-space?" she was tempted to ask him.

Helen told her he didn't have a stake in it anymore, but Kathleen wanted to talk to Steven about their son. She knew he probably would say the changes in Bobby were signs of some meaningful phase he was going through, a period of adjustment perhaps not unlike his own. He might even approve of his son's retreat from the material world, from the *maya* and *duhka* of it all. She had long ago concluded Steven was in love with his own maladjustment; he had a crush on his anxieties. After all these months of their being apart, this aspect of her husband still drove her crazy. In other words, she sadly concluded, part of her still loved him.

Despite Helen's urgings, she wasn't dating anyone. The mere prospect of it wearied her, not because she cherished some ideal of how it had been with Steven (ha!) but because she was busy and felt barren. A blunt thrill was to be had in openly defying desire on those rare occasions when it arose. Besides, masturbating in the bath was undignified.

Her father certainly didn't encourage her to play the field. He all but told her she had finally found her niche in life, rearing a nice boy and keeping a nice little house in the nicest country in the world.

"I like your colour, Kathy, your complexion," he said. "It reminds me of when you were a baby and your mother and I tried to decide which was softer, your face or your behind. Your hair was straight and thin and fire-engine red. Your thirties are going to suit you. You know who you look like, don't you? You know who you remind me of. . ."

Her father coughed too much, tired too easily, and the sight in his remaining eye was fading. She secretly wondered if he didn't miss his son-in-law, if Steven hadn't provided him a reason to keep his mind sharp after his courtroom days were over. Often he reminisced at length about her mother, his devotion pouring forth in minutiae, like rainwater carefully collected in small jars. His blood pressure was also a problem. Even his glass eye bothered him. He complained of periodic bursts of bright light in the otherwise empty socket. One afternoon he fell asleep on his verandah and woke up after dark, confused and shivering. She almost wished she and Steven were still together, for her father's sake.

Maybe it wasn't good not to be held by another person in an

intimate way for a long time. Maybe she and her father were wrong and Helen was right: Maybe what she needed was some carnal knowledge. Maybe Bobby sensed her present carnal ignorance and felt more alive in the company of his father. She had no way of knowing.

That evening at the supper table, as Robert dutifully ate his frozen green beans, trying to swallow them before his tastebuds had a chance to fire a signal to his brain, Kathleen gently interrogated her son. The Thursday nights with his dad (why Thursdays, she asked herself a million times; why not Fridays?) were a terrible mystery to her.

"I've told you. We watch TV or go out."

"Is it fun?"

"Sure."

"How much fun?"

"Mom. . ."

"Rate it on a a scale of one to ten."

"That's *stu*-pid."

"Humour me. Is it more than seven? Less than four?"

"I can't just think of a number. What difference does it make?"

"Okay, okay," Kathleen said. "Let's assume it's around seven."

"It's probably more like eight," Robert said.

"We'll round it off to seven point five. How does that sound?"

"Sometimes it's nine."

"Okay, eight it is."

"Sometimes it's two or three."

"Two or three? When is it two or three?"

"Sometimes."

"What I mean is why is it two or three?"

"I don't know. He asks things about you."

Kathleen put down her fork. "What does he ask about me?"

"He wants to know if I'm happy here at home with you, and if you're treating me nice. He says I can be honest with him, and if there's any trouble at home I should come to him and tell him about it. He wants to know what things we do together and if I have fun doing them with you."

The prying bastard.

"But most of the time we just watch TV or go to the show, and that's fun."

The meddling son of a bitch. She stabbed her pork chop. Robert grimly gathered the last of his green beans.

"I bought you chocolate-ripple ice cream today," she said. She watched her son drink his milk. "And some seedless oranges for your lunch." She watched the boy start to gnaw on the bone of his pork chop. "Does your father buy seedless oranges?"

"I dunno," Robert said.

"Well, are there any seedless orange in his refrigerator?"

"Not when I'm there. Maybe he runs out of them."

"Does he cook you good suppers?"

"We usually order a pizza. Sometimes we just go to the show and eat popcorn and licorice."

"That's not a good meal."

"It's a great meal," Robert disagreed.

Kathleen placed her knife and fork on her plate, rose from the table and carried her plate to the sink. She set the plate in the sink and said, "Does your dad have a woman who comes in and cooks his meals for him sometimes?"

"No. There's this girl named Carol who works in his office at the 4P. But I've never seen her cook anything."

"A girl?"

"She's younger than you."

"How much younger?"

"I don't know, Ma," Robert said irritably.

"Is she nice?"

"I've only seen her a couple of times," he said, dropping what was left of the bone onto the plate. "I think they're just friends."

"He's never mentioned girlfriends to you?"

"I thought people had girlfriends *before* they were married."

"That's true. But if husbands and wives separate, they're allowed to have girlfriends and boyfriends again. Sometimes they separate because one of them already has a girlfriend or boyfriend, or wants to have one, or maybe two or three."

"You can have more than one?"

"Some people have a whole bunch," Kathleen said.

"What for?"

"I guess because none of them is special. Or maybe all of them are special, but in different ways."

Robert turned his fork over and over on his plate. "Do you have a boyfriend?"

"No."

"But you could if you wanted."

"If I wanted," Kathleen said.

Robert turned his fork over and over along the edge of the table and said, "What about Dad?"

"What *about* Dad?"

"If you had a boyfriend, what would that make Dad?"

Kathleen shrugged. "What do you mean?"

"He's your husband."

"Technically, yes, but. . ."

"You can't have a husband and a boyfriend at the same time."

"Your father and I are separated, Bobby. We don't—"

"I know that, Ma." The fork fell off the table and clanged on the tile floor. "But he's still your husband."

"Technically. Until we're divorced."

"Divorced?"

"I'm not saying we're getting divorced. Hasn't your dad ever talked to you about any of this?"

"Sure he has," Robert said. "He said he needed a bit of time by himself, then he'd probably come home. He never once said he was going to get divorced. Never once."

"That's interesting, Bobby," *the prick,* "since your dad was the one who—" *walked out of the marriage,* she left unsaid, *and first brought up the topic of divorce— over the telephone, naturally.*

"You want to get divorced, don't you? Because Dad is so impossible."

Kathleen wanted to tell her son she wasn't the first to bring it up. Probably Steven believed telling a lie about a future reconciliation was the best thing for him. She wasn't the one who decided to separate— though it wasn't at all a bad idea in retrospect. Of course, he didn't flat-out say he wanted a divorce. He never said anything flat-out. He said he just wanted to reason the thing through, to use some adult common sense. As far as she was concerned, he could take his adult common sense and shove it diagonally up his ga-ga. "It's too soon to think about it," she told Robert instead.

After dinner, she contemplated scotch-taping a little note to her refrigerator door. The note would have said:

THE SERPENT GAVE HER AN APPLE,
BUT IT'S ADAM WHO SCREWED EVE.

She was relieved when the open sores of '74 changed to the dull aches of '75. But it didn't stop her wondering what were the right moves, which of his parents her son liked best, and what Robert possibly hoped to gain by hiding out from the world— other than peace of mind.

Steven further complicated matters that Christmas by personally supervising the installation of a private telephone in Robert's room.

. . .

This confused individual, P.W. said to himself, *is not the real me. The real me is relaxing somewhere a little ways off, puttering around my house and not lying on a couch at Kathleen's waiting for the grey October afternoon to deepen into suppertime. I have so many things I need to do. There are so many things. . . Did I remember to pick up fuses, 25s and 30s? Of course I didn't. My stove won't work without them. Polly, I don't think I've been eating enough. I don't remember all my meals. Did I eat something this morning? Toast and cranberry jam. Two toasts, with a little butter on them, and some cranberry jam. No, there was no jam left. When did I last get groceries? I don't have any groceries. Is this the medication or is it me? It's not me. I'm somewhere else, the serene master of my destiny. I'm not lying here fretting about fuses and groceries. You didn't cash your pension cheque, you didn't take it out of the envelope and cash it. You don't even know if it came. . . Then again, Kathleen gave me lunch. Soup and a sandwich. Was I also here for breakfast? Maybe I gave her the cheque.*

He heard a car pull into the driveway, craned his neck and saw a red Camaro. He sat up. It had been months since he'd seen Steven. It seemed strange that he'd bother to knock, but P.W. opened the door anyway.

"Hello— oh hi," said Steven.

"Hiyo yourself."

"Kathleen says you haven't been feeling all that well."

"When did she tell you that?"

"A couple of weeks ago. She said you were spending a lot of time in bed."

"She forced me to stay in bed, and it was for three days, or four at most. She thinks I'm not eating enough."

Steven was shocked to see how much P.W. looked like an old man. *You should be in bed right now,* he wanted to say, as though such an intimacy had once been a part of their relationship. "I just hope you're starting to feel better."

"Me too," P.W. said. *You could use a square meal yourself, and a haircut, but what concern is that of mine.* "Did you want to come in, or. . ."

"Actually, I can't stay," Steven said. "Do you know if Bob is ready to go?"

"He went out with his mother to buy a pair of winter boots. I was expecting them back by now, and Kathleen to have put supper on. She must have run into somebody. Probably she ran into Helen. Helen never stops talking, except to light a cigarette."

"I know what you mean."

P.W. wanted to tell him to come in and sit down and they'd chat a while. It had been ages since they'd had a chat or badgered each other about anything, like the old days. Perhaps there were outstanding grievances. He couldn't remember precisely how it all came to an end. His past was constantly evaporating behind him now, like the vapour trail a 747 leaves at thirty-five thousand feet. *What's my name? My name is... my name is Jose Jimenez, ho ho ho. As for this young fellow*: "You can wait inside if you like."

Steven weighed the invitation. "I wouldn't want to disturb you."

"I'm beyond needing anyone to disturb me," said P.W. "At this stage of my life I'm perfectly capable of disturbing myself."

Steven smiled. "Is that so."

"They say senility breeds indifference, but I don't care one way or the other. All I really care is that we close this door, because the draft is filling the house."

Steven made a move to step inside. Then something insignificant—perhaps the barometric pressure—changed infinitesimally, and inside was no longer the place for him to be.

"Actually, I should drop by my office for a few minutes. Could you have Bob call me at home—at my apartment—when he gets back?"

"I could do that," P.W. said, wondering why he was letting the chance for company slip through his fingers. In the old days he would have bullied his way into control of the situation. Was this indifference or impotence?

"Good. Thanks a lot," Steven said, backing away from the door. "You take care."

This raging, confused, powerless individual is not the real me.

"How come you don't say ridiculous things anymore?"

Steven stopped. "Pardon?"

"How come you don't say ridiculous things anymore? You used to say such ridiculous things."

Stephen chuckled.

"Go on: Say something ridiculous, for old times' sake."

"Like what?"

"Like why you ever wanted to marry Kathleen in the first place." *Oopsy-daisy.*

Steven looked down the street, took a couple of breaths. "I loved her. She loved me. Two good reasons. Ridiculous enough for you?"

"Nowadays love is like an OHIP policy. If it expires you either renew your coverage or go looking for a better plan."

"Nowadays love is honest," Steven replied. "Nobody glosses over the truth anymore."

The same feeling as a pinched nerve in the temple, hot and sharp: "I never glossed over a thing in my life. That's alot of horseshit and you know it. Y-you... That's just a lot of h-horseshit."

A taxi turned into the driveway behind the Camaro. Ansel Bedrosian honked the horn and waved. "Sorry sorry sorry," Kathleen sang as she and Robert got out of the cab. "There was a sale, but I didn't think it would be that crowded." She turned to Robert. "I'll hold your supper until you get back from picking up pumpkins, but you'd better hurry because you still have homework to do." She turned to her father. "What are you doing standing out in the cold? I thought you were supposed to have a nap."

"We were talking," Steven said.

"Oh yeah? What about?"

"None of your b-business," her father said— miffed, he guessed, about supper.

"Good," said Kathleen. "I don't want to know."

"You're dying to know," said P.W.

"I'm dying to get out of these heels. Let's go inside."

After Steven and the boy left in the Camaro and he was ordered to go to the living room, lie down and stay there, P.W. only half-listened to Kathleen's narration of the winter-boot story. A haunting incompleteness hung over the day. *Nothing is happening naturally, Polly,* he told his wife. *Did it happen naturally for you?* He wanted it to be natural, ineffable, as in great stories. How dared they inflict their frantic aimlessness on his big scene? Knocks on doors, boot sales, office visits: Damn them all.

He could blame himself for not filling the shoes Steven Rosseter may have wanted him to fill ten years ago. But the real problem was with them, with their generation. He told his daughter so at length that evening, after stewing through supper. A generation ignorant of adversity and therefore uncomfortable with happiness and prosperity. A g-generation that thought it had the monopoly on both the questions and the answers. That was the problem.

"Daddy, I hardly think you can—"

"Listen me out, Kathy. M-Maybe we let you down by encouraging you to dream so much. But now you're letting yourselves and your children down by refusing to wake up."

"You're generalizing," Kathleen said.

"I'll be specific, then: Your grandfather, Sean Amadeus O'Hagan, was n-nine years old when he took his place in the world. His identity was handed to him. He had no say in the matter. It wasn't something he went out looking for, like some g-golden fleece."

"Things have changed since then," Kathleen said.

"They've changed, all right. Now you spend your whole life t-trying to design an identity for yourself. You'll let marriage rot, you'll let the family rot, you'll let your kids rot while you look for the ideal identity. It's not something you put together from a k-kit, for God's sake. Most of it's imposed at birth and the rest of it's right out that door, where the world waits to put a label on you whether you like it or not."

"I don't agree and I wish you'd calm down," Kathleen said.

"Of course you don't agree. You're all too busy looking for some tiny r-remnant of a group you can identify with."

"Daddy, will you please sit down."

Hot and sharp, just like a pinched nerve.

"In a world so full of little groups and little sub-groups that even a non-conformist can feel he belongs, nobody belongs. Can't any of you s-see that? Everything cancels itself. The lowest common denominator isn't even common anymore, just lowest. Nobody—" he coughed, "s-sees—" he coughed again, "that", and doubled over in a cascade of hacks.

"Jesus God, Daddy." She helped him back to his chair. "That's enough."

"It's n-never enough," P.W. wheezed. He took a hankie from his back pocket and passed it over his lips. *Never enough.*

"You're not supposed to get excited. You're supposed to rest."

"And then," he continued, "you ask yourself why the kids are the way they are. You've provided for their every material need, including s-several they didn't even know about. You've given them quality time every day. You've read books on how to parent, so help me Jesus, because p-parent is a verb now, and being good at parenting is almost as important as the resale value of your home. You've— you've— you've. . ." He coughed something up into his hankie.

"Please, Daddy."

"I'll tell you a secret, Kathy," he said, lowering himself into a chair. "When you're so busy looking for yourselves, you get in other people's way. And when that starts to happen, innocent people pay the price. K-kids pay the price."

"I don't want to go on with this," Kathleen said.

"All right," P.W. said. He was done anyway.

"You're short-selling us. Steven and me."

"I thought you didn't want to go on."

"I don't. But Steven always said you underestimated him, and God knows he didn't think that much of himself to begin with."

P.W. wiped his forehead with his hankie and took a shallow breath. "I wanted him to come in today, you know."

"What do you mean?"

"When he came by for the boy. I think he wanted to come in and talk a bit. But he didn't. I didn't give him the right signal, or it wasn't obvious enough to suit him."

"He asks about you," Kathleen said.

"Does he?"

"That's what Bobby says."

"Do I ask about him?"

"Not often. But I think you think about him."

He was never cut out to have a son. He never knew how to handle him, what to say. "Do I? I'm n-not always aware of what I think." He didn't like to wish a lot of things had turned out differently, but he did. He never expected he would be the type to regret so much so late. "Talking, too. I just t-talk. Always have. It was my profession." Maybe he wasn't supposed to handle him at all, just try to be with him in some happy way. Not that Kathleen was able to. But marriage can be the hardest thing of all. He made for the front closet to get his overcoat.

"Please stay here tonight, Daddy. I don't think you should be alone."

"There's one bed in the world that I sleep in." His bed, Polly's bed, their bed.

"I know," Kathleen said, locking her arm into his and squeezing it as they stepped out onto the landing. "Maybe I should walk with you this time."

"Give my love to the boy," he said and stepped into the darkness.

It was a still night and a short walk. He liked to walk, even when he didn't feel up to it. O'Hagan sturbborness flowed in his veins, all the way from Cork to here. It wasn't regret that weighted him down. It was the blunt certainty that, no matter what, some business would always be left unfinished, an ache tempered by the knowledge that it really was impossible to complete all the business, to claim all of the emotional luggage on time. Then his mind just shut down for a while and left him in blessed silence, his bloodstream humming faintly in his ears.

. . .

While Giles Robert Rosseter examined his cuticles and more or less listened, Miss Hornung gave a talk on the origins of Hallowe'en to her Grade 5 class. The previous evening, he and his father had painstakingly carved two jack-o'-lanterns after selecting a pair of shapely pumpkins from the stock outside D'Agostino's. One was for his house; the other was to grace the living room window of his grandfather's house.

"There are evil (slap) people in this world," Miss Hornung concluded. "When you are out trick-or-treating tonight, beware (slap) of treats from strangers on the street. Have your mother or some other responsible adult (slap) inspect each and every item you receive. Cut open your apples before biting into them; there may be a razor (slap) blade inside. Look out for bits of glass (slap) in your candied popcorn. Be mindful of drunken (slap) drivers (slap). Under no (slap) circumstances should you accept a stranger's (slap) invitation into his car or house. If you are given a treat in the form of a tablet (slap) or capsule (slap), hand it over immediately to your mother or some other responsible adult (slap)."

Eddie Laverty let escape an expansive yawn. Miss Hornung glared at him. "Do you find this tiresome, Mr. Laverty?"

"No, ma'am. But you make it seem like grownups have all the fun on Hallowe'en."

Some of his classmates laughed. Robert continued to examine his cuticles.

"Perhaps," said Miss Hornung, "you'd care to pursue this impertinent point with Mr. Brunk (slap)."

Someone knocked softly on the door. Miss Hornung glared at Eddie as she crossed the front of the classroom. Students near the door glimpsed Mr. Brunk in the hallway and passed the news along after Miss Hornung stepped into the hall.

"Are you in for it now, Eddie Lavatory," said the boy seated next to him. Miss Hornung stepped back into the class before Eddie could deliver his rejoinder.

"Giles Rosseter," she said, "will you come here, please. Mr. Brunk would like to have a word with you."

"What's up?" Eddie whispered as Robert passed his desk. .Robert shrugged.

Mr. Brunk, a solemn disciplinarian, looked more solemn than usual. "Your mother just called. She needs you at home. I've already notified Miss Hornung, so you won't be needing a note. You can collect your things and be on your way."

Some of the students complained about Roosterbrains being let out early as he gathered his books and went to get his coat from the vestibule at the back of the class. "Silence (clap)," Miss Hornung ordered.

The four blocks from school to home gave Robert a chance to plot the evening's route. He'd start with Merrick Street West, where his doctor and his dentist lived. Last Hallowe'en, his dentist put two quarters in his bag in lieu of something that might decay his teeth. He bought ten grape jawbreakers with the money. The people who lived on Merrick Street West were generally well-to-do. Eddie would want to cover his own territory, Birch Street, first. So the two boys could meet up by Saint John's Church and complete their trick-or-treating together, finishing up with his grandfather who always gave them packages of Rosebuds, because he knew they were the boys' favourite candy. Then they would go to Robert's house and sort through their loot while his mother prepared tacos which were a Hallowe'en tradition in the Rosseter home for as long as he could remember. Then Eddie's father would come for Eddie and Robert would smuggle a few chocolate bars up to his room, get into his bed and continue to fill his face.

His father's Camaro in the driveway was a strange sight that triggered memories of a time when the Camaro belonged in the driveway.

His mother and father were sitting in the living room. His father rose, his mother remained seated. Robert took off his coat and dropped it at the foot of the stairs.

"It's Grampa," Kathleen said.

"Where is he?"

"Now Bobby. . ." Steven began.

"He's dead," Kathleen said.

"Grampa?"

Kathleen nodded.

"Grampa."

"Now Bob. . ."

"No way," said Robert.

Dust on the leaves of the umbrella tree in the corner of the living room. Outside, a crack in the windshield of his father's Camaro. Across the street, a man taking a hose out of his garage.

Steven came toward him.

"No way," said Robert.

The man closing his garage door and heading around to the

backyard with the hose.

"I know it's never—"

"Don't touch me," Robert said. "Nobody touch me."

. . .

The children of Presley trick-or-treated as usual on Hallowe'en night 1975, even though no slack-toothed jack-o'-lantern adorned the porch of the Rosseters' semi-detached house or the living room window of Preston Wilhelm O'Hagan's home. Most of the neighbourhood children had been instructed by their parents not to knock on the doors of these houses. The local radio station, CHPY, reported only a couple of serious incidents of vandalism, one of which was an attempt to topple Isaac Presley's totem pole.

Mr. Cutler had discovered the body late that afternoon, after dropping by to borrow a rake. Kathleen's doctor told her it was a massive stroke. Her father hadn't suffered, had lived a long and fruitful life, was perfectly lucid right to the end, and so on. Kathleen thanked him and he left.

In the evening, after it was agreed he would spend the night in the spare room, Steven placed the two carved pumpkins in a garbage bag on the back porch. From the bedroom, where he'd been hiding out since dinner, Robert watched Batmen, Draculae, werewolves and Richard Nixons skip past on the street, lugging shopping bags and pillow cases. By the time Kathleen ordered him to join them downstairs, most of the kids were home and wet snow had begun to fall.

Robert's first taste of the grandest inconvenience of all left him in a state of numbness that lingered into a dismal All Souls' Day, rain falling in sheets, dead and rotting leaves clogging storm sewers all over town. Steven and Kathleen quietly discussed whether to take him with them to the funeral home. Kathleen said funeral homes were morbid. Steven said their son needed to face death. She eventually deferred to him.

The warm broadloomed funeral home felt to Robert more like a cinema lobby than a church. He almost imagined he could smell popcorn.

Kathleen took Robert's navy blue overcoat, hung it up, took off her own coat, dropped a hanger which landed soundlessly on the carpet, bent down to pick it up, sighed, managed to insert the hanger in the arms of her coat, hung up the coat, took a deep breath, straightened her black skirt and started to cry.

"Mommy. . ."

"It's okay," she said. A tall man in a dark suit stood guard at the entrance to the room. From up a flight of stairs, in a lounge where coffee was served, came the sound of a forced laugh. Kathleen made a final adjustment to her skirt and wiped her eyes. "Let's go," she said.

Kathleen's Aunt Alice looked noble in her favourite winter dress. She greeted the three Rosseters and hugged Kathleen a long time. Out of the corner of his eye Robert saw the casket in the back of the room, amid floral tributes from legal colleagues, friends and relatives. The wood of the casket was more polished even than the coffee table at home. Aunt Alice led Kathleen toward it.

"Come on, Bob," Steven whispered. Indistinct kin milled in small groups around the room. They nodded gravely at Steven, smiled sympathetically at Robert. He felt as though he were a part of some sad parade, marching to music no one cared to hear. . .

Now who is this man with the kind face the colour of paper ashes, done up in somebody's best clothes and lying in all that shiny white stuff?

". . .peaceful," someone said.

These hands that whittled arrows for his bow, made iced tea and Kool-Aid on hot summer days, folded newspapers expertly, dispensed endless quarters and dimes, sometimes looked and felt like warm, time-smoothed bones in his own hand: Who made them this way? Who is this? The question swirled in his head, over and over again, until it was forced out his mouth, syllables flattened by outrage and despair:

"Whoisthis"

—green prayer beads twined around fingers that threaded needles to mend old pairs of socks—

"Bobby. . ."

But he was gone by then, up the stairs, not out the door, to the small lounge. No one took notice of the boy in his blazer and bow tie. He went to a window and looked out: Spindly bare trees swayed against a backdrop of featureless grey. He couldn't see his house from here, or the schoolyard. He couldn't see any familiar landmark. But that little girl in the yellow raincoat and high black boots, that was Stella, from his class. Stella wore glasses and was always slow gathering her books together after the bell rang. Now she was high-stepping through the puddles, walking home alone in the rain with her schoolbag bouncing on her back. If you waved at her she would wave back at you. Hi, Stella. You look so all by yourself jumping through those puddles.

One day last spring, Stella made a stained-glass collage out of thin coloured paper that broke even Miss Hornung's heart. She hung it up in the window. No one knew what Stella's artwork depicted, but Robert stared at it for the entire afternoon, mesmerized, as though it offered the answer to an important question he hadn't yet asked.

* * *

6

> The best estimate is that the universe is eighteen billion years old. Civilization is a garden planted in the wrong season.
>
> —Theodore Ng

The city, in a fairly concerted way by Presley standards, mourned the passing of a long-time resident. Stanley Laverty took a day off from his editorial-writing chores at the *Gleaner* to draft an exhaustive obituary. The paper ran a two-column photograph of P.W., taken in the early '50s, above the obit. PROMINENT PRESLEYITE PASSES, said the headline on page two.

Stanley Laverty had been at most a casual acquaintance of Preston Wilhelm O'Hagan's, but he felt he understood the old man, much as he felt he understood just about everyone in the city of Presley with the possible exception of his son Eddie. In an editorial the previous year on mercury pollution in the Kekagami River, he wrote: "The river flowing through our fair community is its soul, and the dynamic spirit of community togetherness is its heart." Preston Wilhelm O'Hagan now took the place of "community togetherness" as the "shining symbol" of Presley's heart. A notion seemed to have sprung up overnight among citizens who had taken little or no notice of him in his lifetime that people like Preston Wilhelm O'Hagan were what the city of Presley was all about.

Eddie Laverty, who had known the old man well, took exception to the obituary.

"Mr. O'Hagan always treated me nicely, but he didn't like any kind of bullshit," he told his father.

"Bullshit? —Mother, I can't believe I'm hearing this from my own son in my own house. Bullshit? You don't use words like that in this house, in front of your mother and your little sister."

"Bullshit bullshit bullshit bullshit," Eddie said. Stanley Laverty took a swing at him with the back of his hand but Eddie ducked it and bolted out of the room, deftly pulling his jacket from the coatrack on his way out the door.

"Mother, I don't need this," Stanley Laverty said as he carefully clipped the obit for his scrapbook. Maybe he would wire a copy to the *Canadian Press*, just in case. "The boy is 'way off base. Totally inappropriate."

"He was close to Mr. O'Hagan," Mrs. Laverty said.

"We all were. It's a blow to the entire community."

Eddie mourned P.W. by walking to his once-stately home, boldly climbing the stairs and sitting down on the verandah floor, where they used to play poker. Eddie imagined great pink clouds in the distance, billowing to heaven, forming the soft floor of a place where there was always peace, where Mr. O'Hagan could rest for a while if he wanted. A neighbour eventually came and told Eddie to go away.

Robert didn't feel the need to mourn. Within a day or two he had successfully enshrined the living memory of his grandfather in a specific compartment of his brain. Here he existed in a kind of suspended animation, forever available as company when Robert felt the need. He liked to think he had absolute control over this abstract fragment of his grandfather. Robert read him the obituary in the *Gleaner* and they worked together on the crossword puzzle and cryptoquote. His grandfather knew the name of every obscure river in Africa; Robert confirmed them with his atlas. They toiled together on his homework. P.W. suggested mathematics was a waste of time, so Robert put the book away and went downstairs to watch television.

At night, P.W. roamed freely in Robert's dreams. His voice was loud but indistinct, like a radio playing in another room. His back was turned to the boy as he walked down the grey halls of dream memory, even through the door that led to Thanksgiving Day 1970. Sometimes Robert heard laughter, sometimes an admonition, sometimes just a great silent presence in the dim space beyond his closed eyelids. He wished he could follow his grandfather deeper into the dreams, into the past.

Steven Rosseter mourned his marriage. Instead of bringing him and Kathleen closer together, P.W.'s death made them more fully aware that an era was over. It had actually come to an end two years previously, but such are the strange rules of time and memory that Hallowe'en 1975 was how they came to mark the true moment of their separation. It was as though P.W. had been the bonding agent in their relationship from the very start, at the turkey and bean banquet of 1963. His going made their coming apart suddenly official and less easily reversible.

After the funeral and the get-togethers were over and the visitors had all left town, Steven knocked on Kathleen's door late one night and begged her to let him spend the night. He felt empty inside, he couldn't sleep, he dreaded the day when he would die without having a chance to say goodbye or that he cared, or to hear someone say they cared about him. He wouldn't ask her to make love. He just wanted to lie with her this one time.

Kathleen let him stay over. They slept together in the bed they had shared for nine years. In the middle of the night she was awakened by Steven's hand between her thighs. She was aroused but he was fast asleep. She took his hand away and just held it.

...

Kathleen mourned her father by taking up her life again, which struck her as a peculiar way of mourning. Robert observed that she allowed herself to express grief only when she thought no one was looking, as though she were ashamed of it. But he was looking. There was a new brassy but brittle quality to her that reminded him of Helen Munsinger, who dropped by frequently in the weeks after the funeral for coffee and Benson & Hedges. Helen made a point of telling Robert he was a good-looking young buck and would be turning heads in no time.

"Turning what heads?" Robert irritably wanted to know.

"Female heads."

"Female heads are dumb," he said.

"Whose female heads are dumb?"

"All female heads."

"Surely not your mother's head?"

"My mother's head isn't female."

"It isn't?" Kathleen said.

"What is it, then?" Helen asked.

"Just a head," he shrugged.

"And my head. . .?"

"Another head," and another shrug.

"Is that a compliment?"

A third shrug.

"What a charmer," Helen said, turning to Kathleen. "Did he inherit it from your side of the family?"

"Robert's been a bit contrary lately. Haven't you, Robert?"

"No I haven't."

"But even if you're contrary, you're not allowed to be contrary with guests."

"I wasn't being contrary," Robert said.

"Oh yes you were," his mother said. "Helen gave you a compliment and you responded rudely."

Helen butted her cigarette. "It wasn't rude, Kath. He was just playing around."

"It was rude."

"Now who's being contrary?" Robert said.

"Jesus God," Kathleen exclaimed, using her coffee cup as a gavel.

"I wasn't being—"

"Why don't we just leave it at that," Helen suggested.

Robert exited stage right. Kathleen sighed.

Helen lit another cigarette. "You two are starting to drive each other crazy. You need to get out more, to loosen up a bit. You could use adult male company."

"What could I use it for?"

"You're joking."

"What can men give me?"

"You're putting me on."

"I'm serious. What do I need from men?"

"Physiotherapy, for one thing," Helen said. "Think of it as a humanitarian gesture toward men if you don't like the idea of physiotherapy. Somebody has to straighten them out."

"I'm not up to it just now," Kathleen said.

"That's the problem. You have to fight that apathy. God knows an awful lot of men aren't worth the effort, but it's time for you to start inflicting yourself on the world again."

"You make it sound so romantic," Kathleen grumbled.

"Romantic, hell. I'm talking about a survival strategy: first aid; life skills. Leave romance to the dreamers."

"But what if I'm a dreamer?"

"Then for God's sake wake up."

From January to the summer of 1976, Helen referred several male candidates to Kathleen. She dated a few of them, usually with Helen and her escort of the moment in tow. Helen fancied her outspokenness at least as attractive as her brown eyes and long legs, but most of her dates found her too stridently opinionated by 11 o'clock, just when they were starting to feel mellow. The evenings tended to peter out regardless of with how much panache Helene wore her scarves and other accessories. The simple fact was that most men lacked the sheer carnal appetite to bother cracking what they knew was a facade.

Kathleen eventually insisted she should go on dates alone. At first Helen balked, but Kathleen was able to convince her this was the only way she could ever get back on her feet again now that all the men in her life were gone.

Some of the men Kathleen dated were pleasant, considerate, mature, generous, good listeners and well-behaved. Others were tense, brooding, insincere, volatile and overbearing. Vic Martin, whose personality neatly straddled the two groups, asked her out one night that summer. He was an engineer with the Ontario Ministry of Transportation and Communications. Helen was introduced to him by one of her fleeting boyfriends, and she promptly introduced him to Kathleen, who had never dated a man with a cleft chin. That he seemed as jumpy and out of sorts about their first date as she was endeared him to Kathleen. They had dinner at Chow's Chow and saw *A Clockwork Orange*. Neither of them knew when to laugh and when to recoil in horror, but they came out of the movie in a strangely buoyant mood. Vic took her to the

Riverview Hotel, where they sipped on brown cows while he told her about Addie, his ex-wife, who was addicted to Valium and once threatened to cut his balls off and fry them in vegetable oil. (She's better these days, he said.) They had a couple more brown cows and Kathleen told him about her husband, Steven, who wanted to go with his friend Ansel into the bush and live in a wooden pyramid for a few months. They had another brown cow, got giggly and tested each other on trivia. After agreeing that Perez Prado was the only recording artist ever to successfully convert a country-and-western tune into a cha-cha, Vic drove her home. Reluctant to let the mood die, Kathleen asked him in. She poured them some white wine and put on a record— not too loud because Bobby was in bed. The Who's "Baba O'Riley" came over the stereo. It wasn't exactly mood music, but what the hell.

"Your son's record?"

"Actually it's mine," Kathleen said. "There's a story behind it but it's a long story."

"Addie used to like the Who," Vic said. "Did you say there was a story behind it?"

"Behind what?"

"I don't know. Whatever was in front of it."

Vic and Kathleen looked at each other and burst out laughing.

"We must have had more brown cows than we ordered."

"It was that bloody movie," Vic said. "The stuff Alex and his broogs were drinking at the Milk Bar."

"Droogs, Victor. Alex and his droogs."

"Whatever."

She poured them some more wine. She noticed that Vic was starting to list in her direction on the couch.

"You've got marvellous hair," he said, as though semi-conscious.

"I need to cut it," she said.

"Don't you dare," he said, slipping his hand under her hair to caress her nape.

"You don't think so?"

His kiss was wet and imprecise. She tried at first to be more composed, then allowed herself to be as wet and imprecise. His mouth tasted the same as hers, of spring rolls, brown cows and wine. She couldn't tell where his tongue ended and hers began, so there was nothing specific for her to resist even if she had wanted to. She kept her eyes closed as he began to unbutton her blouse. By the time his hand reached her bra hook, not knowing Vic much better than the man who read her gas metre made no difference. Suddenly, as though it had slipped her mind for a couple of years, she was filled with a yearning to go all the way. She lay back on the couch and found nothing awkward or unfamiliar about the unbuttoning and unzipping, except to recall that Steven had never been particular about whether she was dressed or undressed. She found nothing confining or adolescent about the couch, except that it reminded her of an evening drive to Lake Mead in Steven's Camaro and of a crazy session in the back seat for the sheer hell of it. She found nothing clammy or alien about Vic's hands, his odour, his breath. They consoled her in a way she had seemingly forgotten—in a way men, without saying anything or even being aware of it themselves, allowed their paternal instinct to surface as long as they weren't conscious of it. When she gently took hold of him to guide into her, she was surprised to feel the warm rubberiness of a condom. "When did you put this on?" she breathed, but he didn't answer because now she was opening up to him, slowly, slowly, because it had been so long, that incomparable pleasurepain of momentary resistance and gradual surrender. "Does it hurt?" he said from somewhere above her face. No. Yes. No. Pleasurepain.

My love, she wanted to say. She let the words slip back down into her. For a time they hardly moved. The coarse upholstery of the couch tickled as he slowly gently easily moved inside her. Their bodies were running things now, so their minds were free to float. She let her head dangle over the end of the couch, fixed her closed eyes on a ceiling she couldn't see. O to be anybody again, just an organism on the road to an orgasm, with pauses along the way to savor the scenery. . .

When I was three I thought my Daddy was God. I have always wanted to be a pilot. I am scared of hot metal ever since I saw the slag heap one night in Sudbury. My son knows things about me he doesn't say. I am guilty of things. When I was nine I actually thought my Daddy was God.

I thought—

I thought—

Every fibre in her tautened, then uncoiled in magnificent concert:

"Jesus God. . .!"

It had been a long time.

Upstairs, Robert's eyes opened. He rolled out of bed, found the doorknob in the total darkness and stepped softly down the hall to the top of the stairs. In the living room shadows he thought he could see someone lying on the couch and bits of clothing on the floor. He was about to call down when his mother giggled; then came the deep, muffled sound of a male voice. His mother laughed, more openly this time. Robert tiptoed back to his room and climbed into bed.

Downstairs, the lovemaking had partly sobered them up and the atmosphere was gradually reverting to early-evening awkwardness. Kathleen wished Vic would vanish peacefully into the night— not that she didn't want to see him again, but so as not to break a private spell.

"I better get going," he eventually said, sensing her detachment. Their parting embrace was forced, unsynchronized, no longer part of the evening's lexicon. Kathleen realized she had forgotten his last name, but couldn't very well ask him at this point in their relationship.

"Can I call you?" Vic said.

"Do that." She smiled at him, amused more by her own warm indifference than by anything he was saying or intimating.

Before turning in, after washing up and brushing her teeth, Kathleen checked on her son. As usual, he had kicked most of the covers from his bed. She put them back after noting how quickly he was growing.

Her own bed seemed larger than usual, and vaguely uncomfortable, like the times she and Steven made love then war, and he fled to the sofa for the night, leaving the residue of his affection to grow cold on the sheets.

...

Nonchalance lingered into the next day. Morning sunlight and the smell of coffee and toast warmed her. She was a slice of golden toast on a delicate silver rack next to a china cup and saucer. She was perfect spotless utensils on a snowwhite tablecloth, pure orange juice in a crystal glass, four parallel strips of crisp bacon next to two fresh eggs, sunnyside up. She was, for the moment, ideal.

Robert, in tartan housecoat and blue striped pyjamas, dipped a piece of toast into his egg yolk. "Was Dad here last night?"

Kathleen suspended a piece of toast at her mouth. "No," she said, her lips frozen in an involuntary O. "Why do you ask?"

"Just wondering," Robert mumbled through a mouthful of egg and toast. *Go, boy,* his grandfather inside him commanded. "I thought I heard you call for help last night. It woke me up."

Kathleen took a sip of coffee. "You must have been dreaming."

"No," Robert said.

"Would you like some more orange juice?"

Robert shook his head as he drained his glass. "You were downstairs at the time," he said, setting the glass on the table and wiping his mouth with the back of his hand.

"What time?"

"When you called out for help." He sopped up the last of the egg yolk with a piece of toast.

"How would you know that?"

"I got out of bed."

Kathleen started wiping the counter with the dishcloth. In the morning sunlight the counter never looked perfectly clean. Come to think of it, dust showed everywhere in the sunlight. It was a wonder anyone could breathe. "You mean you checked in my room," she said.

"No," said Robert, spreading marmalade on his last toast.

"Then what do you mean?" she said, watching a robin hiphop across the driveway to the foot of the bastard maple.

"I saw you in the living room."

The robin disappeared under the Cutlers' hedge. Kathleen felt her face flush.

"I heard you laugh, and there was someone down there with you," he said. "I was just wondering if it was Dad."

"It wasn't," Kathleen said, clearing her throat.

"Anybody I know?" he said as his mother leaned over to take his plate away.

"What do you mean?"

"I mean do I know him— the man you were screwing around with?"

"Wha. . ."

That's something worth knowing, his grandfather inside him said. *It's not an unreasonable question. You're entitled to know certain things about your mother. Don't let her—*

"Take that word back."

"What word?"

Clashplatteratterratter: The plate dropped to the floor and was forgotten. "You know what word."

"What's the right word for what you were doing?"

Kip: A slap on his cheek. Silent welling of tears in two pairs of eyes.

"There is no 'right' word and you know it."

"I was just. . ."

"You were just. . .?"

"I was just. . ." (*Can't help you now.*)

"You want to humiliate me, and you have. You want to make me feel cheap, and you have. Now what? Where do you go from here?"

"I was— I was just. . ." He sounded lame and pathetic and unlike his grandfather.

"What have you got against me? Does your father say things about me? What does he say?"

"He doesn't say anything," Robert said, perfectly abject.

"Then what have you got against me?"

". . ."

"Why rob me of my happiness? I don't try to rob you of yours." Kathleen walked out of the kitchen, leaving the plate on the floor and the dirty dishes on the table and counter.

His grandfather also was gone. Maybe he had never been there at all. Robert stared at the hardening stains of egg yolk on his mother's plate until tears blurred his vision. Now there would be no alternative. Now he would have to be sad. For Grampa, who had the indecency to fade into the past. And for Dad, who had somehow faded into the present.

He found his mother on the back stoop, in her green velvet housecoat, fastening a clip to a garbage bag. The morning sun was warm even from ninety-three million miles away, but not as warm as she was when he wrapped his arms around her midriff and clung to her.

Eventually she pried his arms apart. "Here," she said, lifting the bag, "you put the garbage out."

Kathleen and Vic saw each other again a few times, and even made love once at his apartment, but not with the innocent abandon of that first night. On what turned out to be their final date, Vic was dispirited most of the evening and lunged at Kathleen after pulling the car into the driveway. She struck him on the side of the head and fled into the house, where the tears flowed hot and self-accusing. She had known it would be a mistake to see him after that first night, to try to create order out of something so random. Her father would never have understood. But her father was not with her anymore, and wasn't that fact the source of some small liberation within her? The tears flowed again. Would there have been a Vic at all had her father still been overseeing her life from a few houses away? Sooner or later yes, yes. And why would it have been so different to have thrashed with Steven on the sofa, as though the rings they exchanged thirteen and a half years ago somehow codified desire, put a tasteful frame around their separate loneliness, made everything not only possible but permissible? The past no longer provided sufficient proof that she was still alive.

. . .

To Eddie Laverty, the future offered growing proof that he was dead. He started to get into household chemicals not long after he stopped joining his family for the evening rosary. He stopped joining his family for the evening rosary not long after they started to suspect he was getting into household chemicals. Eddie felt God had let everybody down by allowing his dog to follow Mr. O'Hagan into the great land of pink clouds.

Eddie's dog liked to drink water from the toilet bowl in the middle of the night. Because the Laverty toilet leaked and hissed noisily for a half-hour after it was flushed, the rule was that no one was to flush it after bedtime. To prevent Shemp from drinking copious amounts of human pee, the toilet lid was to be kept closed. One night, Eddie staggered out of bed to empty his bladder and forgot to close the lid afterward. Shemp took full advantage of this oversight and lapped vigorously through the night. The next day, he sniffed around the backyard at some length, then skulked behind the garbage cans and stayed there all afternoon. By the time Rose Laverty came out to investigate, Shemp had died. It didn't take long for Eddie to conclude he was next on the list.

The family said several special Hail Marys for Shemp that evening. Eddie didn't disclose his evidently fatal oversight of the night before. They might have been able to reassure him about it, to tell him Shemp was fourteen years old, had dermatitis, his kidneys were shot, and that dogs don't die from drinking human urine. But Robert was the only one to whom Eddie confessed his fatal error.

"How do you know for sure that Shemp drank your piss?" Robert reasonably inquired.

"I just know," Eddie said.

"How?"

"I just do. I remember forgetting to close the stupid lid that night. Dogs don't know any better. Once I saw a dog eat its own shit. They don't know any better."

Of course, Robert couldn't be entirely certain that dogs didn't die from urine intoxication. Perhaps the piss in Eddie's pot had indeed been fatal.

The incident preyed on Eddie, acted as a catalyst for all his growing doubts. Robert saw the changes in his friend. They had countless arguments over the scoring of their football games. At home, Eddie complained about his meals and made his mother promise never to buy apple juice. For three weeks running he wet the bed, a development his parents found especially troubling since the boy had no previous history of it— not that a lifelong habit of peeing the bed would have been any less disconcerting in the long run.

One endless afternoon that summer, his father caught up in his busy schedule at the *Gleaner*, his mother off grocery shopping, the two boys' senses dulled by several hours of game shows and soaps, Eddie recommended they sniff some Fleecy.

"What for?" said Robert.

"For the hell of it."

"Get serious."

"I am serious. Do you know the guy from Laurier Senior

Elementary who delivers the paper? He sniffs Fleecy all the time. He says it gives him a real lift."

"So what?"

"So let's try it."

"What for?"

"For a while. Jesus Christ, Rosseter, what's the matter with you?"

"What's the matter with *you*?"

"Nothing's the matter with me," Eddie said. Robert glumly followed him into the kitchen. "At least I've got an adventurous spirit." He opened the cupboard doors under the sink and jostled the various aerosol and pump-action detergents, polishes, stains, bleaches, cleansers, spot removers, insect repellents, plant foods, flea killers, leather treatments, waterproofing solutions, shoe polishes, cross-country ski waxes, lawn mower oils, herbicides, fertilizers and starches. "You're not chikenshit, are you?"

Robert didn't answer. He just watched, transfixed, as more of Eddie's body disappeared under the sink amid toppling metal cans. He gazed despondently out the window, watched the little boy next door climb up into the family car and start honking the horn.

"Damn," Eddie said from deep in the cupboard. "Goddamn." He backed out, to the accompaniment of more falling cans, with a narrow cardboard container in his hand.

"Wouldn't you goddamn well know it? My mother uses Bounce."

Later, Robert beheld the demoralizing tableau of his best friend, sprawled on a vinyl easy chair, a wad of fabric-softener tissue stopped up each young nostril, gazing in dumb thrall at *Days Of Our Lives*.

In a moment of morbid lucidity during the winter of 1977, Eddie decided he would not survive his thirteenth birthday. He telephoned the news to Robert.

"Leave me alone, Lavatory," Robert said.

"I'm serious. It's going to happen."

"You've been sniffing Bounce again."

"No way. I've kicked that stuff. It doesn't do anything anyway, you know that. Mark my words. It's going to happen."

"Fine. Best of luck." Click.

Sunday, 23 May 1977, was a fair but cool day. At lunch the

Laverty family gathered to eat hot dogs and brownies, Eddie's two favourites. Friends were not invited. Stanley Laverty had decreed no more birthday parties the year Caroline accidentally set fire to the kitchen tablecloth. Eddie received a record by KC And The Sunshine Band, an NHL encyclopedia and a ten-dollar bill. He tried hard to appear delighted, though he was certain his hours were numbered. Nevertheless he ate three hot dogs and a handful of warm brownies. His charade worked: None of his family seemed in the least aware of his imminent demise.

After lunch he called Robert, who was either too polite to allude to the importance of the day or had forgotten. They agreed to meet at their usual spot, a field on the banks of the Kekagami, to throw the football around.

Although Robert hadn't had lunch yet, Eddie hurried over to the field. He wanted to walk around a while on his own, to have a final taste of this special place. Few kids played here because of all the humps and holes hidden by the tall grass. Robert and Eddie knew every last one and designed their plays around them. Eddie had the field all to himself on this windbreaker day, the clouds high and cold. He stretched out at the base of a lombardy poplar they used as a goal-line and was disappointed to discover nothing all that special about the afternoon. Across the river, grey smoke plumed horizontally from the 4P mill. Not far from his left ankle, garbage flies buzzed around a fresh dog turd. An SAC bomber soundlessly traced a vapour trail across the sky. Someone had meant to throw a grocery cart into the Kekagami but it was mired in mud near the bank. Traffic on the Trans-Canada hummed the way it always did. Eddie stood up and pissed on the lombardy poplar.

Robert finally showed up with the football.

"Today's my birthday," Eddie told him solemnly. "I'm thirteen."

"So what do you want me to do about it?" Robert said. They began to toss the ball back and forth.

"This is the day. This is it."

"Big deal," said Robert. "Go for a long one: Old Faithful."

Old Faithful was their most ingenious play. It called for Eddie to wander away to the right side, then to break sharply to the left at a mad dash, at which point Robert lobbed the ball as high and far as possible. Eddie's job was to catch up with it.

"So long, friend," Eddie said, trotting off to the right. "Good-bye and good luck." He broke to the left and bolted.

Giles Robert Rosseter threw an exceptional pass that afternoon. Eddie couldn't have felt more alive tracking the graceful, spiralling pigskin. This was the summing up he had awaited. He would have liked his life to flash before his eyes, but he was too busy running like mad as the football began to arc earthward. He gave it his best, but the ball eluded him by a couple of strides. He fell dramatically into the tall grass, turned onto his back, made the sign of the cross just in case, took one last look at the cold high clouds sliding across the sky and closed his eyes. . .

Nothing happened.

"What a throw!" he heard Robert exult from far away. He opened his eyes, saw the sky as it was before, pale and thin, sighed and picked himself off the ground.

"Nice play, Roosterbrains. Look."

Eddie pointed to the river, where the football, already well out of reach, had begun its long, inexorable journey to Lake Superior and, ultimately, the great Atlantic desert.

. . .

And so, instead of culminating in one tidy epiphany, the summer of 1977 was no more or less enervating than any of the other thirteen summers Robert Rosseter and Eddie Laverty had abided. Young men fought forest fires in the bush while hundreds of Presleyites camped on the cleared hillside overlooking the city and the river. Robert and Eddie thoroughly explored the world on their bicycles that summer. The bush, the river, the city itself didn't seem the same to them anymore. A stand of charred trees from some previous season's fire was no longer something to fear in the twilight. The weathered old storefronts of downtown Presley looked more tired than imposing. And the once-mysterious Kekagami was merely muddy, shallow and boring.

That August, a young couple from Iroquois Falls moved into Preston O'Hagan's house. One of the first things they did was to have the sagging verandah demolished. They built a cedar deck in the backyard and parked their gas barbecue where Pauline O'Hagan had raised marigolds. Robert passed by the scene of the desecration every Thursday evening on his bicycle while riding to his father's apartment. Eddie suggested they get their hands on some dynamite and blow what was left of the house to bits, to honour the old man.

Robert took long drives with his father in his beloved Camaro. Steven liked to take dirt roads in the lazy summer twilight when the air was still and the lush limbs of trees hung over farmhouses, derelict automobiles and rusted snowmobiles on rickety wooden trailers. It reminded Steven of the curiously detached sense of belonging he had carried through his childhood, of men who grunted at boys, of mongrel dogs forever out of doors and sniffing the wind for excitement, of young girls with quart baskets of wild blueberries, women sweeping wooden steps leading to torn screen doors, and houseflies buzzing on plastic tablecloths.

Steven pulled the Camaro over to the side of the road and took his son on foot past ramshackle homesteads where outcrops of sheer granite made a mockery of the farm machinery parked back of the houses. Can there have been a livelihood more futile than to domesticate such land? When the corn grew tall and full in the summer, the farmers laughed back at the granite. It was a relationship Steven felt he understood.

"I might like to buy some land around here and make a go of it," he said to his son as they followed a dirt road in the direction of an outsized orange moon rising above the trees. "I might like to move out here and get in touch with things."

Robert knew better than to say anything. Instead he marvelled at how certain pebbles on the road seemed to glow as though they were made of mercury. He glanced behind him: The Camaro had disappeared around a bend in the road. Crickets pulsed happily in the moonlight.

"I talked to some people downtown about buying a bit of land and some equipment. What's best about this kind of life is that there aren't any people to hassle you. You deal honestly with the land. I know some people who moved out here, friends of Ansel's. They're raising chickens and sheep already. They'd like to buy a few head of buffalo and let them range freely. Can't you just picture buffalo roaming?"

"And deers and antelopes playing," Robert said.

"It's time we start undoing all the damage we've done and give the land back to the land. I wish you could have seen the place I grew up in. Uncle Edgar had a farm and my dad helped him with it. They've sold it since, but it was really something when I was your age."

"I thought you grew up in the Soo."

"I did. But Uncle Edgar had a farm near Bruce Mines and we spent a lot of time there. Or I did, in the summer. My father travelled a lot in the summer, he—I spent a lot of time with my aunt and uncle. Anyway, I wish you could've seen the place. You'd understand why it stays in my mind."

They turned around and headed back to the car. Venus was prominent in the western sky. Robert reflected on things that stayed in his mind. Since his father was in a nostalgic mood, the boy asked him about Thanksgiving Day 1970.

"Why would you want to talk about that?" Steven said. "I was talking about what I was going to do."

"I want to know why it sticks in my head."

"How should I know? Ask your mother; she's the one with the memory. I guess because of the moose and all. Weird things can make a dent in your memory."

"I want to know what happened."

"I killed a moose. I shot it."

"After that."

"Nothing. I don't even remember. You should be looking ahead. You're starting high school in September. If I buy some land out here you can spend part of the year with me. We'll raise chickens and watch the sun go down, things like that."

"You had an argument with Mom."

"When?"

"That day."

Steven sighed.

"Tell me what it was about, Dad."

"Take a look at that farmhouse over there. Do you see where they've built their coop for maximum sunlight? And that's a greenhouse they're putting up. I bet they dug their well not far from there. Some people around here still use divining rods to find good groundwater. What they do is they take a piece of. . ."

One day he would find out all he needed to know. Of this

Robert was certain. He had no idea where the knowledge would lead him, but he had to go there.

The same applied to Presley High & Vocational School. On a sultry Labour Day, Robert and Eddie pedalled their ten-speeds across town to scout their new territory.

"Did you hear about Miss Hornung?" Eddie said as they coasted along Riverside Road. "She's teaching at PH&VS this year. She follows us around like a fuckin' snotball."

They pulled up in front of the building.

"It looks like a jail," Robert said after a while.

"It *is* a jail," said Eddie, leaning forward on his handlebars. "My Dad said this is the start of a whole new phase in my life. I told him he should write an editorial about it. I say this place is just a bigger cage than the one they had us in, and the girls here all have tits. So what?"

"Do you want to have a look at the football field?"

"What for? I already know what a football field looks like. Let's get out of here, Rosseter. We've still got a whole afternoon of summer left."

Eddie sped away. But Robert lingered.

* * *

II

(1977-1982)

7

> Who says youth is wasted on the young? Would you knowingly re-enter the danger zone of danger zones?
>
> —Theodore Ng

Giles Robert Rosseter decided to decontaminate his room that fall. One of the few remaining visible props was an alarm clock that didn't work properly. He awoke bolt upright in the dead of night whenever it stopped ticking, even though he'd wound the shit out of it before going to sleep. What his eyes beheld in the pale, diffuse streetlight was nobody's room. There was nothing anywhere, not even a mess.

But a visitor gingerly opening the door of Robert's closet would have spied, in a heap, a faded framed photograph of Preston Wilhelm O'Hagan, the half-finished chassis of a plastic model Camaro, a toy telescope, microscope, stereoscope, periscope, kaleidoscope and camera, a small jar containing dead houseflies, a Montreal Expos cap, a Magnajector, games of Monopoly, Careers and Mille Bornes, granite-hard pieces of Dubble Bubble gum, oils, acrylics, watercolours, sketch pads, Laurentian colouring pencils, an "official" CFL football, a fluorescent frisbee, the *Star Wars* novelization, one of his mother's old notebooks containing drawings of cats and cardinals, a Christmas issue of *Ideals*, graph paper, four incomplete geometry sets, an Ansonville T-shirt (he didn't know anyone from Ansonville and had never been there), an unopened wood-burning kit that once belonged to his father, a *Mad* magazine pocketbook of Don Martin cartoons and, very near the back, a stuffed panda with one eye missing. Years ago, the panda had inspired him to compose a rhyme:

Little Johnny Panda Bear
Was going to the market.
He took his little motorcar
But found no place to park it.

Had the cord been long enough he would have stored his private telephone in the closet, so invigorating was the absence of personal property. It was just a room now.

Robert had no such control over the crowded, ammoniated corridors of Presley High & Vocational School. Jostled by older students as they rushed to their sweethearts' lockers, football practice or chemistry class, Robert's body adopted a cool but self-deprecating slouch. He practised the slouch at home. It struck him as just the right kind of swaggering defensiveness to get him safely through high school. Occasionally he asked Eddie Laverty to slouch with him down to the river for lunch period, to eat their egg-salad sandwiches in peace, crumple the wax paper, chuck it into the Kekagami and watch it float away on the glassy brown water. But Eddie preferred to spend lunch across the street from the school at Korner Variety & Grill, where the fries were greasy, the jukebox relentless and the corner booth suitably removed from the real world. Robert admired Eddie's ability to fit in even when he didn't fit in at all, his peculiar aptitude for seeking out the edge of the world and staking a claim. Robert, meanwhile, slouched with his back to his locker, like someone more or less trying not to fall off the ledge of a very tall building.

One Friday evening in March of 1978, he stared into the bathroom mirror at his face raw from scrubbing and after-shave lotioning and cologning, every strand of hair in place, every freckle and pimple on his forehead, nose and chin neutralized by Clearasil. He stared at his nice navy cords and nice shirt with navy checks, his nice navy socks and navy haircut and face. He was about to leave for the first bona fide party of his adolescence and he looked like he belonged in a Woolco window, or on the deck of a frigate. Just as well, he shrugged.

Robert was aware of the evening's hazards, but Sue-Ann Reilly's mother was an occasional tennis partner of his mother's, so Kathleen had been adamant about his attendance at the party.

"You spend too much time cooped up in that empty room of yours," she said. "You don't get enough exercise and you don't have enough colour in your cheeks. You don't socialize enough with people your own age. All work and no plays makes Giles a dull boy."

"Please don't call me Giles," said Robert.

He resisted his mother's offer to chauffeur him to Sue-Ann's house. "Her house is only a few blocks away," he said while slipping on his nice navy all-weather jacket. "Besides, the fresh air will put some colour in my cheeks." The fresh air might also blunt the severe pleat Kathleen had ironed into his navy trousers.

Kathleen couldn't help noticing the fragrance of Old Spice—Steven's fragrance— in the hall after she presented her cheek for a kiss. This made her wistful.

Robert briskly walked the nineteen blocks to the Reilly home. His martial footsteps rang out in the crisp spring night. He proceeded to the tune of Colonel Bogey's March. He was William Holden (or was it Jack Hawkins or Trevor Howard?) about to collapse dead on the detonator that would blow shards of broken bridge all over the shallow River Kwai. He could hear the train a-comin', scarin' the shit out of monkeys and macaws. *Must get to detonator. Blow bridge. Little time. Movie almost over.*

A woman opened the front door.

"Mrs. Reilly?"

"I used to be," the woman said. "Call me Jocelyn. You're Giles Rosseter, aren't you?"

"Robert," said Robert, nodding.

The interior of the house glowed an eerie, uncongenial yellow. Someone had recently fried a minute steak with too much garlic powder on it. The former Mrs. Reilly took Robert's jacket.

"How's your mom?" she said. Her breath smelled of liquor.

"She's fine, very fine," Robert said.

"Quite the tennis player, your mom is."

Robert nodded. The pleat in his trousers was as severe as ever.

"The kids are downstairs, through the door on your right."

Robert felt the bass-heavy throbbing of music through the floor. It sounded like the boiler room of a mammoth ocean liner—perhaps the Titanic. When he opened the door, the anonymous throbbing became the *Saturday Night Fever* soundtrack. The smell of dirty laundry and flat beer intensified as he descended the stairs. Sue-Ann Reilly and her friends had placed two long, narrow couches against opposite walls of the basement. On one of the couches sat two boys, neither of them Eddie Laverty. On the opposite couch sat four girls, including Sue-Ann Reilly.

"Hi Giles," Sue-Ann said. The three girls next to her found her remark uproariously funny.

"Ha— ha— ha— ha— stayin' alive!" the Bee Gees enthused. Robert assumed a position on the boys' couch. He glanced at his fly to see if it was the source of the girls' amusement.

He noticed all the girls had their stockinged feet tucked under their legs. He understood why: It was bloody freezing in this basement. He looked it over, ran a hand along the surface of the ersatz Spanish provincial coffee table.

"This is a nice basement," he said.

"Pardon?" said Sue-Ann Reilly. The music was dense and obnoxious.

"I said you have a nice basement."

"It's not a *basement*," said Sue-Ann Reilly. "It's a rec room." The other girls laughed.

"My parents call ours a family room," said the boy who occupied the far right of the couch. Robert didn't know his name.

"Pardon?" said Sue-Ann Reilly, irritably.

"Does everybody have enough Coke and ginger ale?" the former Mrs. Reilly called down from the top of the stairs.

"Pardon?"

She descended a couple of steps. "Sue-Ann, will you please turn down the stereo. I was asking if everyone had enough pop."

Assorted polite affimatives were murmured. Even Robert agreed, though no one had yet offered him anything to drink.

"Is anybody cold?" the former Mrs. Reilly wanted to know.

Assorted polite negatives.

"If you need anything," she said, "just give me a shout."

Silence.

"And Sue-Ann, don't be playing the stereo too loud."

"God," Sue-Ann Reilly said. The former Mrs. Reilly disappeared back up the stairs.

"Hey, Sue-Ann," whispered the Brezinski youth, a hefty boy who occupied the better part of the left half of the couch, "don't you have anything harder?"

"Harder than what?" said Sue-Ann Reilly.

"Than panther piss," the Brezinski youth replied with a snigger, hoisting his glass of ginger ale and looking to his male comrades for approval. Two of the three girls next to Sue-Ann Reilly laughed. Sue-Ann Reilly made a face at the Brezinski youth. (He was her next-door neighbour; she couldn't not have invited him.)

Robert examined his cuticles at length. So far the party was going remarkably well. Once the girls had safely returned to their private chatter he relaxed even more. He felt almost smug by the time Eddie Laverty and a handful of other classmates showed up. Due to the overflow, some girls were forced to sit on fold-out chairs on either side of their couch. The overflow boys preserved the symmetry on the boys' side of the room.

Robert was on his second ginger ale. Actual conversations were taking place, occasionally between boy and girl. It was pushing ten o'clock and no one had yet suggested dancing. He had his fingers crossed. With luck it would be too late by the time anyone worked up the nerve, and he would be home-free.

"*...You should be dancin',*" the Bee Gees admonished. The topic of conversation among several of the girls was creepy Mr. Quesnel, the history teacher who was always burping under his breath. Eddie dragged his chair close to Robert, who had yet to budge from his place on the couch, though the ginger ale had long ago made its way to his bladder.

"What kind of party is this?" Eddie said. "It's like school."

"It's not so bad," Robert whispered, hoping it would encourage Eddie to whisper.

"I had more fun at my First Communion. Look at those scrags. They don't even know how to mix."

Robert glanced across the room. "I don't see you talking to any of them."

Eddie glared at him. "This party wasn't my idea. I'm not the one that's running it. You're supposed to do something at parties, not sit around like *sta*-tues."

Sue-Ann Reilly, who had begun to sulk when she realized dreamboat Barrett "Bat" Masterson wasn't going to show, overheard the tail end of Eddie Laverty's tirade. It didn't help her disposition. This wasn't her idea of a party, either. She thought the boys were all being super-yucky, expecially the Brezinski youth, who was so sweaty she could smell him from across the room. "You guys are just a bunch of spazzes," she said, which put an abrupt end to all conversation. "This is the last time I invite any of you to a party."

Robert's mouth went suddenly dry. The record came to an end, adding silence to the tension. Everything had been going so well until Eddie opened his big fat mouth. Instinct told him to take control of the situation before it got completely out of hand.

"I'm having fun, Sue-Ann," he volunteered. "I think your party has been a—"

"All you ever do is stare at your fingernails," Sue-Ann Reilly snarled. "What do *you* know?"

So much for instinct.

"You're no Lola Falana yourself, Sue-Ann," the Brezinski youth interjected. Everyone immediately regretted this peculiar remark, because now Sue-Ann Reilly was on the verge of tears. Robert needed desperately to scratch his crotch. He hadn't up to then considered that being invited to a party entailed any specific responsibility to be sociable. The evening had been wearing on so smoothly, but now anything could happen. (Did he smell B.O. in the room? Definitely. The sweat stains on the Brezinski youth's sport shirt had spread as far as his ribs.)

"Let's *do* something," Eddie said. "That's what parties are for."

The girls conferred. Maxine Duguard, Sue-Ann Reilly's best friend, suggested they play spin-the-bottle. Her suggestion took even the Brezinski youth by surprise.

"Sounds good to me," said Eddie, who by now had become the boys' spokesman by default. Robert offered no opinion. He wished he were marching home to the strains of Colonel Bogey's March.

Andrea Veraldi, who wore braces, volunteered to keep watch for the former Mrs. Reilly at the top of the stairs. Sue-Ann Reilly took an empty ginger ale bottle from the bar, ran to the stereo and flipped the record over."Okay," she said, "who starts?"

"You do," said Eddie.

Sue-Ann Reilly didn't seem to mind. She pushed the coffee table out of the way, kneeled in the neutral zone between the couches and spun the bottle. It came to a stop pointing at Maxine Duguard.

"Haw haw haw," said the Brezinski youth. "Now this I gotta see. 'Lesbe friends and go homo.' Haw haw."

"Shut up, you big geek," Sue-Ann Reilly said. She spun the bottle a second time. It ended up more or less pointing at Eddie Laverty. Robert felt a bead of sweat trickle down from his left amrpit. All eyes were on Sue-Ann Reilly as she gracefully rose, crossed the floor to where Eddie was sitting, cupped his face in her hands and planted a long, emphatic kiss on his mouth.

The girls squealed, the boys roared. Even the Brezinski youth acknowledged Sue-Ann Reilly's pluck.

Robert was spellbound. It was as though a thousand veils had been withdrawn from between himself and his hostess. The entire room, perhaps the entire cosmos, was suddenly crystalline and immediate— nothing more so than the mild flush on the lightly freckled face of Sue-Ann Reilly. Robert was agog. He knew in his soul, at that precise moment, he had never seen anyone as beautiful.

A rap on the door broke the spell. Andrea Veraldi all but toppled down the stairs in an effort to get out of the way.

"Time to go, kids," said the former Mrs. Reilly. "It's going on eleven."

"Aw *Mom*?"

"Come on, Sue-Ann. That was the deal."

"I should get going anyway, I've got bowling in the morning," the Brezinski youth muttered. Others agreed. Robert didn't know what to think anymore.

"Give us one more minute, Mom," Sue-Ann Reilly said.

"All right, but that's it." The door closed.

"Time for one last spin. Here." Sue-Ann Reilly handed the bottle to Maxine Duguard, who blushed, kneeled and spun. Robert was certain he wanted out of this one. So were all the other boys. Maxine was gangly and had a moustache. The boys flinched each time the bottleneck crossed their territory. Trapped in some weird travesty of time and space, the bottle seemed to spin for geological ages before slowing and finally coming to rest pointing at Robert.

"Ho ho ho, Roosterbrains," the Brezinski youth chortled.

"What a way to cap off an evening."

"Shut up, Fatso," Sue-Ann Reilly snapped.

"*You* shut up, Skinnyso," the Brezinski youth shot back.

Robert was inert, as though welded to the ersatz Spanish provincial couch. Maxine Duguard was no less enervated.

"Come on, you guys," whined Sue-Ann Reilly. "We haven't got all night."

"I bet Roosterbrains wished he had," the Brezinski youth said with a laugh.

"Listen, Brezinski," Robert said, turning to face his portly antagonist, "if you call me Roosterbrains one more time, I swear I'm gonna. . ."

Maxine rose from the couch. Robert watched transfixed as she came toward him. She stopped, bent forward and closed her eyes. He closed his. Eventually his mouth made contact with a wall of clenched teeth, as though he were kissing the keyboard of a toy piano.

. . .

Robert's sex education had been spotty at best. When he was ten years old, his newly-single father took it upon himself to elucidate the facts of life. Robert had never made any specific inquiries, which Steven interpreted as evidence of distressful inhibitions unconsciously induced by the boy's sexually straitjacketed mother. Over ice cream cones in the Dairy Queen parking lot one August evening, Steven began by disussing puberty, then girls (for whom Robert professed no interest), then sex.

"The way a woman has a baby," he said, "is that the man puts his penis into the woman's vagina, and sperm from the man's penis spurts into the vagina and fertilizes her egg. A foetus forms in the woman's womb and nine months later a baby is born."

"How does the man get his penis into the woman?" Robert inquired, dutifully warming to the subject while chipping flakes of solid chocolate dip from the soft ice cream.

"The man's penis gets hard and the woman's vagina gets soft and wet when they're making love. That makes it easy for the penis to go into the vagina."

"Then what?" said Robert, licking distractedly.

"Then the man moves his penis around inside the vagina until the sperm spurts out of his penis."

"How long does that take?"

"It varies from person to person. The average is maybe five minutes."

"How does he get his penis to move around?"

"By moving his hips back and forth, in and out, like people do with a hula hoop, only he's lying down on top of the woman."

Robert tried to picture that; it struck him as comical.

"What makes the penis hard?"

"Blood from other parts of the body flows into it," Steven said, "and it stiffens."

"Is that what's called a boner?"

"Right."

"How come blood goes into the boner?"

"That automatically happens when the man is sexually excited."

"Why?"

"To make the penis hard," Steven said.

Robert stopped licking. "How does blood make a penis hard?"

"Well," Steven said, "I guess it. . . it makes the penis more dense or something. I'm not sure. But that's what happens when a man gets excited."

Robert gnawed on the edge of the cone. "If the man's penis gets hard when it's excited, how come the woman's vagina gets soft?"

"That's so the man and woman can make love together, and the sperm can fertilize the egg."

Robert gnawed some more, then said, "That's *stu*-pid. The man has to do all the work, and then his blood spurts out all over the woman."

"Not his blood, Bob, his sperm. And when the sperm is released, it feels really nice." He bit down on his cone with a crunch.

"But you said the penis fills up with blood."

"That's not what comes out of it when the man ejaculates. The blood isn't in the little tube that sends the sperm into the vagina."

"What does 'ejaculate' mean?"

"That's when the sperm comes out of the little tube."

"You said the sperm comes out of the penis."

"It does, it does," said Steven. "There's a little tube inside the penis— not the part of it that has the blood— that carries the sperm from your balls into her vagina."

"My *balls*?" Robert said.

"That's where the sperm is made, the same way a woman's ovaries make eggs. It's called the scrotum."

"Do the man's balls get hard when he's excited?"

"They don't have to get hard."

"They just go into the woman the way they are?"

"They don't go into the woman," said Steven, who was beginning to regret having raised the subject. "All they do is manufacture the sperm for the penis when it goes into the woman. It's the sperm that goes to the ovaries to fertilize the woman's eggs."

"Where are the woman's ovaries?"

"They're up her vagina, in the Fallopian tubes or something. I'm not sure."

"How come my balls aren't in my Fallopian tubes?"

"Because you don't have a vagina," Steven sighed, "you have a penis. All men have penises. . . Some women wish they had penises."

"They do? Why?"

"I guess they'd like to feel what it's like when it's hard."

"That's *stu*-pid," Robert said, popping the last of his cone into his mouth. "I hope my penis never gets hard."

"You'll change your mind," said Steven, wiping his hands.

"So what happens after the sperm comes out of the penis?"

"The penis eventually gets soft again, then the man slides it out of the woman and they both go to sleep."

"What if it's the middle of the day?"

"Usually people make love at night."

"Why?"

"Because that's when they're in bed," Steven said.

When he was very young, Robert wandered into his parents' bedroom early one Sunday morning because he felt sick. His mother was lying on top of his father, under the blankets. The strands of her red hair seemed to slither over her bare back, like Medusa's. "I've got a fever," he announced. His mother reacted with a look of surprise, but said nothing. He couldn't see his father's face under his mother's, but he heard his voice say, "Go back to bed for a little while and we'll check in on you in a couple of minutes." Robert obeyed. Back in his bed, staring at the ceiling that seemed to swim above him, he wondered how his parents could sleep that way.

"Does the woman ever lie on top when they're making love?" Robert now pertinently asked.

"Some women like to," Steven said.

"Did you and Mom ever make love?"

"That should be obvious, since you're here to ask the question. All married people make love."

"Do you and Carol What'shername make love?" Robert asked, licking sticky ice cream from his wrist.

Steven dug into his pocket for his car keys. "That's none of your business," he said.

"How come?"

"Because it isn't."

So ended Robert's sex education.

If love was just a horizontal hula dance, all sweat and blood and sperm, how did it pertain to the curious ache he carried into the day after the party at Sue-Ann Reilly's house some four years later? Why were his pulse rate, galvanic skin response, heart and soul now seemingly under the control of someone he didn't even know?

By evening, he had dragged Eddie into his cogitation. They huddled together in a booth at D'Agostino's, pulling hard on chocolate malts. Robert was searching for newer, more clever ways to ask Eddie a simple enough question: What did kissing Sue-Ann Reilly feel like?

"You know what it's like," Eddie replied. "You kissed Maxine Duguard, didn't you?"

"That's not what I mean," Robert said with an impatience born of utter desperation. "What I mean is. . ."

"What?"

"What I mean is. . ."

He hadn't imagined confusion could burn so intensely. What he meant was: To kiss someone's soul— the sort of mystical hula dance you might want to write a sonnet about, or strum a lute in medieval moonlight. "I don't know what I mean," he finally admitted.

"You sure have been going on about it," Eddie said.

"I know," Rosseter agreed, as though commenting on the mental condition of a mutual acquaintance.

"Don't tell me you have a crush on Sue-Ann."

"Drop dead," said Robert as dismissively as possible.

Crush: The word was rife with unpleasant associations. Infatuation gnawed at him because he was incapable of identifying it as such and had no sound reasons for suffering it at all. He knew as much as he needed to know about the hot lubricated mechanics of sex. He knew where babies came from. What he didn't know was where love came from. It was as though an unimaginable amount of what P.W. called emotional luggage had miraculously accumulated overnight and evolved into a black hole, from the enormous gravity of which not even the light of intellect could escape.

"Forget about her," Eddie said. "She's crazy about Bat Masterson. Everybody knows that."

"What do I care?" said Robert as convincingly as possible. He sucked on the dregs of his malt. *Sluuuuuuuuu*... Christ, he couldn't even summon a reasonable likeness of her in his mind. He couldn't remember what colour eyes she had, or what she smelled like. But something about her, some unseen but overwhelming distillation of her, was vivid and ubiquitous. This manifestation of Sue-Ann Reilly had a life of its own, apart from whatever the real Sue-Ann Reilly was about. This phantom of her was a foreign substance preying on the soft tissue of his libido, overpowering antibodies in its relentless campaign to conquer his ego. Robert shuddered at the thought of the havoc actually getting to know her might wreak. *Sluuuuu. Sluuuuuuuuuu*...

"Stop that fuckin' noise," Eddie commanded. "You look like a guppy when you do it. A guppy with fish and tail rot, waiting to go to belly-up. Jesus, there's nothing more pathetic than a guy a girl has power over."

"What power?" said Robert as innocently as possible.

"'What power?'" Eddie mimicked.

"What do you mean, 'power'?"

"I mean power."

"What kind of power?"

"*Power* power."

"Shit," Robert said.

At school on Monday morning, he wandered nonchalantly over to Sue-Ann Reilly's desk and thanked her for the party.

"It was fun."

"Yeah, well, no thanks to you spazzes," Sue-Ann Reilly said, turning her back on him.

Nevertheless, he floated through classrooms and corridors the rest of the day.

. . .

Robert would long recall the vicissitudes of that first love as though it were only yesterday. Already, he had a bad habit of existing out of time. Twenty years ago was often the day after tomorrow. The third Wednesday of next month was sometimes Thanksgiving Day 1970. Time was made of thin glare ice; there was no sense trusting even the smallest fraction of it.

Early in his twenties, when he began reading the philosophers, he found his personal time-space orientation validated by savants from as long ago as classical Greece. So much was arbitrary. His existence was based on a number of tenuous circumstantial links—a couple of pounds of arbitrary sausage in a metaphysical meat store. Things could just as easily have gone quite another way. He liked to picture the scenarios:

In one alternate universe Robert was never conceived. Steven Rosseter was killed in a fiery car crash and Kathleen O'Hagan entered a convent to the chagrin of Preston Wilhelm O'Hagan, who was on retainer to a number of Toronto-Hamilton-Buffalo underworld figures.

In one alternate universe Robert was a Thalidomide baby.

In one alternate universe Robert married Sue-Ann Reilly and they converted to Scientology after their twin daughters, Sheila and Cilla, were struck and killed outside Rivoli, Italy, by a syphilitic priest driving a lime-green Fiat.

In one alternate universe, all the circumstances of Robert's life were identical to those of this life, except for one detail: Hop Sing didn't have his hair lopped off by desperadoes.

Robert speculated that the phenomenon called *déjà-vu* was actually the leakage of an almost identical alternate universe into his own. In that other universe, time was flowing fractionally more slowly, hence the feeling that he had already lived through a particular moment. Clairvoyance was caused by the opposite phenomenon, the leakage from an alternate universe on a time-track slightly in advance of his own. Human memory was forever suspect, as were sensory perception and the conventional definitions of sanity. Robert's efforts to extricate himself from the passive, invisible clutches of Sue-Ann Reilly weren't working precisely because inner space was as deadly and convoluted as the external world. It wasn't just a jungle out there; it was a jungle everywhere and everywhen, filtered through one fraudulent sensation after another.

What if he were to fight Sue-Ann Reilly's absurd spell over him by consciously distracting his untrustworthy senses? What if he were to cultivate a rigourous fixation on someone else? Into what parallel universe would such a strategy propel him? Suddenly, he needed to know.

Cynthia Thomas was fifteen and slightly overripe, having failed her first year of high school. Her favourite top, one she wore seemingly three days out of five, was a quasi-fishnet affair through which, under salutary lighting conditions such as those of the drama club meeting room or the cafeteria, her commodious flesh-toned brassiere was plainly visible. Robert studied her brassiere from a safe distance while eating his salmon sandwich. He meditated on matters pertaining to mass, weight, inertia, body temperature, perspiration and other bodily secretions he more or less understood. In his imagination he subjected Cynthia Thomas' brassiere to a battery of scientific tests: Was it biodegradable? did it chafe? would she not be more comfortable out of it? would she kindly remove it so that he could send it to the lab for more thorough analysis?

A few tables down from Cynthia Thomas, Sue-Ann Reilly held court with her girlfriends. Robert discreetly examined her upper torso: a pair of unspectacular bumps under an azure sweater. The conclusion was clear. To rid himself of a more long-term slavery, he was compelled to harness his id to the melons of Cynthia Thomas.

The latter had just finished her plate of french fries and was on her way out of the cafeteria alongside a girl Robert didn't know. Without forethought he abandoned his fruit cup and blazed a diagonal trail to the door, where they converged.

"Hello there, Cynthia," he heard himself declaim.

"Bobby, hi," Cynthia Thomas said, surprised.

His heart was in his constricted throat. Now what?

"I was wondering whether..." He felt his face get warm. Cynthia Thomas grandly swept auburn hair out of her eyes with one deft flick of her head. "...I could borrow your math notes. My mind was wandering in class this morning and..."

"You want to borrow my math notes?"

"I thought maybe I could copy the—"

"I'm not very good at math, Bobby," Cynthia Thomas said with an incredulous laugh.

"Well, I... well, you know, it's... I just... you know..."

Cynthia Thomas glanced at her friend. "You really want my math notes?" she said, squinting.

Robert nodded.

"Okay," she said with a mystified shrug. "It's in my locker. Come on, Janie."

The two girls rushed down the corridor to the lockers. Robert evaporated against the wall. He couldn't have chosen a more lame pretext for talking to her. From an academic standpoint, Cynthia Thomas was dolt of dolts. He righted himself and drifted just outside the cafeteria. He prayed to the gods of all universes that this ludicrous transaction would be completed before lunch period ended and the others began filing out.

Eons later, Cynthia Thomas came bobbing back up the corridor. "Here," she said breathlesly, handing him the notebook. "But I don't think it'll be any help."

Robert was about to say something incoherent in the way of thanks when the bell rang above his head. He flinched.

"We've got to run," Cynthia Thomas said. "Hornung takes a hairy if we're late for Health. 'Bye."

Robert bowed.

Health class. God damn: What he would have given to observe her from a darkened room, through a two-way mirror, talking about scrotums. He watched in a daze, clutching the pink notebook, as the others made their way back to class. Sue-Ann Reilly swept by, glanced conspicuously at the pink notebook and levelled a glare at Robert that would have crushed the skull of a large rat.

That night, up in his sterilized room, he carefully removed the scribbler from his bag, switched off his desk lamp, climbed into bed and turned on the reading light. The cover was standard enough:

CYNTHIA THOMAS
LEVEL ONE ARITHMETIC

Did anybody call it arithmetic anymore?

He opened the notebook. Long divisions, like upside down Towers of Babel, tailed off into minuscule collections of numbers that had little to do with the original problem. The neatest, most impressive of all the work was *Let x represent*, which Cynthia Thomas had inscribed at the bottom of the page in florid longhand. He turned the page and saw more of the same, except she had taken to practising her ornate longhand in the margin. From top to bottom

of the page was her signature. Looking more closely, he noticed that the

CYNTHIA THOMAS
CYNTHIA THOMAS
CYNTHIA THOMAS

evolved about halfway down the page into

CYNTHIA BREZINSKI
CYNTHIA BREZINSKI
CYNTHIA BREZINSKI

and concluded in a slightly more tentative

CYNTHIA THOMAS-BREZINSKI
CYNTHIA THOMAS-BREZINSKI
CYNTHIA THOMAS-BREZINSKI

The Brezinski youth! Robert was astonished.

Few other pages had markings of any interest, with no longhand in the margins except for a small, rococo

CYNTHIA BREZINSKI-THOMAS

on the back page.

Robert closed the notebook and brought it up to his nose. It smelled vaguely of perfume and foundation, like his mother's makeup drawer. He closed his eyes and imagined he was sniffing Cynthia Thomas' brassiere. He felt a stirring in his pyjama bottoms. There was a knock on the door and his mother poked her head in.

"I'm going to bed now, honey."

Robert abashedly set the scribbler down. "I wish you'd knock before coming in."

"I did knock."

"Well you should knock harder."

"I'll try to remember that." Kathleen said. "Have you brushed your teeth?"

"For God's sake, Ma, I'm not a child."

"Sorry, sorry." She closed the door and called out "good night" from the hall.

On the back of Cynthia Thomas' notebook, in the bottom right-hand corner, he spied a tiny inscription in red ink:

C.T.
L.
T.B.Y.

It amazed him that even Cynthia Thomas apparently didn't know the Christian name of the object of her love. Brezinski kept it secret and the school authorities complied with his wishes. He was known simply as "the Brezinski youth".

Cynthia Thomas' evident attraction to someone else didn't disappoint him. If anything, it freed him to focus his senses on lascivious thoughts of her without being compelled to regret any possible exploitation or misunderstanding of intentions. This he now did with gusto, drinking her scent from the paper and willing the fragrance to assume physical contours in his imagination. This proved even more tantalizing and dangerous than the time he and Eddie found a withered, sepia copy of *Fotorrific* behind a billboard near D'Agostino's. The boys raced on their ten-speeds to a deserted picnic area near the Kekagami, where they feasted their eyes on newsprint-quality photographs of women with newsprint-quality bodies whose poses suggested sundry vile delights. Pure danger was the stimulant that time; the tingling sensation was generalized over his whole body. The time he happened upon the *Penthouse* magazines neatly stacked in his father's linen closet, he was too busy disvovering that women had a hairy V on their crotch to feel much of anything. Though he was able to glean more raw anatomical information from *Penthouse*, he preferred the rotting little yellow pamphlet.

But now, lying in his bed with the light out and not a creature stirring all through the house, he felt no sense of danger— merely the deepening of a sensation that was still unfamilar to him. He held the scribbler against his face. He brought his hand down to his pyjama bottoms and was startled by his own hot solidity. Waves of pleasure emanated up to his brain and back down again.

His bed was the furthest point from anywhere in the world. He floated slowly into a half-sleep, where voices he didn't recognize whispered words he didn't know, a distant piano played and radiant colours combined into the bright pulsating light of the PH&VS cafeteria. All alone like a mirage in the blinding distance was Cynthia Thomas. He floated in her direction, or she and the rest of the world to him. In front of her, on a plate, a Westphaler sausage, red and alive, grew more dense and substantial. She leered a *Fotorrific* leer, said You Want Them Don't You?, cupped her hands on them, said Take Them Giles Robert Rosseter For Your Very Own To Have And To Hold So Help You God I Do. Two boa constrictors slithered down her milkwhite collarbone and under her blouse. Hands found ground zero and no bra. These were the Mercator Globes of the World, twin suns, Betelgeuse in distant space. The Creator moulded and kneaded the primeval mass, and by the time He discovered it was the Westphaler sausage He was fondling and not the Mercator Globes, He was moltengranite and there was no postponing the Big Bang:

Let. . . there. . . be. . . L I F E !

When his malfunctioning alarm clock rang shortly before dawn, Giles Robert awoke to the crusty remnants of a warm goo gone stonecold in his pyjama bottoms and on the cover of a pink mathematics notebook, property of Cynthia Thomas.

. . .

By the time the first light leaked into his room, Robert had decided he was sick and would not leave his bed for a couple of days. By then, with any luck, the incriminating stains would have evaporated or simply have faded from the sheets and the notebook. At this point, he wasn't entirely sure the stuff was dead. For all he knew, millions of tiny tadpoles wriggled this minute in the crotch of his flannel pyjamas, the potential population of the Western Hemisphere swimming frantically in search of a familar Fallopian landmark.

"You don't have a temperature," said Kathleen, frowning over her son, who clutched the bedspread to his chin.

"It's some kind of flu. I feel terrible. Believe me."

"I believe you," Kathleen said, "but I can't imagine what it might be. Maybe I should call Doctor Paine's office. They might be able to—"

"It's not that serious," Robert quickly interjected. "A couple of days in bed and I'll be fine."

"You think so?"

"It's just some kind of forty-eight hour virus."

"I don't know of any forty-eight hour virus, Bobby, but tell you what: Stay in bed this morning and I'll look in on you at noon. We'll play it by ear from there."

"Sounds good, Ma. But I'm pretty sure it's one of those two-day things. Dad always gets it. He spends two days in bed and then he's fine, like he was never sick at all. It's weird."

After his mother was safely out of the house, Robert folded back the bedcovers for a more thorough inspection of the problem. It wasn't as bad as he had first feared; the beige sheets had all but absorbed the stain. A coarse brush would take care of any residual crustiness. The pyjama bottoms were a more serious problem: He would have to spirit them into the laundry hamper and hope for the best. Cynthia Thomas' math notebook was worst of all— bent, folded and irreparably stained. In a sudden fit of perverse self-assurance, he tentatively decided to give the notebook, stains and all, back to her. He'd tell her he spilled lemon spread on it and was willing to defray the cost of a new notebook.

First things first: He stripped off his pyjamas and stuffed them deep into the laundry hamper, found a suede brush in the kitchen closet and went to work on the sheets. Then he put on a fresh pair of pyjamas and jumped back into bed, pondered the biological implications of the night before and patiently awaited his mother's return to share the amazing news of his recovery.

"I'm glad to hear it," Kathleen said. "I see you changed your pyjamas."

Robert had foreseen the question. "They got all sweaty and uncomfortable. I must have sweated the virus off or something. I put them in the hamper."

"Good. I was going to put a load of wash on before going back to work. Maybe you'd better stay in bed this afternoon, just to be safe."

"If you say so." *A load of wash?*

Sorting through the dirty clothes downstairs, Kathleen came upon her son's pyjamas, tucked down near the bottom of the hamper where an old orange cardigan of Steven's had been lying for years. She spotted the stain. Her reaction perplexed her. She wondered what dream had caused it, who or what was responsible. Had she and/or Steven adequately filled him on on the birds and the bees? (She knew she hadn't.) Was he terribly embarrassed, or afraid he was dying of some horrible disease? She wished she could call Steven to confer with him but he was away on some other plane of consciousness, a twin-engine aircraft trailing thick black smoke through clouds of purest white. *Bon voyage*, Steven. Her father wouldn't have been much help, either. A lecherous uncle from Red Lake itemized the birds and the bees to her one summer afternoon in 1958. From the day she made the mistake of telling her father about it, he refused to speak to his brother-in-law. P.W. had consoled himself for his own errors of omission by concluding it would have been easier to broach the subject of sex with a son than a daughter. Kathleen's mother was out of the question, he realized. To her, sex was something you indulged in on those rare occasions when you forgot your better self. Making love was no more nor less than a mystery to be tolerated from generation to generation. It also happened to have been one of her husband's bad habits.

Kathleen couldn't have imagined either of her parents preaching about sex, let alone practising it. Staring at her son's soiled pyjamas made the subject no less alien to her now. It made her feel alone, and filled her with the weary realization that her boy was growing into seasons that pointed her own life in the direction of something finite and beyond her control.

They sat together that evening in front of the television. Kathleen leafed through a folder describing a revolutionary new merchandising program called the Bernardy System. Robert read a Philip K. Dick novel about androids. The TV set was off. She put her booklet down and gave her son a big hug, bigger than usual.

"Hey, what gives?" Robert said, squirming.

"Everything gives," his mother said.

* * *

8

> So much of what we fear is externally programmed, yet so few of us fear the programming itself. We rail against being cogs even as we refine the machinery. What strange beings we are.
>
> —Theodore Ng

Kathleen had little time to coach her son in his marathon wrestling match with his hormones now that she had joined the Bernardy System. Soon she would have more time, she told herself again and again. Maybe they'd go away on a holiday. Right now she was up to her ears in work.

More than once she attempted to explain to her son the intricate workings of the Bernardy System, whereby the simple ability to motivate others in their spare time translated into the prospect of untold riches. Robert wasn't surprised it was Helen Munsinger who had talked her into attending a couple of introductory sessions at the community centre. Helen always liked to be on the cutting edge. From his mother's breathless explanations he was able to deduce that the Bernardy System was a highly structured sales network devoted to household products said to be of a calibre vastly superior to that of the brands available in stores. Even had she found the philosophy of the System unappealing, Kathleen swore she would have been sold on the the way its non-abrasive cleanser, for example, went to work on her bathtub, removing stains she had long ago given up for permanent.

"Helen laughed when I showed her the part of the tub I cleaned with Bernardy cleanser and the part I cleaned with my old cleanser. Have you noticed the tub lately, Bobby? The difference is absolutely amazing. It gleams. And Bernardy cleanser doesn't cost that much more, really, when you take into account that you don't have to use as much of it. After seeing the bathtub, I was a believer."

Robert couldn't help but admire the minds behind the System, whoever they were. Cleanliness, godliness, easy money: How could the concept possibly fail? Even Helen Munsinger, who at first had suspected gender manipulation by the male-dominated managerial level of the System, now rose to the its defence.

"Manipulation is in the eye of the manipulee," she said. "Who's getting rich off who, Kath? Who really has the upper hand? We can drop out of the System any time we like; we can do as little or as much work as we want. The stuffed shirts who think they run the System can't do that. We're not tied to it at all. There's sexual justice in that. Think of all of us selling Bernardy products of our own free will, making new business contacts and meeting new people, while the stuffed shirts grow old and fat in their panelled offices, their arteries clogging by the day. It seems so right."

To prevent its sales army and civilian targets from becoming complacent, the System regularly introduced lines of new improved household products. The day Kathleen was designated to host a meeting of the Presley and district sales network, she left work early, cut the crusts from dainty sandwiches of egg salad, salmon, devilled ham and mock turkey, filled a borrowed coffee urn with Nabob, stocked up on wine and beer, and bought a magnum of Canadian champagne to celebrate her network's fulfillment of some esoteric quota projection drawn up by the regional office in Thunder Bay.

Robert spent most of that evening in his room, half-listening to a talk show about Zero Population Growth on a Minneapolis radio station. Occasionally he heard laughter and the clink of glasses. Later, after the coffee and sweets had induced quiet discussion of the business at hand, he crept into the hallway and listened to the group from the top of the stairs. Conspiratorial satisfaction hung in the air. They were like overconfident Christians in the catacombs of Rome. They found strength in their number and optimism in the certainty that the System was the vanguard of an imminent golden age of co-operative capitalism— a form of responsible private prosperity that even Karl Marx would have had to admire. They were entrepreneurs in their spare time, paving the way for the 1980s. "And the thing that's so wonderful is we're truly helping others," one of them said.

Robert crept down the stairs and hung a hard right toward the kitchen in search of a snack. The former Mrs. Reilly, weaving slightly by the sink as she tried to pop the cork of a bottle of white wine, spotted him before he could make an about-face.

"I could use your help," she said, extending the bottle to him.

Robert silently took the bottle from her. All her fellow entrepreneurs had graduated to coffee; he wondered if she intended to drink the whole bottle herself. He tugged hard on the corckscrew but it didn't give.

"They put those corks in so tight it's a wonder any of them ever come out," the former Mrs. Reilly said. She took her glass from the counter and sipped. The wine in it was red.

"You have to pull on it in a certain. . . way," Robert said, feigning expertise. The corkscrew came out of the bottle without a pop. He handed the bottle to her.

The former Mrs. Reilly tilted the bottle to her glass, but no wine poured out. "You're Giles," she said, still pouring. "A friend of Sue-Ann's. Remember me? I'm Jocelyn."

"I prefer Robert," he said, gravely watching the wine in the bottle defy gravity.

"She's told me a little bit about you," the former Mrs. Reilly said, still pouring. "You're a big boy. Do you play football or hockey?"

"I think there's something wrong with the bottle," Robert said, moving toward her. She looked at him, at the bottle, and laughed an adolescent laugh.

"Bobby," she said, putting her hand on his chest, "you left half of the cork in the bottle." She leaned forward, until her flushed face and fermented breath were only a few centimetres from him. "You pulled it out so hard you broke it in two."

"What do I do now?" Robert said, paralysed by the unfamiliarity of the entire situation.

"Get a little knife and we'll shove the cork down into the bottle. Where does your mother keep her little knives?"

Robert diplomatically backed away from her toward the utensil drawer. Fishing around for a knife, he could feel the former Mrs. Reilly's unfocused gaze on his back.

"So do you play football?" she said.

"Not at school. My friend and I sometimes throw a ball around." He found a slender steak knife and handed it to her.

"We better push it in together," she said, sliding the knife into the neck of the bottle. "Put your hand around mine and when I say push, push."

Robert obeyed. Her hand was surprisingly warm. Her entire body, next to him, was surprisingly warm.

"Okay, push," she said, twisting her body toward him until they were belly to belly. The cork fell soundlessly into the bottle. Robert could smell not only the wine in the bottle and on her breath, but pleasant perfume, shampoo and soap. She leaned forward and kissed him lightly beside the mouth. "Thank you, honey," she said, touching his cheek, and disappeared into the living room with the bottle and her glass.

Adults, Robert grumbled to himself. *Think they own kids. Touchy touchy kissy kissy. Honey sweetheart. Help me with this, help me with that. Dirty old woman. Paw paw peck peck. Jesus.*

He retired to his room and longed for the spirit of P.W. O'Hagan to ooze out of the walls and put a scare into all the women downstairs. He'd tell them the Bernardy System was nothing more than a ploy by businessmen to capitalize on women's subconscious desire to return to their mothers' state of grace, gabbing about household cleansers and small appliances in broadloomed living rooms.

Change, change, change, yet no change: That was the ultimate state of things. Eventually everyone turned into an automaton, drawn this way and pushed that way by unseen forces, reduced by various mysterious instincts to the condition of bumper cars in an amusement park. Free will was nothing more than a rumour. The best a person could hope for was to avoid being sideswiped. To that end, Robert used his continuing carnal desire for Cynthia Thomas as a counterforce to his unfounded spiritual devotion to Sue-Ann Reilly (notwithstanding her dirty old mother). But he doubted he would recognize the moment when the proper balance was achieved. Besides, what good was such a balance if it only meant being frozen in space at an equal distance from two heavenly bodies?

Instead of boldly returning Cynthia Thomas' shot-spotted mathematics notebook to her, he manufactured a sheepish story to the effect that his mother had mistaken her notebook for a magazine and thrown it into the garbage. He lent Cynthia Thomas his own scribbler to recopy the work he ostensibly had copied from her. She of course understood little of his work, so he was forced to endure the ridicule and envy of classmates as he tutored Cynthia Thomas in math problems he wasn't supposed to have understood in the first place. During these lunch-period sessions, as Cynthia Thomas devoured her fries and Robert nibbled on a Mille Feuilles, lust and good intentions inevitably blended into a state of constant mortification. He considered it a form of penance for sins he didn't yet comprehend.

As for Sue-Ann Reilly, he could only wait for her power to wear off, like radioactivity. He tried to keep out of her way the rest of that year at school, but couldn't help stealing glances of her lengthening brown hair and delicately blossoming body in the hallway when she was at her locker, or out in front of the school at the end of the day when she kibitzed with friends while waiting for the bus. Sometimes watching Sue-Ann Reilly from a distance was physically painful.

More than once, he sketched her. One such drawing he didn't throw away, in the hope that she would consequently be frozen in the past. Instead, this artistic homage seemed to drive her that much deeper into his future.

Summer holidays, first term, Christmas, second term: Sue-Ann Sue-Ann Sue-Ann. Fear and desire spanned '78 and '79. Change, change, change, yet no change. By the summer of 1979, Robert was in a prolonged state of restless anticipation. A primeval dread ate at him as the gravitational pull of the rest of the world grew more powerful. What with the record store and the Bernardy System, his mother was seldom home, but Robert derived little comfort from the solitude. He roamed from room to room, banana sandwich in hand, as though his home were the Louvre. The only part of it that contained original art was the basement, where faded crayon scrawls like the stick-figures in the caves at Altamira offered intriguing clues from prehistory. *This was me?* he said to himself while examining what was left of a fresco. The living room, where his father once cultivated and discarded pipe- smoking, seemed to sing of days when the *Saturday Star* was strewn over every available piece of furniture. *Better Homes* was always neatly placed on the coffee table for scrutiny by Kathleen as soon as there was peace. The homes in *Better Homes,* Robert recalled, resembled opulent waiting rooms. In those homes there was always time enough to read *Better Homes,* but of course there was no need to do so, since those homes were demonstrably better already. The Rosseter living room now gave off neglect, or indifference at best. It was tidy— tidier in fact than Robert ever remembered— but so was the moon. Gone from the dining room the Rosseters had made into a den were Steven's paperback collection and pine chess-checkers table. Gone was the smell of Preston Wilhelm O'Hagan's Sunday cigars. Only the little television, surrounded on a shelf by Kathleen's knick-knacks, had survived that hectic era when arguments and all the other familiar sounds of domestic life filled the home.

Memories chased Robert into the kitchen. Its stillness and southern exposure propelled him back to the diffuse, preternatural light of Thanksgiving Day 1970, to a memory that wasn't a memory yet begged remembering.

Anticipation and dread carried Rosster out onto the comatose streets of Presley. As he walked, he imagined his eyes were a Panavision camera and the world was a movie set full of actors. The movie was

ROSSETER

starring
G. ROBERT ROSSETER

produced and directed by
G. ROBERT ROSSETER

filmed on location in

ROSSETERVILLE

and if nothing overly cinematic happened— which was usually the case— the opening credits rolled forever, listing the special-effects teams, second-unit crew, grips, gaffers, gofers, wranglers, foley artists and best boys. If still nothing of any visual interest transpired, it was obviously an experimental film that explored the subtle effects of real time projected on a screen, as in

3 AUGUST 1979

a film by g. robert rosseter

Where is Eddie Laverty these days? the filmmaker asked himself. Changing, changing, changing, yet not changing. Eddie moved in a different circle now. In fact, Eddie moved in several different circles, or epicycles, at once. Perhaps his ambition was to discover the ultimate vicious circle and become the Magellan of teenage discontent. They didn't see much of each other that summer. Walking through downtown Presley, past the wheelbarrow display in front of the Home Hardware, the table of cheap underwear and socks outside Wiseman's Men's And Boys' Wear, and the reduced-to-clear reels and rods in the window of Devillers' Sport & Tobacco Shop, Robert fancied Eddie Laverty had become one of those grizzled men of indeterminate age who regularly staked a square metre of parkette at the corner of Main and Church, stretched out on the sunscorched grass as though rehearsing for full-fledged bumhood, and pretended to enjoy the fact that there was nothing in the world to do. For that matter, Eddie could be one of the newly laid-off workers from the 4P who lounged on benches at the foot of Isaac Presley's totem pole, or one of the young Indians who wandered hopefully into town late Friday afternoons and pretended there was more to do in Presley than on the reserve.

For the purpose of the movie already in progress, Eddie Laverty was Everyboy, coming of age in a city that had fallen asleep. Being Everyboy, it was his duty to summon all junior citizens to the Main-Church Parkette and to say to them: "There's no truth to the stories you've been told about an exciting world awaiting you. This is all there is. What we have to do now is return our overdue dreams to the public library, be happy dreaming the same dream as everbody else, and pretend none of it is a dream. *(Peggy Lee singing "Is That All There Is?" comes over the soundtrack.)* Look at me: I tried to do things my way and now they've made me Everyboy and I have to work for them to straighten you out. (*Tears well in Eddie's eyes as the camera closes in.)* I don't want to be Everyboy. Would somebody here please take my place? How about you? (*Stares into the lens of the camera.)* Yeah, you, Roosterbrains." (*Cut.*)

Where is Eddie? the filmmaker asked himself, suddenly sad.

He continued walking to where the storefronts grew vacant and derelict. Loneliness turned to elation when he spotted the familiar red Camaro parked outside a narrow two-storey building. The ground-floor window displayed sepia sheet-music and used harmonicas of various sizes and shapes. A handwritten sign in the second-floor window said NG MISSION. Robert wondered what an "Ng" was. He leaned against the Camaro and ran his hand along a dent in the passenger door. Had his father taken up the harmonica?

When Steven finally emerged onto the street from the stairs that led to the second floor, Robert quickly altered the movie credits to

DAD

starring
STEVEN ROSSETER

introducing
G. ROBERT ROSSETER
as The Kid

"Bob," Steven said, surprised. "What are you doing here?"

"Taking a walk. You?"

Steven shrugged. "Just running a few errands. Can I give you a lift somewhere?"

Robert could sense his father's unease. "I don't know," he said. "What's the Ng Mission?"

Steven looked up at the window and back at his son. "It's this organization I belong to. I can give you a ride home if you want."

"Where are you going?"

"Home, probably. Did you— do you want to come over for a

while."

"Okay," Robert said, trying to conceal his pleasure.

"You'll have to get in on my side. That door doesn't open anymore."

"Were you in an accident?" Robert asked as he clambered across the bucket seats.

"Nothing serious," said Steven. "The cop insisted I lost control but I didn't. The road was wet and I was trying to avoid a porcupine. I fishtailed into a telephone pole."

"When did this happen?"

"About a month ago. I've been meaning to mention it but I thought your mother would get upset." He steered the car out onto the street.

"When did you join that church?"

Steven smiled. "It's not a church. I would've told you about it sooner but it's been hectic at work with the layoffs and everything. I signed up a few weeks ago. It's just this group of people who get together a couple of times a week to talk about things."

Steven said Ansel Bedrosian had heard about Theodore Ng from an old friend in Toronto who attended a weekend retreat in Cheektowaga, New York, and came away a believer.

"Actually, believer is the wrong word. Mister Ng isn't interested in a particular faith. He always says he's just muddling along, like the rest of us. But he has all these insights that he shares with anybody who'll listen. Ansel's friend sent him a copy of one of Mister Ng's cassettes. We got together one Friday night to listen to it and it just blew us away."

The high-grade Colombian marijuana Ansel had purchased earlier in the day may have contributed to their sense of wonder, but subsequent listens to other cassettes confirmed Steven's opinion that Theodore Ng was perhaps the most important man in North America. His apprenticeship climaxed on a weekend in Minneapolis, when the charismastic Mister Ng mesmerized him, Ansel and several hundred others for a full ninety minutes with a piece of extemporaneous genius on the potentially mundane theme of To Thine Own Self Be True.

"Mister Ng was in tears, I was in tears, Ansel was in tears, the people sitting next to us were in tears. What he said in a nutshell that night was that instead of constantly striving to be somebody or something, we should learn to accept exactly what we are, warts and all. If we can learn to accept what we are, then we naturally start to become the somebody or thing we have been trying so hard to become."

"That doesn't sound so profound," Robert said.

"I'm no good at paraphrasing. You'll have to listen to one of his tapes to understand the feelings he can arouse in people."

"Is he a hypnotist or something?"

Steven laughed. "The only thing he has ever called himself, and what he thinks we should aspire to be, is a SAP."

"A sap. Great," said Robert, gazing out the window.

"It stands for Self-Assurance Programmer. Mister Ng says our emotional life is like a complex computer program that needs de-bugging from time to time. A trained SAP learns the key routines to de-bug his and other people's emotional programs. That's what we do when we get together at the Mission. We listen to Mister Ng's cassettes and talk about what's bugging us."

"I bet Mister Ng is from India and he has a fleet of Cadillacs," Robert said.

"Theodore Ng was born in Akron, Ohio on March 23, 1939," Steven said, as though reading from a printout. "He left school when he was 17 and took a job in his father's restaurant. He became manager of the first McDonald's in Akron and eventually was promoted to the McDonald Corp. head office in Oak Brook, Illinois. In August, 1974, he resigned from that company and emigrated to Canada. He believed the American dream died with the re-election, resignation and pardon of Richard Nixon. He thought his alternative dream might become the Canadian dream. He lives in Vancouver, British Columbia, with his wife Cora and three children, Lester, Charles and Renata."

"I didn't need a whole biography," Robert said, his mood darkening as the Camaro pulled into the parking lot of his father's apartment building. Steven was oblivious to the remark.

"I wasn't planning on having you over for a little while yet, but the world works in mysterious ways, so what the hell." He guided the Camaro into its parking space.

The first thing Robert noticed about his father's apartment was that his favourite Edward Hopper print, the one of a sunlit room of a house seemingly drifting at sea, had vanished and been replaced by a much smaller, modestly framed photograph of a pudgy man of Oriental descent in a business suit.

"Who's that?" Robert said.

"Guess," said Steven.

"What's he doing there instead of the Hopper painting?"

"Mister Ng is on my wall for inspiration and clarity," Steven said. "He's responsible for the new me."

"What new you?"

"Mister Ng does remarkable work with a lot of people, Bob. He's worthy of a place of honour in my home."

Robert moved closer to the photograph. Steven joined him. Robert listened to his father's breathing— rapid, shallow, vaguely impatient. "Mister Ng is my guide," Steven said softly.

"Where's the Hopper painting?" Robert asked, his eyes glued to the man in the frame with the congenial expression.

"In the bedroom."

"Why didn't you leave the Hopper painting here and put Mister Ng in the bedroom?"

"Because Mister Ng belongs in my living room. Think of it, Bob: In just a few short years, he has singlehandedly built up a multinational franchise of non-profit, non-denominational encounter missions that exist to help others help themselves instead of just feeding them meat byproduct. All he asks in return is an open mind. Even if our soul lives forever, there's just one chance to make things right in this life. Mister Ng writes rules for right now, not the day after tomorrow. I've been running too long on negative energy, looking for something and not knowing what it is or where to look. Mister Ng took that load off my back. He multiplied my capacity to love. Because of him I can love you better."

"Shit, Dad," said Robert, scowling.

"What's wrong? For once I'm being direct with you, telling you exactly what I feel."

"There's direct and then there's. . . meat byproduct," Robert said, wandering forlornly over to the couch and collapsing onto it.

"I'm not trying to snow you. I'm being rocksolid for the first time in my life. You're just not used to it."

"Okay, Dad," Robert sighed. "Rocksolid it is. Whatever pleases you."

Steven turned to look at his son. "Forget it," he said with a wave of the hand. "Let's talk about something unimportant. It's easier that way."

"I was just trying to understand what—"

"No, Bob. You're right. I was coming on too strong, as usual. I want you to accept too much too soon. I haven't seen you in a while because I was afraid you wouldn't understand the changes in me. That's all right. Mister Ng says the message always finds its own course and its own pace. Can I get you some ginger ale?"

"What's Mister Ng's message?"

"I'll get you some ginger ale," Steven said, disappearing into the kitchen. By now, Robert had of course forgotten this was all part of a movie called *Dad*. He seemed to forget it was a movie whenever anything happened. He had seen less of his father that summer than ever before. He assumed they were just growing apart. Once or twice he wondered why it didn't bother him more, or why he wasn't more aware of being bothered. What was his father to him now other than a living snapshot in some photo album of the mind, the leading man in a midsummer film feature? Is this what happened to all families, regardless of whether the parents split up? Past a certain point, what were parents for? He glanced at the inscrutable smiling face of Theodore Ng and sniffed the air. "What smells?"

"Pardon?" said Steven from the kitchen.

"Something smells. What are you cooking?"

Steven reappeared carrying a saucer with a smoking grey cone on it. "Incense, son. An offering to the First Mover." He placed the saucer on the coffee table

"It smells like insect repellent," Robert said. "I hope you're not burning it on my account."

"I'm burning it on all our accounts," Steven said. "I'm a real accountant now." He went back to the kitchen, returned with two glasses of ginger ale, set them on the coffee table and sat down on the worn-out recliner he expropriated years ago from the matrimonial home. "How's your mom?"

"Fine," Robert said.

"And Eddie?"

"Fine, I guess; I don't see him around much. So what's Mister Ng's message?"

Steven smiled, leaned forward, tapped the incense cone, sat back and said, "In thirty words or less?"

"If possible."

"Then let me ask you a question: Can you imagine living a life devoid of purpose, meaning or direction?"

"Yes," said Robert.

"Can you imagine," Steven continued, "the pain of being cut off from a higher awareness of the Primary Life Force?"

"Yes."

"That's the story of my life, Bob. No reflection on you or your mother. I've been doing a lot of hard thinking on my own these past few weeks. Ansel and the others have been a big help. I've come to the conclusion that I've been knotted up since as long as I can remember. When Ansel and I went to that Ng Mission retreat in the Twin Cities, it was like I was thrown off my horse on the road to Damascus."

"That's a good thing?" Robert inquired.

"It was like starting life all over again. . . Like your first kiss."

"Ha," Robert responded involuntarily, recalling Maxine Duguard's wall of teeth.

"What's so funny?"

"Nothing. I'm sorry. It has nothing to do with anything."

"You think this is all a joke. 'There goes Dad on another one of his stupid tangents.'"

"That's not what I think.""I wonder why nobody close to me takes me seriously."

"I take you seriously," Robert said. "I want to know what Mister Ng's message is."

"No you don't," Steven said, staring at the incense smoke, "and I think I know why, deep down. Confession is supposed to be good for the soul, so here goes: The truth is I haven't been much of a father to you."

Robert sat up. "Come off it, Dad."

"I wasn't much of a husband to your mother, either, though she'd probably never tell you that. But Bobby," Steven said, shifting his gaze from the plume of smoke to his son, "I've changed. God love us, I've changed. All I'm asking is that you forgive me."

Robert stared incredulously at his father. "Forgive what? There's nothing to forgive."

"You know there is," Steven said. "I've been alone in my own little world all these years, begrudging everybody who trespassed on it. Now that I've come this far out of it that I can level with you I need you to acknowledge that. I need everybody to acknowledge that."

"What for?"

"So I can change. So I can start over again."

Robert felt the first wave of indifference wash over him. It made him feel guilty, which only added to his resentment.

"You're so melodramatic, Dad. All you ever want to do is change. I don't know why you always think you have to change so much."

"You don't grow if you don't change," Steven said. "Sometimes you can't love unless you're willing to change."

"That's baloney."

Steven took a breath. "Since when are you an authority on baloney?"

"I grew up on the stuff," Robert replied.

"You wouldn't know baloney if it came up and slapped you on the face."

"I know what I know. You think you have to change all the time, but that's not the way it is."

"I can prove to you that you don't know baloney: Did you ever realize that your grandfather didn't give a shit about me, never cared one way or the other?"

Robert sat up straight. "Grampa never said a word against you."

"You were young, you don't remember. He had all sorts of ways of making me feel I wasn't part of the family. He put me down in front of you, then he'd take your hand and walk away as if he was your father and I was an uninvited guest from out of town. He's the one who helped turn your mother against me."

"That's not true, Dad," Robert warned.

"How do you know?"

"Grampa wouldn't have done something like that."

"You don't remember."

"I remember a lot. Grampa never once—"

"You don't remember anything."

"Let me speak, Dad."

"You don't know the half of what went on."

"Let me speak."

"You've got some precious idea in your head that's got nothing to do with what really went on. But you won't even listen to what I have to say."

"Then you tell me what went on," Robert said, rising from the couch. "Why don't you start with that Thanksgiving when you got drunk after you shot the moose. Tell me what you were talking about that day."

Steven smiled. "You still stick up for him, after all this time."

"Tell me what you said."

"He's been gone how many years? and your first loyalty is still to him."

"You can't tell me, can you?"

"You were always blind to his faults."

"You can't come clean at all. Your little Chinese friend on the wall can't do a thing for you."

Steven lunged out of the recliner and rammed his son back onto the couch.

"Get off me. . ."

Robert felt a blow to the side of his head and struck his father in the eye with his fist. They grappled inconclusively for a while, tugging on loose bits of clothing and hearing each other's breathing. Someone's foot caught a leg of the coffee table and overturned it, along with the incense. Eventually they toppled onto the floor—Steven heavily, on his elbow.

"Jesus *Christ*."

Steven let go of his son and clutched his right hand. His palm burned and his elbow was numb. He got up on one knee and hurried over to the kitchen sink to pour cold water on his hand. Robert stayed on the floor, felt the side of his head for blood but his hand came away dry.

"Jesus," his father repeated from the kitchen.

Robert got up from the floor and advanced as far as the kitchen doorway.

". . .Are you all right?"

"No, I'm not all right. I think I broke my elbow."

"Can an elbow break?"

"Why not? It's bone and cartilage, like everything else." He shut off the tap.

Robert took a step forward. "Dad, I'm. . ."

"Don't even start," Steven said. "You're not in a position to forgive me and I'm not in a position to put up with you ridiculing what's important to me now."

"I don't know what I'm supposed to forgive."

"It doesn't matter anymore, because the past is the past. Someday we'll understand each other perfectly and nothing will ever have to be said. Until that day, let's you and I get together now and then to play Monopoly or go to a movie. Let's just carry on like before, you your way and me mine. Your grandfather died when he did because he didn't want to have to see me any other way than he always did. That's fine, that's his business. You may think I haven't changed but I have and that's what counts. We live in different worlds now. What's all mush to you is rocksolid to me. I can accept that. I hope you can."

"I don't know what you're talking about," Robert said softly.

Steven massaged his palm. "Not to worry. Mister Ng says the process of asking and receiving forgiveness is essential to rebirth. So I stay unborn a little while longer; I can live with that."

Undulating sheets of smoke hung in the living room as the forgotten incense cone burned a black dent into the hardwood floor. The late afternoon had darkened.

"How's your head?"

"I'm sorry, Dad," Robert said, stifling tears.

"Me too," Steven said. "I'm sorry too."

His hand stopped hurting after his son left, and he eventually was able to bend his arm. There was no permanent damage. The floor was a different story. He put out the incense cone like a cigarette on the sidewalk, with one sandaled foot. The floor didn't belong to him; he was just a lodger here. He could set this whole place on fire and he wouldn't miss a blessed thing. Moira, from the mission, was coming over later. She was interested in tantric sex. She said sex was the ideal form of physical meditation. She wanted to see the pyramid Steven had helped Ansel build on land they leased from the 4P. He took her there one bright day in May and after a few glasses of wine they made love on a blanket he had thrown down to cover the mouse shit, dead flies and dryrot. She said he wasn't paying enough attention, he might as well be jerking off. He laughed at that, because she was right. Nothing she said hurt him. "You're just a lodger in your body," she said. "You ought to treat your body with more respect." He asked if he could sublet hers for another fifteen minutes. She didn't think that was funny but she went along. He tried a second time to stuff all his loneliness inside her, there in the shelter of a pyramid made of barnwood and scavenged two-by-fours. She said the second time was better, but he wasn't interested in her approval. Kath was the only one who seemed to understand. "There's something so sad about sex," she remarked once after they had made love, when Bobby was still a baby.

. . .

Robert asked his mother about his father and grandfather, but she didn't warm to the subject. She told him they got along just fine. They had the occasional argument, like all in-laws, but they were close. Why? Had his father said something to him about it? He shook his head. She said she ran into his father downtown yesterday. His father had a black eye. Did he know anything about his father's black eye?

He shook his head a second time. He asked her about his grandfather but she told him she had an awful lot of Bernardy orders to fill. There wasn't enough time in a day, was there, she said. No, he agreed. The older he got, the more quickly the river of time flowed past the present to the great sea of forgetfulness. What had become of those endless afternoons of yore in his sun-dappled backyard? He had no idea, but he longed for them with an intensity that surprised him.

Another school year was upon him. Fallen leaves clogged storm sewers again, municipal campaigns got underway amid calls for the dismantling of Isaac Presley's totem pole, and Sue-Ann Reilly had put on weight in all the right places. He felt a need to get close to Eddie Laverty again. Perhaps it was simply a matter of crossing the ecliptic of Eddie's peculiar orbit more often. The only topic that never failed to make Eddie smile was P.W. O'Hagan. These wistful talks made him feel Eddie was his brother, or at least his first cousin. And if they ran out of stories about P.W., there was always the Sue-Ann Reilly mess. Eddie listened attentively one wet October afternoon at D'Agostino's as Robert tried to unravel his confusion.

Sue-Ann Reilly had asked him to the first dance of the school year, just when her spell over him was beginning to wear off. He had dilly-dallied on the way home that afternoon, savouring the musk of rain-sodden leaves in the rare autumn sunshine, singing

"Slip Sliding Away" to himself and stepping carefully over all the cracks in the sidewalk. Runoff from the morning's rain trickled down curbs; leaves glistened on bright wet asphalt. He felt unconsciously optimistic, like a kid again— fifteen going on nothing. His mother had left a cordial note on the kitchen table:

> WON'T BE HOME TIL AROUND TEN. MEAT LOAF IN THE FRIG TO HEAT UP. PLEASE REMEMBER TO TAKE OUT GARBAGE. WHAT A NICE DAY!
> M.

Had Sue-Ann Reilly's telephone call come a few months earlier, he might have been paralyzed by panic and joy. Even now, it dazed him.

"You're kidding me," he said into the telephone.

"What's the matter? Don't you want to go?" Her voice was sweet singsong over the telephone line. He was transfigured by it, re-programmed to throw all caution to the wind.

"I don't have all day," she said, but he wanted to prolong the moment.

"Who's all going?"

She explained that her mother would drive a gang of them to the school but she wouldn't be able to pick them up after the dance because she had to work the midnight shift at the nursing home.

"Is Eddie going?"

"Eddie who? Eddie Lavatory? How should I know? Yes or no, Bobby. Hurry up."

". . .I'll call you right back," he said.

"What for?"

"I'll just be a minute," he promised and hung up.

He paced the kitchen, closed his fists tight and bit his lower lip. He whistled a melody he didn't recognize. He opened the refrigerator, inspected its contents and took out an apple. He put the apple on the table and checked to see if there was a bottle of ginger ale in the cupboard. He took the apple from the table and put it back in the refrigerator. He took out a carton of milk and placed it on the table, took the Pop Tarts out of the cupboard, placed a knife, fork and plate on the table, went to the telephone book, leafed through the Rs, memorized a number, paced some more, then stopped and dialed.

Sue-Anne Reilly was unusually affable with him the rest of that week. He hoped Eddie was going to the dance.

His first dance with Sue-Ann Reilly was "Danny's All-Star Joint". She seemed to look everywhere but at him. Bat Masterson went out to smoke a cigarette every few minutes. Sue-Ann Reilly was talked into taking a long drag. She inhaled and coughed blue smoke. He laughed but turned down a drag. Sue-Ann Reilly danced a few times with Bat Masterson. Cynthia Thomas glided over to the Brezinski youth and asked him to dance. It was a slow one: "Don't Let The Sun Go Down On Me". The Brezinski youth's loutish buddies whooped at the couple as they lurched across the dance floor. Two seniors were caught smoking grass in the boys' washroom. The police came. Sue-Ann Reilly and the others milled in the hallway while the two students were led out. Maxine Duguard asked him to dance a slow one with her. Sue-Ann Reilly pushed him onto the dance floor after her friend. "When I Need You". Maxine spoke at length about her history project on the deportation of the Acadians. Her breath smelled of peanut butter. Eventually she shut up and clutched him close. His hands went numb on her pointy shoulder blades. She held on for dear life as they traced awkward figure-zeroes in the middle of the dance floor. Her hair felt like steel wool against his cheek. He was sweating heavily by the time the song ended. He was told Bat and Sue-Ann had gone out to smoke another cigarette. Maxine stayed close to him while the deejay complained that there weren't enough kids on the dance floor. The deejay put on a Bob Marley tune, "Is This Love?", to punish all the non-dancers. Warren Pearce pogoed across the vacant gymnasium floor, then did his customary homosexual impression which was cut short by the advent of Miss Hornung wearing a smart two-piece outfit none of the students had seen on her before. The Brezinski youth staggered over to where Cynthia Thomas was standing and asked her to dance the next slow one with him. Jason Gaudet, who had been discussing the sad state of pop music with the deejay, requested something by the Clash. The deejay laughed and put on Donna Summer, "Hot Stuff". Dancers poured onto the floor. Bat and Sue-Ann, back from their cigarette break, did a variation on the tango which everyone enjoyed. He heard a rumour that the Brezinski youth was carrying a mickey of Canadian Club. Miss Hornung caught two seniors petting in the shadows under the stairs near the side door. "This is not a bordello," she informed them. Cynthia Thomas wandered over to him and said hi. Her breath smelled of C.C. straight from the bottle. The Brezinski youth took to yelling "boogie 'til you puke" as he staggered from one clot of dancers to another. Bat and Sue-Ann went out for another ostensible cigarette. "Blue Bayou" came on. He idly asked Cynthia Thomas to dance. Her breasts felt like artillery shells. There was no give. He had expected them to be soft. "I like you," she whispered, touching his ear with her warm wet lip. After the song she vanished. The star of the senior basketball team thrilled everyone with his footwork as "Motherless Children" roared out of the speakers. *"Father will do the best he can when the mother is dead. . ."* Maxine Duguard waited for him to ask her to dance, but he excused himself and went into the hall, where Miss Hornung was upbraiding the Brezinski youth. He examined the trophies and plaques locked in a glass cabinet outside the principal's office. He recognized few names. He watched Jason Gaudet call his parents to come and take him home to his microscope and record collection. He heard the deejay exhort the dancers. From the hall the music boomed and echoed, like it was already a morning memory of the night before. He wondered where Eddie was. He drifted back into the gym. Bat was holding court, telling a stupid joke about the shape of Japanese vaginas. At eleven-twenty, Sue-Ann Reilly took him by the hand and led him out onto the dance floor. *"Lod ah miss you chal,"* Mick Jagger sang. She asked him why he hadn't spent more time with Maxine, who had gone to get her coat. He said he didn't come to dance with Maxine. She said he could have made more of an effort to be sociable with everyone. He let that pass. At ten to twelve the former Mrs. Reilly arrived to take them home. He sat in the back with Bat Masterson and three others. Sue-Ann Reilly said goodnight when he got out of the car in front of his house, but it was Maxine Duguard who turned and waved sadly to him as the car pulled away from the curb and faded down the dark street.

"That's it?" said Eddie Laverty. "That's the whole story?"

"I had a strange dream that same night."

He was by a lake with his friends. Some of them were wearing hip-waders. Sue-Ann Reilly stripped down to her bra and panties and joined them in the water. The others stood in the shallows but she waded into deeper water. A few of them skipped rocks on the glassy grey surface of the lake. He looked at Sue-Ann Reilly from the shore. The air was dead, as though they were in an impossibly large room. He spotted a rowboat further out from shore. His grandfather was in the rowboat, clutching a fishing rod. As the boat drifted closer, he saw that it was a rosary in his grandfather's hands. The water was the colour of the sky was the colour of the sand was the colour of the old man's face as he said it's beautiful here, but the words were spoken through the voice of Sue-Ann Reilly, who slipped under the water. The lake turned glassy again and stayed that way. *Wish,* said the empty rowboat as it came ashore.

"What's that got to do with anything?" said Eddie, sucking on the dregs of his milkshake.

Robert shrugged. "It must mean something."

"That's like English class, where you're supposed to find deep meaning in bits of catshit. That just throws you off the real story."

"Which is?"

"Which is that Sue-Ann Reilly couldn't care less about you. She was trying to set you up with Maxine. You've gotta be blind or something."

Blind or a marionette, Robert said to himself— a bleep on a long-range homing device Sue-Ann Reilly keeps in her room to monitor him and make sure he doesn't wander out of range. "There's got to be some meaning to that dream," he said.

"Why?" said Eddie, sliding his glass away from him. "You just want there to be more, so you can compare and contrast it on an exam question. Same thing with my father and everybody else. Nobody's satisfied that things are what they are. It's not important enough that way. People have to make everything more complicated. That's what your dream is about— wanting to make some kind of epic out of a shitty little episode with a cunning broad. The Rime Of The Ancient Rosseter."

"What about your clouds, then?" Robert said. "How do you explain them?"

"My what?"

"Those pink clouds you used to talk about all the time."

Eddie gazed blankly at his friend, then chuckled and paradiddled on the table with his fingers, more or less to the beat of the jukebox. "Those clouds. They're something I was born with.

I haven't thought about them in a while, but they're as real as this place or anywhere else."

"What if I said my dream was as real?"

"It isn't, is it?"

No. And neither was Sue-Ann Reilly.

"There are lots of things in my head that are more real than any of this," Eddie said, looking around. "Sometimes what's really real takes over and I forget about everything else, just black it out." He took the straw from his glass, sucked on it, started drumming with it, set it down and went on.

"Last Sunday, on the way home from Thunder Bay with my father, I played that rhyme game we used to play with your dad. Remember? I took every word I could think of and rhymed it in my head. It was probably because of this word-association thing I did the day before with my Uncle Cecil. While you were on your blind deaf and dumb date, I was trapped in a little room in Thunder Bay with Uncle Cecil. My father thought it would be a good idea to visit him for a weekend so we could have a long talk. He's a psychologist. I didn't have any say in it. I sat in Uncle Cecil's study while he asked me one ridiculous question after another: What do I think about my parents, what do I think about my little sister, what do I think about school, about the teachers, about girls, about God, life, death. You name it, he asked me. There I am, trying to answer all these pointless questions, and Uncle Cecil is chewing on a pencil and not saying anything, not even taking notes, just nodding nodding nodding. Then he tells me he's going to say a word and I'm supposed to answer with the first word that comes into my head. That's when I remembered the rhyme game we used to play when we went for drives with your dad. Uncle Cecil said 'life' so I said 'knife'. He said 'father' and I said 'bother'. 'Mother'-'smother', 'rules'-'fools'— on and on like that. Then he said 'happiness' and I couldn't think of a single solitary word that rhymed with it. Finally I just told him my mind was a blank. This made him really serious. He said we didn't have to play the game anymore, and he came over and put his arm around my shoulder. It was time for supper anyway. The reason I wasn't at the dance, saving you from Sue-Ann Reilly and Maxine Duguard, is because my father thinks I'm emotionally disturbed. He doesn't have enough imagination to understand why his only son might not want to grow up to be like him. They're the ones who are emotionally disturbed— my father,

Uncle Cecil, that whole generation. They're too old to be young and too young to be old. They never had minds of their own and now they're trying to tell me I'm losing mine to make them feel better about their own. How's about we split another milkshake?"

"No thanks," Robert said. "You go ahead."

Eddie raised his glass to catch the attention of someone behind the counter, then resumed his tabletop drumming. "You might as well let Rolly Easterbrook sell you acid in the gym. You come into this world with your parents' scrambled chromosomes anyway."

"Rolly Easterbrook sells acid in the gym?"

"He sells whatever's going, at lunch and during spares. Christ, Rosseter, get your head out of the sand."

"Have you ever bought anything from him?"

"This and that. Now and then."

"Like what?"

"This and that. A bit. Not much."

"Jesus," Robert said.

"What? What's the problem?"

"You use the stuff by yourself?"

"So what?" said Eddie.

Robert watched his friend drink his milkshake. The music on the jukebox was more insistent than he remembered it having been. The fluorescent lights above the booths were too bright. People in other booths were talking much more frantically than in the days of *real somebitch.* The future wasn't turning out the way he thought it would.

"You know what my real problem is," Eddie said, almost to himself. "My real problem is I can't be honest with anybody about what my real problem is."

"What's your real problem?"

"I just told you."

"You said you can't be honest about your real problem."

"Right."

"What is it?"

"What is what?"

"Your real problem."

"I just told you. I can't be honest."

"Honest about what, for God's sake?"

"About my real problem." He stared solemnly at Robert for a moment, then burst out laughing. "Jesus, Rosseter, it's simple enough."

"Drop dead," said Robert.

"I'm telling the truth."

"Drop dead."

"If I'd been in your shoes at the dance I would have made up some story instead of admitting I was used by a girl that way. And the story would have kept getting more and more complicated to protect the truth, until I didn't know who or what I was protecting and forgot what the real story was. That's my problem. Do you know what I mean?"

Robert knew exactly what Eddie meant. It sickened him to think that his friend would agonize over a theoretical lie, whereas he had fabricated a story about what happened after the dance without any evident distress.

When the former Mrs. Reilly arrived unexpectedly at the school at ten to twelve, it was left to him to break the news that her daughter was nowhere to be found. Neither was Maxine Duguard. (Neither was Bat Masterson, but he didn't tell her that. Dishonesty has so many different levels.)

"I guess that leaves you and me," Mrs. Reilly said. He couldn't smell liquor on her breath, but she seemed unsteady on her feet. He shrugged and said, "I can get a ride with somebody else."

"No no," she said. "I decided to book off sick tonight. I can give you a ride. Come on. "

The former Mrs. Reilly drove at a funereal pace, slowing for stop signs not long after clearing the previous intersection. "Sue-Ann and a couple of other girls are sleeping over at Maxine's house tonight. She could have had the common decency to stay with you until the end of the dance. Weren't you her date?"

"I guess so."

"She asked you out, didn't she?"

"Uh-huh," he said. He just wanted to go home.

"You poor dear." She put her hand on his leg. He didn't mind this time. He was covered in a thick coat of apathy. He watched silently as she drove past the street where she was supposed to turn to take him to his house. He glanced down at her hand on his leg. It was a small hand, just like Sue-Ann's, except there were no rings on it. Sue-Ann must have inherited her imperious manner from her dad. Her mother was quite a congenial woman and preferable company at the end of a dismaying Saturday night. *Fuck them all. Fuck Bat Masterson, who's probably fucking Sue-Ann Reilly.*

"I haven't seen your mother in ages," the former Mrs. Reilly said. "Is she still selling Bernardy products?"

"A bit," he said. He boldly rested his hand against hers. "People aren't ordering as much as they used to." Her hand lightly stroked his thigh. "People need only so many vegetable containers."

"That's true," she said, running her hand up his thigh. "Besides, they spray the vegetables in supermarkets with this chemical that keeps them from going rancid a lot longer."

"I wonder if it has any effect on the nutritional value of the vegetables," Robert said as her hand slid further up. He was certain she could hear his wildly beating heart.

"Supposedly not," she said, stopping short of his crotch. "Supposedly the chemicals lock in the flavour, vitamins and minerals."

The car jolted up the curb and into the former Mrs. Reilly's driveway at an impractical angle. She switched off the engine and gazed tenderly at him. "Would you like a hot chocolate or a glass of pop?"

"Maybe," he said.

"All right, then."

She stumbled up one of the steps to the front door. He took her arm and helped her the rest of the way. She handed him the key to the door but it wasn't locked. He followed her in. She turned on the hallway light, took off her coat, went into the living room and sat on the couch. She was wearing a pale green track suit. He hesitated in the doorway, but the unguarded expression on her face told him everything he needed to know. He sat down next to her and put his arm around her. She leaned toward him. He clumsily cupped his hand on her breast and marvelled at its soft warmth. He put his hand on her breast again and she turned to kiss him, not on the side of the mouth like before but inside it, with her tongue. He squeezed her breast hard. "Mmaf mmurts," she said. He slid his hand under her track top. "Mmaif," she said, moved away from him and deftly pulled the top over her head. He was astounded by her erect nipples. She sat back. At first he didn't move, because he felt dizzy and bewildered. "This is weird," he managed to say, but fell forward, as though by gravity, until his mouth eventually found a nipple. For a long, blessed time he suckled, more like a baby son than a lover.

* * *

9

> Misery has a way of being egalitarian in the long run. You must believe your lot in life is somehow comparable to that of the men, women and children who poured out of the boxcars at Auschwitz-Birkenau, whose ashes drifted back across Europe and still dim the sun all over the world.
>
> —Theodore Ng

He measured the summer of 1980 by the movement and evolution of afternoon thunderheads that swelled to magnificent proportions, only to be neutralized in the evening by the strong stationary high pressure system that had spawned them. Somewhere it's raining hard, he said to himself, as if knowing this enabled him to share in the release. Some August afternoons grew so dull and heavy in the still heat and insect hiss that it took all of his imagination to convince himself time hadn't come to a full stop. Was the sensation of time a purely subjective phenomenon, governed by the mind rather than any universal physical laws? He toyed with that idea while hiking through dense bush with Eddie Laverty and Bat Masterson. That morning, Steven had picked them up and driven them as far as the wooden pyramid where he was spending his holidays. Robert was grateful there were no portraits of Mister Ng hanging at forty-five degree angles from the sloped wooden walls.

"Far out," Bat Masterson said after stepping through the trap door into the one-room pyramid. "How come there aren't any windows?"

"Ansel forgot to build them into the plans," Steven said. "Besides, he figured the intrinsic powers of the pyramid would be sapped by windows. That's what he said afterward, anyway."

"What powers does it have?" Eddie asked.

"Curative, mostly. It's good for warts. It keeps razor blades and scissors sharp. And I sleep like a rock."

"It removes warts?" Eddie said.

"Gradually," Steven said. "Not overnight."

"Far out," Bat Masterson said. "Where do you sleep?"

"On the floor," Steven said, "after we've swept up the mouse shit. We use a couple of kerosene lamps for reading at night, and a kerosene stove to cook on. We'll probably dig an outhouse pit this fall."

"What do you do for water?" Eddie asked.

"We bring it in from the city, and there's a cistern near the road."

"Far out," Bat Masterson said.

"He's a lot more enthusiastic about the place than you are," Steven said to his son.

The boys were heading deeper into the bush on foot. They blazed a trail through dry undergrowth in search of a clearing for their tent. Their motive was convenience more than camaraderie. Bat Masterson owned the tent and Eddie Laverty wanted desperately out of the house— but not alone with Bat Masterson. Robert had agreed to the idea of a weekend camping trip before he was told Bat Masterson would be tagging along.

"Do you suppose we have much further to go?" said Bat Masterson, who was lugging the canvas tent.

"How should I know," Robert said. He disliked Bat Masterson not only because of Sue-Ann Reilly; he disliked the very idea of Bat

Masterson—someone who was dashing and aware of it, a braggart who was never alone, who was seen by others as being immensely popular, yet who had no real friends. He jostled the sleeping bags and camping tools.

"I knew I shoulda brung my Junior Woodchucker's Manual," Bat Masterson said. Eddie snorted and tried to raise the cooler of supplies onto his head. The lid slipped off, and cans of beans, packages of bacon and a Kellogg's six-pack tumbled out of it. While Eddie and Robert put the supplies back in the cooler, Bat Masterson stared up at the treetops. They formed an almost opaque canopy. "You know," he said, "I think I've been here before. I think I took my second cousin for a hike here last summer. She's only thirteen but built like a Playboy bunny. She lives in Montreal and her parents have been all over the world. She couldn't keep her hands off me. The tops of the trees around here look familiar."

Robert sighed. Eddie tried to secure the lid of the cooler.

"I'm not kidding," Bat Masterson said. "We had sandwiches and a few bottles of my father's Heineken we smuggled out of the house. I think it was somewhere around here she said she wanted to do it."

"Do what?" Robert said.

Bat Masterson grinned. "*It,* Roosterbrains. She wanted to do *it.*"

"Don't call me Roosterbrains."

"So what did you do?" said Eddie, the faithful prompter, at once repelled and compelled by Bat Masterson's tall tale.

"Well, first we necked for a while. This was my second cousin, you've got to remember. I guess French-kissing comes naturally to Montrealers. She had a tongue on her like an eel."

"All my cousins are boys," Eddie said. "If any of them wanted to do it with me, they never let on."

"What about you, Rosseter?" Bat Masterson inquired.

"What *about* me?" Robert said.

"Did you ever get it on with any of your cousins?"

"What a stupid question," Robert said.

"What a stupid answer," Bat Masterson replied.

"What a stupid conversation," Eddie concluded. "Are we there yet? I've gotta go to the bathroom."

"Go wherever you please," Robert said. "It's not like there's a toilet at the end of the trail."

"I think there's a clearing not too far from here," Bat Masterson said. "I remember my second cousin saying to me we should look for a spot where we could lie down."

"Spare us," Robert said.

They walked in silence across a gully. The undergrowth varied with the tree cover. Eventually they arrived at a large clearing. A few grunts and monosyllables later the campsite was unanimously approved. Bat Masterson put up the faded yellow tent. Eddie was dismayed by the rent in the roof. Robert was too exhausted to react. He wondered why he was already so tired.

"We'll get soaked if it rains," Eddie observed.

Bat Masterson made a face. "Jumping Christ; so there's a little hole in the roof. If you wanted a Winnebago why didn't you say so?"

Out of boredom as much as hunger, the boys decided to prepare supper. Kindling wasn't a problem; soon they had a healthy fire going. Spirits rose accordingly. As Eddie and Bat Masterson took turns burning their hand on the skillet of sizzling shrinking bacon, Robert whittled birch twigs stout enough to hold wieners and marshmallows for a late evening roast.

The boys ate silently but with enthusiasm. In the span of a quarter-hour they devoured ten eggs, a pound of bacon and three large tins of beans and pork. They separately doubted they could stomach the same fare again at breakfast the next morning, but that was still a long way off. For now, they busied themselves with the search for the evening's firewood. The August light started to fade as they wandered through the woods near their campsite. Dusk could almost be heard to descend in the crisp crackling of undergrowth and the snap and hiss of fresh wood turning to smoke and ash.

By the time the boys had collected enough firewood for the rest of the summer, the darkness was almost total and the stand of scotch pine by the tent was pitchblack. Soon the only part of the world that existed beyond dispute was that small radius of space illuminated by the fire. After sleeping bags and incidentals were deployed inside the tent, after the package of wieners and the bag of marshmallows were removed from the cooler, Bat Masterson fished into his hunting jacket pocket and pulled out a large cigarette.

"Maryjane for fearless junior woodfuckers," he said, waving

the joint in the firelight.

"All *right,*" Eddie said. He looked at Robert, who had already fastened a wiener to his stick. "Hey, Bobbyboy."

Robert looked at Bat Masterson. "It looks like a cigar, for God's sake."

Bat Masterson laughed. He took a wooden match and struck it on the fly of his jeans, brought the flaring match to the joint, took a long bug-eyed toke, held it in and passed the joint to Eddie.

"A Havana cigar," Robert said. Bat Masterson spat out a lungful of smoke and laughed. Eddie handed the joint to Robert, who took a long drag.

"Assaboy," Bat Masterson said.

The joint made the rounds countless times before Bat Masterson finally flung the roach into the flames. Robert coughed and laughed.

The fire was burning hard. Robert could swear it was scorching his forehead, pulling the skin tight as a snare drum, cauterizing his lungs. He coughed up a piece of his lung and spat it out. If the skin of his head gets any tighter the front of his face will... the front of his face will come up and off like a rubber mask, a rubber Richard Nixon mask. He coughed up some more lung.

"Fetornly skrebnun," Eddie Lavatory was saying to him. He understood and passed Eddie a wiener and a few marshmallows.

"Marshmellow," said Bat Masterson. "Mellowmarsh. Kforniak ptibi."

"Sragnalt kerveckni," Robert said to Bat Masterson. It seemed to be the funniest thing he ever said. Eddie Lavatory thought so too. "O brendlatun cospui. . ." Eddie said. "Skrebnun."

Robert coughed and coughed. Coughcoughcough, turning himself inside out.

"Wiener philharmoniker," Bat Masterson said as he fished for fire with his allbeef frank on a stick. They watched the flames lick at the stick and the little wiener dangling forlornly from it. They gazed at the wiener til it was black as space and the stick was in flames. "How would you like to live in Wiener and have to wear liederfuckinhosers?" He waved the stick 'til the flames went out, then stood up, walked into the shadows and waved it some more. Embers nightwrote against a wall of blacktree:

NY NANE IJ BARRY MAJTERJON

"Did you see that?" quoth Eddie Laverty.

"See what?"

"Red words," Eddie said. "Look..."

YOU GUYJ ARE

". . .NUTS!" a voice screamed and the red ember flew at them through the black.

"O Jesus," Eddie said.

The smouldering stick landed behind Robert, lay there glowing on the ground like a radioactive rod in heavy water at Chalk River.

"Ftekkliut," Eddie said. Robert didn't get it. His mouth was so dry. His upper palate felt like salt flats to his tongue. Like a cracked land where skulls of wildebeest bake in the sun. A strange yellow light was shining up from his lungs to the top of his throat. His tonsils are these ovaries of his. . . His heartbeat a bass drum someone's kicking.

Ftekkliut. . .

They didn't have a clue how long Bat Masterson had been gone when he appeared from the dark and leaped over and across the flames. "I'm king of the gazelles!" he announced.

Robert felt bleary now, a living fogmammal. Eddie stared at the blue roots of the flames. Bat Masterson threw a big log onto the fire. "*Wo*," they all said as red sparks soared wavelike up to the ink. . .

. . .Girls they knew, girls they didn't know but wanted to, girls who lived in exotic lands far from Presley, girls their friends told stories about, girls who existed in mythology, girls who could never get enough, girls who liked girls, girls who liked Dobermans, girls who lived in magazines, girls who wanted to be politicians, girls with balls, girls whose skin tasted like goat milk.

"What I do is keep a journal," Bat Masterson said. "At the end of every day I have a scoreboard called Broad Of The Day—B.O.T.D. Each day I decide which broad has grabbed my attention the most that day and I name her Broad Of The Day. At the end of every week I choose a B.O.T.W.— Broad Of The Week. Some days more than one broad deserves the award, so I give points to each B.O.T.D. depending on where she places on the list on that day. The B.O.T.W. is the B.O.T.D. with the most points during the week. At the end of every month I also declare a B.O.T.M, who's the B.O.T.D. with the most B.O.T.W. points. Then I can work out averages and calculate who deserves to be named B.O.T.Y—Broad Of The Year."

"Who was your Broad Of The Year for 1979?" Eddie asked.

"You don't know her."

"Did she get a prize?"

"This," Bat Masterson said, clutching his crotch.

Robert felt strangely expansive in the afterglow of the grass. He was tempted to give a lewd account of the Cynthia Thomas Affair, but Bat Masterson continued to hold sway. He set out the facts of his life with the dispassionate precision of a Crown attorney. He said he'd been sexually active since the age of seven, when his friend's thirteen-year-old sister seduced him. From then it was one ribald adventure after another involving ministers' daughters, babysitters, aunts, playground supervisors, Avon representatives, countless schoolmates and at least one teacher.

"By 1988 I'll be in a position to officially announce the Broad Of The Decade. What a day that's gonna be," Bat Masterson said.

Robert and Eddie piled logs onto the fire until the flames towered above them, forced them to retreat and even threatened the tent. Bat Masterson blathered on about his sexual exploits but neither of them listened closely. They had grown bored with his singlemindedness. It was making them sleepy. Yet he blathered on. . .

"We haven't talked about Sue-Ann Reilly and her horny old lady."

Pow! A flying ember traced redyellow ringlets against the black. Eddie looked over at Robert, who was staring at the ground. "Nobody wants to talk about Sue-Ann Reilly," he said. "There's nothing to talk about."

"Oh there's *plen*-ty," said Bat Masterson with a conspiratorial chuckle. "About her and her old lady."

Robert looked directly at Bat Masterson. "I don't want to talk about Sue-Ann Reilly."

"Okay, okay. I'll just tell one story. One that Sue-Ann made me swear I'd never tell. You'll definitely be interested in this one, Rosseter."

"We don't want to hear it," Eddie said.

"Eddie, do you remember the first dance of the year last fall?"

"Masterson. . ."

"When Sue-Ann's mother was supposed to drive us all home?"

"I was out of town," Eddie said. "I think we should be hitting the sack."

"Sue-Ann and I left the dance early and went directly to her house. We figured we'd have it to ourselves until eight the next morning because her old lady was supposed to be working nights that week."

"We don't want to hear about it," Eddie said.

"So there we are, going crazy on her bed, when what do we hear but the front door opening."

"Masterson, if you don't—"

"Sue-Ann jumps out of bed and sees her mother getting out of her car with— guess who with, Eddie?"

"I don't know," Eddie said, helplessly.

"Young Roosterbrains, here," Bat Masterson answered with a grin. "The old lady's fairly tanked up, as per usual, so he's helping her to the door as any gallant gentleman would. Right?"

Bat Masterson paused there, as though waiting to be ordered to stop. Eddie gazed off into the dark. Robert reached for a piece of wood.

"Except he goes into the house with the old lady. Meanwhile, Sue-Ann and I are up in her room, trying to figure out what to do. After it's been quiet for a while, I sneak out of the bedroom to the top of the stairs. I can't see anything. So I sneak down a couple of steps and lo and behold, what do I see? Old Lady Reilly lying starkers on the couch, and Roosterbrains is there with her, trying to figure out what goes where."

Robert was on his feet. He raised the piece of wood high above his head before bringing it down hard. Bat Masterson had just enough time to roll out of the way.

"Jesus Christ. . ."

"I told you not to call me Roosterbrains," Robert said. Eddie grabbed him, but Robert had no strength left anyway. "You're worse than shit, Bastardson," he said. "You're nobody. Zilch."

"Are you crazy?"

"Shut your face," Eddie said. "Shut up."

"He's fucking crazy."

"I said shut up."

So ended their campfire evening. Bat Masterson continued to mutter to himself as they crawled into their sleeping bags. Robert didn't say another word. The flashlight was switched off; the fire cast the merest glow through the canvas. The walls of the tent occasionally rippled in the wind that had come up from the east. Long after the other boys' breathing had turned deep and rhythmic, Robert lay rigid, awake and short of breath. Whitehot fury hacked his thoughts into fragments. They fused with pieces of the forgotten past, shards of long-buried feelings that fit no existing puzzle. The sum of all these fragments was an omnidirectional rage such as he had never tasted. From the depths of potent spells cast by woodsmoke and grass now erupted a furious power. It consumed him.

Bat Masterson and Eddie Laverty farted in their sleep. A sickening sweet smell enveloped the tent. Robert was ovewhelmed with disgust even as his own innards roiled beans and bacon. His stomach and head ached. His chest burned. Sporadic drops of rain pattered on the canvas. Soon the rain began to fall more steadily. Before long a puddle collected in the centre of the tent. Robert grabbed the flashlight and wriggled out of his sleeping bag. He would not spend another minute in the tent. He would walk to his father's pyramid and sleep there for the night. He would leave the two others to fend for themselves; they were each other's friend.

The heavy rain was deafening as it fell through the trees. He had never imagined such darkness. He followed his own trail back in the dull glow of the flashlight. Insects darted in and out of its beam. He had no idea what time it was. Already he was soaked to the bone.

Bat Masterson's bullshit story was true, but that didn't damp his fury. The trail grew less distinct, then there was no trail. The flashlight dimmed. He was surprised to discover he was sobbing. He sounded like an animal. The flashlight died. He threw it as far as he could but didn't hear it hit the ground. The rain drowned all sound. He stumbled through the undergrowth. The smell of the bush, sodden and gone to seed, made him gag. He tripped over something sharp and fell. He turned onto his back and lay still for a while, eyes locked shut against the rain. It was more deafening than ever, so deafening that he was oblivious to his own wailing and to the stab of pain in his left leg.

A small part of him recognized the need to find his father's pyramid. Another small part of him recognized the need to return to the tent. He slowly got to his feet and began walking again. The underbrush scratched his face and arms. Each step shot pain up his left calf. He cried out for help but he could barely hear his own voice.

Minutes or hours later, when the pain in his leg was no longer bearable, the bush more dense than ever and his lungs seemingly ablaze, Robert collapsed on the ground and curled himself into the smallest ball he could be. *I'm a dying moose with nobody to name me.* He let the hiss of the rain urge unconsciousness over him. *I'm a dying moose with. . .*

Less than two hundred metres due north of where he lay, Steven put down his book and dimmed the kerosene lamp on the floor next to his mattress. He closed his eyes. The rain on the sloped walls evoked strange mixed memories of hunting weekends when he was a child in the rugged bushland north of the Soo. The train ride there through the Agawa Canyon, *cathunky cathunky,* the stepping off at mile such-and-such, the keeping up with the men on the rough trail to the cabin, the finding a place to keep out of their way at night when they got drinking, the doing favours for them at all hours, the lying in his youthbed under the sweet forgiving rain on the roof. That's what he remembered.

. . .

. . .we thought it was the thing to do we thought it was the thing to do thought it was the thing to do was the thing to do. . . stop I just wanna sleep leave me alone I have to sleep. . .who is that is that Grampa no it's Dad. . .*it's you Dad you understand just let me be. . .now I can go back to where the tall trees thing to do we thought it was the thing to do we thought it was the thing to do was the thing. . . none of the others can be with me this is my private place it makes me shiver and burn inside* I have to sleep don't touch me don't move me don't don't it's gonna be all right Bobby I'm here now *forgive us our trespassers as we forgive those who despise against us and deliver us our daily breadfruit of thy womb Jesus holy Mother Mary of God prefer us sinners knowing in the hour of our death don't slam the screen door it tires her out* what did he say what did he say it's all my fault shut up Masterson he looks so

pale if I had kept my mouth shut never mind about that now just keep those blankets around him is his skin still blue *gosh Miss Hornung the class is noisy why can't they shut up for a change* shut up he's in bad shape oh Jesus Mr. Rosseter do you see the colour of his what's this about Sue-Ann Reilly's mother we were just talking about girls last night and he and Bat had a bit of an argument and you didn't hear him when he left the tent was it early or late in the night we don't know you don't know how long he was in the bush we were asleep Mr. Rosseter what was the argument about nothing special nothing at all *I have to make them be more quiet in my moving bed goodbye tall trees good soldiers an honour guard.. .Grampa have you caught anything you only fish for relaxation and Mommy made us delicious devilled ham. . .who's there?*—who's there?— *WE ARE TAKING YOU AWAY TO A BLACK PLACE WHERE YOU WILL ROT WE ARE STANDING ON THE ROOF OF THIS CAR AND WE ARE TAKING* somebody's on the roof of the car Dad somebody's on the roof *TIME FOR US TO TAKE YOU AWAY FOREVER* don't let them Dad don't let them who what Jesus I wish it wasn't so far back into town Eddie wrap those blankets around him better I should give him my jacket how could he have spent the whole night no that's okay the blanket will do his mother doesn't even know yet his *MOTHER IS GOING AWAY TO ANOTHER PLACE WHERE THE WORMS ARE* should have known it was going to rain it's not your fault none of us knew or we would have *BURY YOU IN A DEEP HOLE then take me. . . . . .there. . . . . 'Im on my way now I will say goodnight to everybody in alphabetical order beginning with Aaron Aardvark my dearest friend from Australia goodnight Aaron. . . . . .*you don't know. . .he was. . .something on his. . .before Mr. Rosseter but he looks. . .falling asleep oh yes. . . . . .I feel responsible for this I now just try and calm down a little sir I'll take over from here was he unconscious when Jesus God my baby my baby this is his mother my baby oh Jesus God was he unconscious when you I called you as fast as I could excuse me but was he unconscious when you found him he was delirious he kept saying the same words over and over again he kept saying wee tot in walls so thin to do he just went on and on and on and on

. . .

A breathless day, the sky the colour of dough by midmorning. Shopowners closing up at noon. Dogs panting under verandahs in his neighbourhood, arguments breaking out in kitchens and down the street. Nobody moving, no true shade anywhere. Loading up the Camaro in slow motion for the drive to Lake Mead and the hot breeze of afternoon. He, his mother, father, grandfather. Sandwiches and pop in an overnight bag, he in the back seat with his arm out the window all the way to the lake. Grownups talking. Parked cars in treeshade, bare feet on gravel. The beach a sea of bodies standing, sitting, asleep. Jimi Hendrix guitar in the air thick as water, "All Along The Watchtower" from portable radios strewn in the sand. *"There must be some kind of way out of here. . ."* Blankets unfolded, suntan lotion and beachball. His grandfather carrying a lawn chair to the bright shade.

—I'll race you to the water, his father saying. Through an obstacle course of sunbathers at a dead sprint. His father highstepping into the shallows, he pulling up short.

—Come on. What are you waiting for? His father splashing lukewarm water on his arms and legs.

—I don't want to go in.

—Why not?

—I just don't.

—There's nothing to be scared of. Look. It's not deep here at all. It's barely up to my waist.

—I know.

Forgot pail and shovel. Maybe too old for pail and shovel.

—Well, then?

—I don't want to go in.

—Don't be silly, this is what we came for. His father coming back to shore, taking him by the hand, leading him into the water. He breaking free.

—No.

—What's the matter with you? You said you wanted me to teach you how to swim.

—Not now.

—Just give me your hand and I'll guide you.

—No!

His grandfather, barefoot, pants rolled up to his milkwhite calves. Smooth hand on his nape.

—What's wrong?

—Bobby's afraid to go in the water.

—I am not.

—You're acting as if you are.

—Can't you see you're upsetting the boy?

—I'll go in later, Dad.

—Why does he have to go in the water right this minute?

—He told me he wanted to learn how to swim. He wanted me to teach him.

—There's no reason he has to go in the water if he doesn't want to.

—He wants to. He's just being contrary.

—Do you or don't you want to, son?

—I don't.

—There you have it.

His father parting his lips to answer, instead turning for the deeper water, diving into it and swimming out and away, now only a little black dot of a head against the shimmering blinding white. He and his grandfather walking back to the blanket, his mother already lost in a book. A lawn chair leaning against a tree for Grampa.

—Where's your dad? The back of her hand shielding her freckled face from the sun. Fair skin in a maroon swimsuit. A love so fierce it hurt.

—Over there.

Pointing to the water, to the bobbing black dot of Daddy's head. Wishing now he were out there with him, so far from everyone.

. . .

He saw his mother and father holding hands at the foot of the bed. He could have been struck by how right they looked together in the fair afternoon light. He could have reflected on their interlocked hands. But he wasn't of their world.

. . .

His eyes opened again. It was later in the day. Kathleen was at his bedside.

"We'll have to leave soon, darling, but I'll be back this evening." Her Indian red hair, held up by an assortment of combs, was the happiest thing in the room.

Where am I?

"Hang in there, kid," Steven said from the other side of bed. "If you need anything special, let me know. There's a phone on the table. You're sharing it with Mr. Philbin."

What day is it?

Kathleen adjusted his pillow. "Do exactly what Doctor Paine and the nurses tell you to do."

What am I dying of?

"Be sure to finish all your meals," Steven said.

"Yes. And if you have any problems, you can buzz a nurse with the buzzer that's right above your head."

"Your toothbrush and your slippers are in that drawer right next to you."

"I'll be bringing you your sketch pad tomorrow."

"If you have to go to the bathroom, ask a nurse to help you out of bed."

"You'll be fine again in no time."

"But you need to rest."

"Yes. Rest.

"Okay, honey?"

What are they talking about?

. . .

He standing in the doorway while his father pours another glass of Niagara wine. Tears. Tears.

. . .

Steven and Kathleen had dinner at Chow's Chow. Cynthia Thomas brought them menus. He told Kathleen the whole story of how the boys banged on the trap door at dawn and they all went out looking for Bobby and found him unconscious not far from the pyramid. By then the rain had changed to drizzle. He was surprised she didn't blame him for any of it. She was, too.

"Had they been drinking?"

"I don't think so," Steven said.

"So why did he wander off?"

"Eddie said something about an argument Bobby and Bat had about Sue-Ann Reilly and her mother."

"Jocelyn?"

"Apparently. He didn't go into detail and Bat sure didn't want to talk about it. . . What are we going to do about Bobby?"

Kathleen looked at Steven. "Love him, I guess."

"We already do that," Steven said.

"Maybe listen to him. Ever since the separation, I kind of. . . it's been tough knowing what to do. It doesn't come naturally anymore."

"Imagine how I feel," Steven said.

"I know." Surely, she said to herself, if the former husband and wife can resolve their differences and reach a steady state of friendliness, the child of the marriage can make the necessary adjustments, too.

Cynthia Thomas set a platter of beef fried rice on their table. It reminded Steven of their courtship in the summer of 1963. Fried rice, chop suey and honeygarlic chicken in warm greasy cardboard containers. Violet twilight at Lake Mead. Mad passionate endless aimless necking. He always was able to recall what her mouth tasted like afterward. Her mouth tasted like Chinese food.

Kathleen O'Hagan, his honeygarlic sweetheart.

"Jesus God, I didn't realize I was so hungry."

"Maybe we ought to do more things together," Steven said.

Kathleen spooned rice onto her place. "How do you mean?"

"The three of us. Maybe we ought to do things together."

"Like what?" she said with her mouth full.

"For instance, maybe next Easter we should go to the turkey and beans banquet."

Kathleen smiled. "I haven't been to one of those in ages."

"Exactly."

"Okay. Let's do that. It's a deal."

"A date," Steven said.

"A date," Kathleen agreed. "A chaperoned date."

"To make sure we behave ourselves."

By the time the coffee arrived they spoke a lot less and wondered a lot more what they were speaking so little about. It reminded Kathleen of their first few months together, when they didn't have to say anything to each other.

Perhaps, thought Kathleen, love, like energy, was subject to the laws of thermodynamics. Perhaps it could be acted upon but neither created nor destroyed.

. . .

After two days of sleep and antibiotics, Robert's strength slowly began to return. The bright sunshine and the reassuring smell of assorted fruit slowly rotting on his bedside table helped a lot. He began to enjoy the enforced isolation of his semi-private room in Riverside Hospital. Patients and staff were more sensitive than the general population to the dangers of contamination by the outside world. He enjoyed putting in his meal orders, insisting upon Jell-O for dessert though he usually got bread pudding. He enjoyed the condescending correctness of the nurses, their predictable use of the first person plural and the reassuring swish of their uniforms. During mid-afternoon lulls he loved to watch other patients trudge past his door. Some of them, like Mr. Philbin in the bed across from him, didn't look at all well. But if they were up and around, it could only mean they were getting better— or not getting worse just yet.

On the afternoon of his third day, Robert slipped into his hospital-issue kimono and took a trudge down the hall to the nearest sunroom, where patients from the geriatric ward communed the hours away. Robert sat across from two elderly men who discoursed at length on lumbago, trapped gas, bowel movements and mucus buildup. Occasionally they gazed at Robert, who stole glimpses of their hairless swollen ankles and bloated insteps. The television in the corner was turned up loud. The dashing young daytime actors looked nervous and suspicious but no one paid them any mind. A happy sleepiness overcame him. If he wanted to, he could stretch out on one of the empty couches in this sunwarmed room. He luxuriated in the freedom of the hospital's impersonal custody. The next day he would bring his sketch pad with him.

Visiting hours were another story. Robert couldn't help feeling they were an invasion of his privacy, an unwanted obstacle in the easy flow of an otherwise totally unremarkable routine. But duty eventually drew him back to his room, where he received Eddie Laverty.

"That was some stunt you pulled," Eddie said after the uneasy niceties were out of the way. Robert said nothing; he peered into Eddie's face as if it were a photograph of someone he'd been asked to identify. "You're lucky, you know. I heard about this guy who was boarding at the College Of St. Vitus who caught something called military tuberculosis and went from totally healthy to dead in a couple of days."

"I had pneumonia, not tuberculosis," Robert said.

"Whatever. They both have to do with the lungs. You might just as easily have caught tuberculosis and died."

"Is this your way of cheering me up?"

"No," Eddie said. "Let's drop it."

Robert let his head roll to the side so that it faced the window, the cool blue sky and the snaking brown Kekagami flowing out of the city limits. His elderly friends were probably trudging out of the sunroom by now, back to their beds and the day's *Gleaner* or *Toronto Star*.

"About Bat," Eddie said.

Robert watched a steam shovel scoop soil and concrete from a sidewalk a couple of blocks away and expel it into a dumptruck.

"About Bat," Eddie repeated. "He says he feels terrible about what happened, but he's sticking to that ridiculous story about you and Sue-Ann's mother. Don't ask me why. He admitted he exaggerates when he tells stories about his sex life, but he says he wasn't exaggerating at all that night. What can I say, other than he's an asshole?"

Robert felt weary and oddly removed from the topic— not so much above it as somewhere beside it, out of mindshot.

"There's an old man in the next ward," he said, "who talks through a tube the doctors put in his throat. He's got a couple of months left to live."

Not long after that, Eddie Laverty left and Robert was free to stare placidly out the window. He watched cars come and go like Dinky Toys in the visitors' parking lot. The cars cast long comical shadows. He watched children ride their bikes on the sidewalks, do wheelies and sudden skidding stops. He watched his father's Camaro pull into the visitors' parking lot. Was it already that late? He wondered about the chemistry of the brain, and what minor changes in his own had occurred in the last few days. He decided to feign sleep because he didn't want to talk to anyone else that day.

By the time Steven stepped quietly into the room, Robert was no longer feigning sleep. He was truly out, and dreamless.

...

The final stage of his convalescence took place at home, as August waned into a windy wet September. Bidding the nurses farewell, making a few final sketches of the old patients as they discussed gout and cancer of the prostate proved a wrenching experience. Saying goodbye to the languid daily arc of the sun and the smell of overripe fruit was not an easy thing.

Kathleen's brand of fussing wasn't nearly as liberating as the detached ministrations of the nurses. She thought her son looked gaunt. She was right. One evening he examined his scrawny frame in the bathroom mirror with the understandable bewilderment of a young man who didn't often look at himself. Who is this guy? he wondered as he stared at his reflection, clad in yellow briefs. Who bought him these yellow gotchies, and why? The boy in the mirror was more than ever a stranger to himself. The hospital had been a marvellous incubator, but he had no idea what it had hatched.

Having missed the first couple of weeks of school, Robert was obliged to see a guidance counsellor to help him select his courses. His counsellor, who had the unfortunate name of Dennis Malarkey, possessed a degree in geography with a minor in library arts. Since there was no teaching position open to him that year, since he professed a keen interest in kids, since the previous year's guidance counsellor had been convicted of possessing marijuana, and since the the board of education was strapped for time and funds, Dennis Malarkey inherited a stuffy little office near the storerooms.

"I see social studies and bookkeeping are your favourite subjects," he said as he leafed through Robert's records. Robert sat glumly on the other side of the desk. He had dreaded this appointment more than the dentist— more, even, than the six weeks of gymnastics he would soon suffer in phys ed.

"Not really," Robert said.

"You certainly have done well in them the past two years. You consistently show your best work in those two subjects."

Robert shrugged. Dennis Malarkey jotted down a few words on a legal-size notepad.

"What are your favourite subjects, then?"

Robert pondered, ticked off a mental list. "Art, I guess," he finally said.

"Art? That's just an elective."

Robert nodded.

Dennis Malarkey looked past Robert for a moment, then said, "I suppose you're too young to remember Jon Gnagy."

"Jon. . .?"

"Gnagy. He was an artist who had a television show and sold learn-to-draw kits. Some of the things he did were brilliant— winter scenes of a mailbox on a country road, a covered bridge; that sort of thing. Brilliant. He was that rare breed of man who was able to combine his interests with a lucrative career. Most artists end up being cab drivers or waiters. Believe me, I've known a few in my time."

Robert nodded.

Dennis Malarkey perused Robert's records. "Your marks in art haven't been spectacular. Why do you suppose that is?"

Robert pondered, then shrugged.

"Have you ever given any thought to a career in commercial art? Of course, you'd have to boost these marks considerably to stand a chance of breaking into that line of work."

"I just like to draw," Robert said, clearing his throat.

Dennis Malarkey scratched another observation on his notepad. "What we're aiming for here," he said with a chuckle, "is something more than just a pastime, Giles. We want to be thinking about something in a bread-winning capacity. Don't get me wrong: I think it's simply wonderful that you have a hobby; Lord knows where we'd be without our artists. All I'm saying is that you've got to set your sights on something practical, something solid you can fall back on if this art thing doesn't pan out— which it doesn't seem to be, judging from your marks. Still and all, Giles, and this bears repeating: A man without a hobby is like a horse without a bridle. That much is a fact."

"Mr. McGirr doesn't let me draw the way I want to draw," Robert said.

Dennis Malarkey smiled generously and said, "More to the point, you don't let yourself draw the way Mr. McGirr asks you to draw."

The appointment ended shortly thereafter. Dennis Malarkey asked Robert to consider two key ideas over the next few weeks— computers and marketing— and to come back before Christmas so they could bounce those ideas around.

What bounced around in Robert's mind instead was the idea of a hobby and a horse and a bridle. There was no lack of time to consider these and other matters. Eddie Laverty's father had decided to pack Eddie off to the College Of St. Vitus that fall in a last-ditch effort to whip him into shape. Robert found school a lonely place full of boisterous peers feigning the best of health. He longed for the comforting corridors of Riverside Hospital, for the reassuring aroma of medication and antiseptic and flowers and chocolate and day-old vomit, all thrown together into the singular fragrance of enforced solitude. Sometimes, when he drew, he reflected on the example of Jon Gnagy, successful artist/teacher/ salesman. One day, while he examined the sketches he had done at Riverside, all the pieces of the puzzle abruptly came together: He could have a career as a hospital artist. His job would consist of visiting hospitals throughout the land, observing patients in various stages of recuperation, and making drawings of them and their environment for the edification of all patients and the healthy public at large.

On a trial basis Robert did sketches from memory of the old men in the sunroom. As the work proceeded, he meditated on the concept of recuperation. It seemed to begin at birth. Surely there was no better place to recuperate, no more womb-like a retreat from the contaminants of life, than a hospital. Granted, some people checked into hospital to die. But wasn't death itself an effective, if somewhat overemphatic, flight from the contagions of the world?

Robert rejoiced. At last: purpose.

* * *

10

> Sign all the cheques you like, love as many enemies as you please. You haven't practised true charity until someone forcibly takes something precious from you and you say, "Very well, may you find a way of practising charity with it."
>
> —Theodore Ng

Unbeknownst to Steven, Kathleen or anyone in his life, Robert took to spending spare weekend time— and even weekday evenings when he could swing it— inside one or the other of Presley's two hospitals, Riverside Civic and Saint Sebastian Among The Arrows. He wished some friend, schoolmate or relative would fall ill to provide a tangible pretext for his visits. At first he pretended he belonged in Riverside by visiting some of the old patients he had befriended. They craved company and were flattered whenever he took out his sketch pad. Often they nodded off while he drew them. Upon completion of a sketch, or if time dictated his departure, Robert gently awakened his subjects. They asked him to call again whenever he could.

The situation was not so simple at Saint Sebastian Among The Arrows. Robert had to remind Sister Sarah, the dwarf-like head nurse, that he was doing research for a school project on the excellence of Presley's hospital system, and would not harass any of the patients nor disturb anyone when Father Laferriere was hearing confessions in the lounge. Sister Sarah liked Robert and eventually allowed him to come and go as he pleased. Thus he became a fixture to the staff of both hospitals, as predictable and invisible as the old women who buzzed for a glass of juice at night.

After two weeks of regular visits, Robert concluded that recording hospital routine as an outsider was not nearly as rewarding as the life of a full-fledged patient with all its affiliated rights and privileges. He examined medical texts in the school library in search of a lingering but not overly debilitating disease to contract so he could take up indefinite residency at Riverside. No such disease jumped off the page at him.

Awaking especially desperate one Saturday morning in November, Robert packed his pyjamas and bathrobe into a paper bag, gave Kathleen his standard story about library work on a school project, and left the house. Kathleen was not disposed to cross-examine her son, particularly now that he seemed to be regaining his pre-pneumonia vigour. Robert changed into his pyjamas in Riverside's ground- floor bathroom and headed casually up to the third-floor sunroom, confident that the weekend skeleton staff would not sense anything untoward. He found two of his old friends lolling in the lounge. He noticed an elastic banbage around the ankle of one of them.

"Hey, Norman Rockwell," said the man with the bandaged ankle. "What are you in for?"

"Nothing serious," Robert said. "Just a few tests. It feels nice to be back."

"Speak for yourself," said the man with the trapped gas. "You couldn't find a nurse on Saturday if you wanted one."

"Are you in your old room?" the other asked.

". . .Actually I don't have a room. I'll be going downstairs for tests, then I imagine I'll go home."

"I've been waiting six months to go home," said the man with the trapped gas. "And I'm not getting any better. I'm getting worse."

"I'm the one who's getting worse," said the man with the

bandaged ankle. "Look at my neck. The skin flakes right off. The doctor says he can't do a thing about it. He doesn't even know what it is."

"It's nothing," said the man with the gas. "Try waking up in the middle of the night with your intestines swollen the size of balloons. Six months I've been cooped up in here."

While the two patients debated their respective conditions, the head nurse down the hall checked the day's records. She knew Robert from his regular visits and had greeted him that morning, mildly surprised that he was now a patient. His name was nowhere on the records. She puzzled over this for a moment. Then it dawned on her. "Louise! Come here a minute."

The two nurses headed together down the hall and stopped at the door into the sunroom. "Look at the Rosseter kid," the head nurse whispered. "Now he's even dressing like a patient. I don't care what you say, I'm making that phone call I should have made weeks ago."

The old man with the bandage around his ankle gingerly unravelled it and said, "Have you ever seen anything like that? Try walking sometime with an ankle like that."

"Trapped gas is worse because you can't see it," the other man said. "I've been six months without a working pancreas."

"Gas can be easily treated," the man with the bad ankle said. "Gout and lumbago are horses of an entirely different colour. . ."

Robert let the two men argue at length. They were oblivious to his sketching. Even he didn't notice, some time later, when two men stepped purposefully into the sunroom. One of them walked up to Robert, took an identification card from the breast pocket of his jacket and dangled it in front of Robert's face.

"My name is Don Chapman. I'm from the *Gleaner*."

Robert jumped to his feet, closed the sketch pad.

"I have reason to believe you're not an actual patient in this hospital."

"Uh. . ."

"I'm also told you've been hanging around here almost every day for the past few weeks."

". . ."

"My colleague here is going to take a couple of pictures while I ask you a few questions."

The late morning sun was just beginning to fill the far side of the room with a dazzling light. The two old men dozed peacefully. Robert straightened his bathrobe. "I think you've got the wrong idea. . ."

"I want to start by saying that what you're doing here, Mr. Rosseter, the fact that you're impersonating a patient when you're not even registered at Riverside—"

"I'm not actually impersonating a patient," Robert said.

"—fills me with nothing but admiration for you."

Robert opened his mouth but no sound came out.

"You don't mind if we take a couple of pictures, do you?"

Robert dumbfoundedly glanced around the room. The two nurses smiled and waved from the doorway.

"Uh. . ."

"Terry, why don't you get a shot of him standing between the two men." The photographer nodded and went to work with one of two cameras dangling from his neck.

"This is going to be a perfect Monday feature," Don Chapman said. "Mr. Rosseter, you've made my day. Now if we could just sit down for a minute so I can ask you a couple of questions. . ."

. . .

Kathleen eased herself into a living room chair. It had been a gruesome day at work, sorting the new wave records from the punk records and the reggae records from the roots records and the progressive bluegrass from the western swing. Whatever happened to the simple days of Grand Funk Railroad and Nana Mouskouri? She felt the music business was gradually pressuring her out of a job, making her feel old and apathetic and behind the times. Damn those kids and their fat allowances and their pretentious adolescent lifestyles. She wished there was another record store in town for them all to frequent.

She sighed and unfolded the *Gleaner*. Her eyes settled on a story boxed in a heavy blue line on the front page:

BOY SAMARITAN BRINGS
EARLY YULE CHEER
TO AREA SHUT-INS

By Donald Chapman
Gleaner Staff Reporter

Some say Christmas is the only time of the year when charity and self-sacrifice become community preoccupations. If that's true, then at least one 16-year-old Presleyite is determined to celebrate the Yule six weeks early.

His name is Giles Rosseter and his hobby is that of self-appointed bearer of good cheer for those less fortunate citizens who spend their days confined to hospital beds.

Giles spends as much of his spare time as possible fraternizing with the ill and the disabled of the community, bringing a spark of life and gaiety to them as only a youth can.

Last Saturday morning, the *Gleaner* caught up with this modern-day Good Samaritan as he was making his rounds at Riverside Civic Hospital. Giles had gone to the trouble of actually wearing hospital clothing, to make the sickly and infirm feel as at ease with him as possible.

Why this admirable and exceptional concern for the welfare of others?

"I don't know, it's just something I do," Giles said in his typical self-effacing manner.

At first he was reluctant to talk about his philanthropic vocation, but he eventually agreed

"Bobby!" Kathleen bellowed.

Robert, who had ensconced himself in his room after school and had emerged just long enough to wolf down his supper and ask if the newspaper had arrived, took a deep breath and walked slowly out of his room.

Kathleen tried in vain to compose herself. Of all the flaming hoops her son had put her through, this was the most death-defying to date.

From the foot of the stairs Robert saw the *Gleaner* in his mother's lap.

"Oh, that," he said.

"Yes, Bobby. That."

Robert managed a lame chuckle. "It's a bit much, isn't it?"

"A bit," Kathleen said.

He chuckled again, shifted his weight from one foot to the other. Kathleen was at a perfect loss. No motherly emotion seemed suitable for the occasion. She finally settled on bewilderment.

"Bobby, what does— I mean, what are. . .?"

"I know what you mean."

"I didn't. . . you never. . . Jesus God, Bobby, what am I supposed to make of this?"

"Ma, this is something I can easily explain if you have the time to listen right to the very end."

"Fire away," she said. Her eyes were glued to the large photograph of her son in his bathrobe, standing between two seated, similarly-clad old men who appeared to be sleeping. She felt dizzy. She felt that anything was probable.

"Okay. I'll start with the two guys in the picture: They're people I met when I was in the hospital. I'm sure I told you about them. They were really nice to me when I was a patient, so I thought I should visit them every now and then just to see how they're doing and to say hello and tell them I'm doing fine. That's about all there is to the whole thing. You know how newspapers sensationalize things."

"Then how do you explain this?" Kathleen said, holding the paper out to him with her index finger pointing to:

> Sister Sarah McKee, the diminutive head nurse at Saint Sebastian Among The Arrows Hospital, said Giles has been a "more or less permanent guest" there in recent weeks.
>
> "This boy obviously has special qualities. And he doesn't confine his charity to any specific ward. Giles roams the entire hospital," Sister Sarah said. "He's been a stirring example for the entire staff here at SSAA."

"Do you have patient-friends at that hospital, too?" Kathleen said, the newspaper trembling noisily in her hands.

"The whole thing was Mr. Malarkey's idea," Robert blurted.

Kathleen let that statement sink in.

"I thought Mr. Malarkey advised you to think about marketing computers or something."

"He did, sort of. But he also said it was important that I have a hobby. He said a man without a hobby is no better than a horse."

"This," Kathleen said in a quavering voice, tapping the newspaper with the back of her hand, "is your hobby?"

Robert nodded. "Hospital artist," he said.

Kathleen gazed at her son. "I see," she said finally, the first hint of resignation in her voice. Robert sensed an opening.

"Newspapers are always making mountains out of molehills. What's so special about me visiting hospitals? People do it every day and nobody writes stories about them. Some guys my age build schooners out of toothpicks inside liquor bottles. That's really crazy. But do you ever see any front-page stories about them?"

"I never meant to imply that what you were doing is crazy," Kathleen said. "I was just... surprised to find out about it this way. You never said a word to me about visiting any hospitals."

"I know. I feel bad about that. I was afraid you wouldn't understand. Do you understand now?"

"Not entirely..."

She stared again at the photograph. Her son looked more embarrassed than demented in it. She knew the basic symptoms of dementia— whites of eyes, froth of mouth and so on. At worst, the expression on Robert's face was one of serene dislocation, as of a saint who carried all the sordid emotional luggage of the world on his fragile shoulders. She cursed that rainy August night in the bush near Steven's ridiculous pyramid. It seemed to have set the boy's life on a new course. Where was the enervated introvert of old? But that wasn't the right attitude. Had she not prayed for the day when he would step decisively into the world and assume his rightful place?

But Jesus God, was this his rightful place?

She fought to unscramble her thoughts. There was nothing to be gained from second-guessing her son's motives. His hobby was... sweet, that's what it was. More boys his age should show such kindness and respect for the elderly and infirm of the world, for the less privileged members of the community.

Buy why her son, she couldn't help thinking. Why not someone else's son?

"Bobby," she said, "I think what you're doing is very interesting. I mean, I think it's commendable. I'm proud that you would think of— of keeping these people company. What I want the most for you is to make sure you get completely well again, to be your old self. I mean, to be like your old self, or at least to be as healthy as you used to be before everything happened, which is not to say that any of this has anything to do with your not being completely healthy or— what I'm trying to say, Bobby, is. . . what do you do when you're at the hospital?"

Robert shrugged. "Not much, really. A few sketches now and then. It passes the time."

"I see," said Kathleen, who was no closer to seeing than when she first set eyes on the photograph of her pyjama-clad son and his two old friends. After Robert excused himself and returned upstairs, she re-read the last paragraph of the article.

> Mayor Spooner was unavailable for comment as of press-time today. But Deputy-Mayor Bud Theriault said Presley City Council would likely discuss some formal way of recognizing Giles' "selfless efforts on behalf of the community" at tonight's regular meeting.

She shuddered.

. . .

In the ensuing forty-eight hours, much emotional luggage was seen to accumulate above the head of Kathleen, Steven and Robert Rosseter. First came the telephone calls from relatives and friends, many of whom were offended that no one had seen fit to inform them of Robert's courage and altruism. Uncle Edgar said the story was featured prominently in the Sault Ste. Marie newspaper.

"I've been all over hell's half-acre telling everybody that Giles Rosseter is my grandnephew, but I never knew him as Giles. You never told me that was his name. I thought his name was Bob."

"Giles is his first name," Steven said into the telephone. "We started calling him by his middle name not long after he was born. He doesn't like the name Giles."

"So why does the paper call him Giles? Surely if they—"

"I don't know," Steven said. "Thanks for calling, Uncle Edgar. I've got to go."

"Where'd you ever come up with a name like Giles?"

"Goodbye, Uncle Edgar."

Kathleen's Aunt Alice said she heard about it over the radio in Wawa. "I knew there'd be a saint in the family one day. Your mother was a bit of a saint, Kathleen, but you probably don't remember. Preston Wilhelm was a fine man in his own way. And now look at your son. You must be just flabbergasted."

"I am," Kathleen said.

"You must have really taught that boy something. I bet Pauline did, too."

"Mommy died before he was born, Aunt Alice."

"It's the sort of thing that gets passed on in the bones, Kathleen. Our Lord works in mysterious ways. I think you know what I mean. You can see for yourself how everything turned out. You can see that Our Lord didn't pass judgment on you or. . . or. . ."

"Steven?"

"Yes, Steven."

"Thanks an awful lot for calling, Aunt Alice."

"You've got to be two proud parents."

"We are, Aunt Alice. Thank you."

"I'm still in shock over it."

"We are too, Aunt Alice. Goodbye."

Eddie Laverty's father sequestered himself in his den that week and composed the editorial of his life, which managed to touch on all the variations he had ever developed on the theme of What This Community Means To Us. He envisioned a piece of work that would take its rightful place alongside "Yes, Virginia" in the pantheon of timeless newspaper commentary. "Presley: What is it?" he began, and proceeded over the next eight hundred words to answer. "Presley is the spirit and endurance of those rough-hewn men who first settled the land; Presley is the symbol of people from all walks of life finding common cause in prosperity and peace; Presley is the Kekagami River, in whose muddy currents drifts the timber that feeds the mills and employs the men; Presley is the Gateway To The Northwest, civic exemplar for all those who choose lives fraught and enriched by the adversity of the elements; and now, for which we can all be thankful, Presley is also Giles Rosseter, Boy Samaritan", and continued in a similar elegaic vein for another six hundred and fifty words.

Stanley Laverty believed it was his editorial, more even than the story itself, that unleashed an avalanche of letters to the editor praising the work of Presley's new favourite son. By the end of the week there was no stopping the Boy Samaritan Phenomenon, as it came to be known. Presley City Council, afraid of being upstaged by the Chamber of Commerce or one of the service clubs, decided with uncustomary haste to present Robert with a Community Service Citation the following Monday. A Toronto television station expressed interest in doing a feature profile on the Boy Samaritan. The executive producer of *Man Alive* called Kathleen on behalf of the CBC to arrange for an interview. Strangely enough, the Soviet news agency *Tass* picked up the story from the UPI wire service, which had transmitted it as a Christmas oddity, and added an editorial postscript of its own explaining that this kind of benevolent behavior on behalf of the community as a whole was such a rarity in capitalist societies that it rated the front pages of Western newspapers. The *Tass* piece engendered the interest of other national news networks and even prompted a widely-circulated comment from a senior U.S. State Department official to the effect that Canada should offer to loan Giles Rosseter to the Soviet government as a "bearer of Christmas cheer in the gulags".

A freelance writer contacted Kathleen in the hope of securing exclusive rights to the Boy Samaritan story for the purpose of a hypothetical instant book he intended to complete by the end of the following week, assuming interest in Robert continued to grow over the next few days. "I'm in a very reactive and unpreditable line of work," the writer explained. "I'm prepared to offer you $500 up front, plus another $2,500 once I've snagged a publisher. We can work out residuals down the road. What do you say? You'd be crazy not to jump at the chance. I know about these things. I make it my business to know."

"Why don't you make it your business to shove your head

longitudinally up your ga-ga?" Kathleen suggested and hung up.

She booked off sick, disconnected the phone and tried to calm herself by stripping wax from every last centimetre of uncarpeted floor in the house. Steven wondered if his son might benefit from psychiatric counselling. Maybe the bout of pneumonia had triggered some mental side effects. Kathleen scoffed, though she couldn't deny that Robert was looking pale and weak and out of it.

"The bloody world needs a psychiatrist," she told Steven while rewaxing the kitchen. "The world is a lot crazier than Bobby could ever be. Fungus and bloodsuckers: That's what the world's made of."

"Bobby is news," Steven said with a shrug.

"Yeah, right," Kathleen said, scratching with her thumbnail at antique bubblegum on the baseboard. "He and some 80-year-old guy in Iran. Jesus God, tell me it's all a dream."

"Believe me, Kath, if I could turn back the hands of time. . ."

"What the hell good would that do?"

"I don't know. Maybe if we could go back six or seven years and redo a few really bad months when we lost track of things, all three of us would be long gone from Presley by now."

"Where would we be?"

"Who knows? Somewhere together. Don't you ever wish that?"

Kathleen gave up on the last bit of gum. "Wishing is too dangerous," she said. "I stopped wishing a long time ago. Once you get in the habit of making wishes, you can't stop. Even if you're convinced you couldn't be any happier, it's impossible to stop new wishes from cropping up. And unless they come true, you know every minute of every day of the rest of your life that you're not as happy as you could be. Wishes are for idiots who think life goes on forever."

"You mean me," Steven said.

"I don't know what I mean."

"My wishes wrecked this marriage."

"Steven," Kathleen said, wiping her forehead with the back of her hand, "have you ever wondered why neither of us has ever filed for a divorce? Do you suppose deep down we're cowardly and we've passed that flaw on to our son?"

"Maybe we're just optimists," Steven said. That almost made her laugh.

After he left, she headed upstairs to be with Robert before

turning in for the night. He was reclining on his bed, sketch pad in hand. His room was strewn with drawings, mostly of jagged lines intersecting at random. He let his hand roam freely over the surface of the paper and deliberately aborted any pattern or rhythm that might represent something. Eventually he crumpled the paper and threw it at the door. It struck Kathleen in the face. He wondered how long she'd been standing there, spying on him.

"Jesus God, you're really going to town." She picked up a couple of sketches and examined them. "What are they supposed to be?"

"Nothing," Robert said.

She studied them a while longer and said, "I think I see an alligator here." She carefully placed the drawings back on the floor where they had been flung, and took one from the corner of the bed.

"I used to draw, ages ago."

"I know."

"You do?"

"Grampa showed me some."

"I loved to draw birds. My favourite bird of all was the cardinal. The male cardinal has the sweetest, saddest song. He perches up on the highest part of the tree and just wails until somebody takes notice. I remember the day I found a dead cardinal on the front lawn. My cat, Misty, had killed it. I loved that cat but I never thought about her the same way after that. A few weeks later Misty was hit by a car. It scared me that I was the only one in my family who understood why Misty had to die. I was nine or ten at the time. Everything happens for a reason, Bobby. You can count on that."

"What if everything happens for the wrong reason?" Robert said. The question stumped Kathleen.

. . .

He had no trouble convincing his mother it would be unwise to return to school until everything blew over. She knew he wasn't sleeping well and had almost no appetite. Although he felt sapped and strangely cut off from both the past and the present, he meditated on the meaning of what had transpired and decided it didn't put him in a very flattering light. The first order of business would be to politely decline the citation from Presley City Council. He didn't deserve a medal. He didn't genuinely care about the patients in the hospital. The fact that his visits might have brightened the days of some of the patients was irrelevant. The motive was all wrong.

Midway through Day Seven of the Boy Samaritan Phenomenon, after Robert had exhausted himself reassuring his father that neither of them was losing his marbles, he called the *Gleaner*.

Cites excessive publicity
'BOY SAMARITAN' CANCELS
FURTHER SHUT-IN VISITS

Robert Rosseter, self-styled Boy Samaritan and subject of international interest, told the *Gleaner* in an exclusive interview yesterday he will visit no more hospitals for an indefinite period.

"My actions have been misunderstood. The attention I've received since your paper printed its misleading article about me makes it impossible for me to continue. I only want to be left alone," Mr. Rosseter said in what appeared to be a prepared statement.

When asked, Mr. Rosseter refused to state how last Monday's exclusive *Gleaner* story had been inaccurate, saying only that he was "not a saint, and please don't call me Giles."

Mayor Spooner was unavailable for comment as of press-time today, but Deputy-Mayor Bud Theriault told the *Gleaner* a special meeting of City Council would likely be scheduled for tonight or tomorrow to come up with an official response to this surprising development.

Although Mr. Rosseter emphasized he would accept no citation from council, Mr. Theriault said the presentation, slated for next Monday evening, is still on.

"I think the best thing right now is for the media

> and the entire community to respect this selfless young man's plea for privacy. He certainly deserves it," Mr. Theriault said.

The following Monday, in the glare of television lights, Deputy-Mayor Theriault, in Mayor Spooner's absence, presented the Community Service Citation, in absentia, to Giles Robert Rosseter, who at that moment was up in his room shivering and sweating and studying the sketches from his hospital period and tearing them up one by one. Safely stored in his desk drawer was a picture of Sue-Ann Reilly, and further back, tucked deeper, darker in a locked box in his head, was Thanksgiving Day 1970 and all the things that made him what he was and what he would become.

Kathleen took him downstairs and made him lie on the couch. He said he was cold so she got a blanket and draped it over him. He still shivered. She went to the kitchen and poured a bottle of ginger ale into a saucepan. Her mother always swore by hot ginger ale. Kathleen stood there, staring into the saucepan, until steam began to rise. When she decided the ginger ale was hot enough that it couldn't possibly taste good, she poured some into a large mug and carried it into the living room.

But the Boy Samaritan was dead. On the couch, in his place, lay a sleeping young man with tousled hair who could actually use a shave.

* * *

11

> All memories are fabrications, whether we know it or not. Those who say they remember well are the biggest fabricators of all.
>
> —Theodore Ng

In the middle of January 1981, the *Gleaner* ran an editor's note advising that no further letters arguing any of the various sides of the Boy Samaritan debate would be published. The last letter was from a widowed pensioner who wrote that saints always toiled best in obscurity and she'd be proud to have the Rosseter boy as a grandson, regardless of whether he ever visited another hospital. "You people in the media have ruined his good works," she concluded.

Presley was back to normal, with the exception that a slate of anti-totem pole candidates had been elected to City Council for the 1981-82 term. Isaac Presley's legendary sub-contracted monument was to be formally dismantled on Dominion Day, with a grand fireworks display to mark the occasion. Not a dissenting peep was heard from the Presley & District Historical Society. In fact, some of its younger members had begun a quiet but effective campaign to blot the legacy of Isaac Presley from the city's annals, or at the very least to spruce it up for the tourist market. Maybe Isaac Presley wasn't a bastard and a cretin but an orphan and learning-disabled. Maybe he didn't bilk the CPR out of millions. Maybe he had nothing to do with the ersatz totem pole that was finally coming down. P.W. O'Hagan would have relished the discussions that accompanied Presley's sudden pressing need to develop a more favourable tourism profile. There was talk of a deep recession around the corner, which didn't do much for the morale of a traditionally depressed area. The Indians in the nearby reserve were drafting land claims and demanding self-government. Presley's francophone community, though small by Northern Ontario standards, was campaigning hard for its own high school. It was as though age-old layers of illusion were suddenly peeling off and the city was showing the world its true face, which had all the character and internal logic of a composite photo.

"One day I'll leave this place and never ever come back," Kathleen said, setting down two Irish coffees on the kitchen table. She and Helen Munsinger were celebrating the official end of the Boy Samaritan Phenomenon. "No one will miss me and it won't make a bit of difference because people don't make any difference in Presley."

"I'll miss you," said Helen after taking a sip of the scalding coffee.

"You won't stay, either. The people who stay are the ones who make sure that the people who leave don't make a difference. Those people who want to tear down the totem pole won't stay for long. That's sort of sad. Maybe that's how a place doesn't change for generations. The people who want things to change end up moving on. My father's the only person I known who never fit in here at all, yet stayed and stayed and stayed."

"I wonder why," Helen said.

"He used to say it didn't matter anymore where you came from or even where you happened to be; as long as you had a television you belonged."

"For whatever belonging is worth."

"For whatever it's worth."

"I think I'm getting depressed," Helen said.

"I think I'm getting drunk," Kathleen said with a laugh.

"So what are you going to do about Bobby?"

Kathleen sighed. "Doctor Paine says he could use a change of scene."

"Brilliant."

"He said I should take him away somewhere, even if only for a few days. He said Bobby was still weak from the pneumonia when the Boy Samaritan stuff started getting out of hand, and he had a relapse. 'The lad can't stay in bed forever.' That's what he said. I told him I'd think of something."

"And you're thinking of taking him away for good."

"No," Kathleen said, staring into her coffee. "Not yet."

Helen butted her Benson & Hedges and gazed out at the dark through a filigree of frost on the window. Upstairs the toilet flushed and footsteps sounded as Robert made his way back to his room.

"Why don't the three of us go away for a while?" Helen said.

"Where?"

"Anywhere. Florida, the Bahamas, Democratic Kampuchea. We could all use a little sun."

"It's not cheap, Helen."

"So?"

"You've been saving for a townhouse."

"Maybe I've been saving for right now. I can buy a townhouse any old time, but right now happens only once in my life. Think about it, Kath. I can sit here making meticulous plans for a tomorrow that never comes. We could all be radiocative ash six months from now. Look at Afghanistan; that whole thing might blow up tomorrow. Ronnie Ray-gun can do whatever he wants with the world whenever he wants, so why can't we? What makes us any less free than he is? Let's just screw it and do what we please with the time we have now before the whole world goes—" she clapped her hands once.

Upstairs, in the enveloping silence of his room, Robert listened to Helen's exhortation through the floor. He had heard a similar message before. Prior to Christmas, prior to all the Boy Samaritan unpleasantness, his history class had studied the Soviet Union in a cursory way. The events leading up to October 1917 were briefly covered, but his ancient teacher of modern history was much more interested in what was going on now. According to his teacher's reading of the current situation, only Russia and America's morbid fear of one another postponed the inevitable nuclear confrontation. The teacher, who was retiring at the end of the year, said he didn't envy the students' generation. He figured the holocaust might not come in his lifetime, but it would certainly come in theirs, and probably in the Middle East.

"I pity you kids," he said cheerfully.

From the vantage point of his bed, Robert imagined tens of thousands of Soviet soldiers massed along the frontier of that country, passing the time by polishing the Iron Curtain with primitive electric buffing machines. Now and then, soldiers thought they heard enemy footsteps and shut off their noisy machines to reconnoitre.

"I really pity you," said his history teacher.

Giles Robert pictured MIRVs and ICBMs criss-crossing in elegant arcs over the Atlantic Ocean on their way to mutually unpronouncable targets in North America and Northern Asia. He pictured families in the United Kingdom of Great Britain setting out lawn chairs and holding impromptu roadside picnics to observe the brilliant display in the evening sky; high-rise dwellers in Copenhagen cowering on their balconies as cruise missiles sweep soundlessly by, the roar of their computer-driven engines in their wake. He pictured the barbecuing of Washington and New York, of Moscow and Leningrad; he imagined how it would look from the moon as the firestorm rages across the American continent, the heat and rumble of the conflagration recorded on instruments as far away as the Falkland Islands. "And North Bay," he said aloud, where the grandfather he had never seen helped build an underground fortress for the Americans— it, too, hot ash for the geiger counters. And the citizens of Paris marvel at the beautiful distant luminosity that was once the Union of Soviet Socialist Republics. But everyone's number will soon be up. No time for the war effort, for Victory Bonds, peace marches, economic sanctions, shuttle diplomacy. No time even for the draft or the stockpiling of Shreddies. This is not a fun war, like the others. This is not a war to inspire patriots and history teachers. "We would be fools not to live for today," he heard Helen say from the kitchen. He pictured people's dogs dying of radiation poisoning in Oregon and Frobisher Bay, ham radios hissing hot static in Gdansk and Ocho Rios, Cuban troops goose-stepping through the ashes of Miami, Belgian reservists sacking what was left of Kiev. Rolphton and Riga are no more. The shadows of incinerated souls on reinforced concrete walls. Digital clocks frozen at 23:23. The vestiges of humanity running madly over the hot coals of the planet, like those miserable Second World War sailors he once saw on TV, making their last stand on the enormous slippery hull of their capsized ship before being sucked down down down, like ants whose hill has been levelled by the whim of a bored little boy on a sleepy summer afternoon (he remembers the time he did that, and the pang afterwards). The proportions of Mutual Assured Destruction are fascinating: two men settling an argument over how many home runs Mickey Mantle hit in 1961 with AK-47s, Aunt Alice pruning her roses with Agent Orange, kids playing dodge-the-neutron-bomb on a quiet residential street. Helen and his history teacher were right. He had written a haiku about it for his neurotic English teacher:

There are snakes in the grass,
There are sharks in the river,
No one is safe.

Even people in hospital weren't safe, though theirs was a richer illusion of shelter. Depressed French intellectuals had spent the better part of the century warning the world of the absurdity at hand. Robert's great leap of doubt was the product of his own sixteen and a half years. In his mind he sketched Presley in ruins with burnt cork. Only the totem pole was left standing. Down in the kitchen, his mother made another Irish coffee for Helen and herself.

"Quality of life," Helen declaimed, emptying the contents of her purse on the table in search of a fresh pack of Benson & Hedges. "That's all there is. It has to be our top priority now because it might be our last chance before other people start calling all the shots. Know what I mean?"

"Vaguely," Kathleen said, setting the two cups down.

"More than ever, we have to decide exactly what we want with our lives. We have to fess up." Helen lit a cigarette, blew out the match. "The trouble is nobody wants to fess up. We used to call it being phony. Remember? Holden Caulfield hated everybody because they were phonies. 'So and so's a phony.' Remember?"

"You made a mess of my table," Kathleen said.

"I'm cleaning it up." Helen said, stuffing an asssortment of cosmetics, pills and perfumes into her purse.

"I'm funny about messes."

"You're a nice lady, Kathleen Rosseter, but are you ever a *phony*."

They both laughed. Upstairs, Robert pictured a pudgy Indochinese man who looked a lot like Mister Ng. The man has assumed global power after the nuclear war. His first priority, once planetary government is established, is to fortify Earth against a possible invasion from outer space.

"Don't you wish you could become a nun?" Helen said after taking a long sip of Irish coffee.

"Jesus God, no," Kathleen replied. "All they ever do is cook meals for priests. Ham and eggs and orange juice, day after day after day."

Technological mutations: second- and third-generation computer systems with the power of telekinesis; weapons systems whose software can pinpoint more than fifty percent of all the matter/anti-matter vector points in the spacetime continuum between here and Tau Ceti; a concise plan for the pre-emptive defence of some thirty-five hundred parsecs of interstellar space—The Man From Indochina knows what to do with these new tools.

"But don't you wish it was fashionable to be a nun? People in the singles bars aren't looking for a husband or a wife or even the old in-out in-out. Most of them don't know it but what they're looking for is love, plain old love like they had when they were kids."

"Love," Kathleen said.

"As soon as a man starts talking, he ruins it for me. As soon as he opens his big fat mouth about his career or, worse yet, the kids he left behind, I can feel myself go dry. To be blessed with a son in such a love-starved, phony world is something really special—even if it's the only thing you've got."

"It's not the only thing I've got," Kathleen protested.

"That's not what I meant. What I meant is it's all you need."

The Man From Indochina has acted not a moment too soon. The Sirians are on the verge of mastering interstellar drive. They would love nothing more than to turn what's left of Earth into a swank theme-planet for those jaded masses on the galactic fringe who've grown bored of ten thousand years of peace and harmony.

"So let me come away with the two of you," Helen said. "I like the idea more and more. In fact, I can't wait."

Luckily for Earth, the Sirians have their hands full with the Tetrans, who have already declared the Sol system their sovereign territory, owing to a series of reconnaissance missions in prehistoric times. But the Sirians and the Tetrans would do well to join forces soon, for the vile Mutrestins, galactic pariahs, are at this moment razing an entire quadrant for the sheer lifeforce-sucking pleasure of it, and they've been salivating over Earth and its neighbouring planets since the days when all the others, Tetrans, Sirians and Earthers alike, lived in trees and subsisted on bananas and ants.

"But where?" said Kathleen.

"Anywhere," said Helen.

The Man From Indochina knows nothing of this galactic tug-of-war, but he is gifted with foresight. He has a favourite parable his father taught him long before the holocaust— the one about the turtle who wore a crash helmet that matched his shell, but whose tender heart proved his undoing, the moral being that you can't hurt anyone with a shield and sooner or later someone will devise a way of puncturing it; or: The best defence is a good offence. You either make peace by fighting back or you accept death. This, too, depressed French intellecuals realized long ago.

"Quality of life," Helen reiterated.

. . .

On the eve of his departure for Barbados, Robert met Eddie Laverty at the playground rink near the banks of the frozen Kekagami River. Eddie had heard about his friend's trip through a mutual acquaintance at the College Of St. Vitus. He phoned Robert to tell him they should get together. Robert was surprised by the call. Eddie sounded sad and broken. They hadn't seen each other in more than three months. It was as if St. Vitus had swallowed Eddie whole.

Eddie arrived first and began blasting slapshot after slapshot off the boards. Someone had haphazardly shovelled a corner of the deserted rink. The recent dusting of snow slowed the puck's progress back to him. Other kids had decided to stay off it altogether rather than ask the alcoholic who manned the dressing-shack to wake up and hand them a shovel. Eddie wished he had a bucket of pucks, like the professionals. He gazed up at the strangely luminous overcast sky. Seemingly every light in town was reflected in the low clouds and snow cover.

"You're fading away," Robert said as he stepped onto the ice.

"You're no Orson Welles yourself," Eddie replied. "To tell you the truth, you look like death warmed over— or is it just this light?"

"I feel okay. What's your excuse?"

Eddie propped hands and chin on the butt of his hockey stick, Ken Dryden-style. "I'm never hungry," he said. "I think I've finally gotten tired of food."

"Starving yourself to death. That's novel."

"While you go off to soak up the sun: Mister Photosynthesis." Eddie took a slapshot. The puck sailed over the boards and into the snowbank. Robert passed his puck across the ice. "Here we are, the Boy Samaritan and Ivan Denisovich. Funny the way things turn out."

"Ivan who?" said Robert.

Eddie took a wrist shot. The puck rolled back to him on end, like a little tire. He redirected it to Robert. "I've been thinking about back when we first met, at Sir Charles Tupper. Remember?"

"We got into trouble with Miss Hornung because we stayed out in the yard after recess. I think we were talking about God."

"Hornung hasn't changed at all," Eddie said. "I've been thinking about those times. You know what?" He took a slapshot. "I really believed in God back then. I mean I really believed. God scared the shit out of me for the longest time, then one day he didn't anymore."

Robert took a shot and went running after the rebound. They silently passed the puck back and forth for a few minutes, pretending they were a pair of New York Islanders closing in on the enemy net late in a game late in the season late in their career. Back, forth, back, forth, slap— the silent distension of mesh in the red glow of the goal judge's light, the roar of the crowd in the smoky popcorny light of Nassau Coliseum.

"I wish it had never happened," Eddie said.

"Wish what had never happened?"

"I wish God had never stopped scaring me."

Robert wanted to laugh but didn't. An ambulance siren wailed somewhere downriver. "So start believing again," he said, aware of how lame the suggestion was, yet compelled to say something.

"Flick a switch, right? Or take a couple of aspirin and call Jesus in the morning. Believing doesn't mean anything. All those Hail Marys my family floated up to heaven? God isn't interested in them. God isn't listening. God doesn't know or care." He took a slapshot; the puck struck a flaw in the boards with a surprising bang. "I bought the old ideas when I was a little kid because I didn't know any better and I counted on others to guide me. Then one day everything changed and I was left with what was handed down to me when I was too young to figure things out for myself, and now I'm stuck with somebody else's God who doesn't hear or see, so I blather to myself at bedtime. Hail Eddie, full of grace, the Force be with you. In my sleep I see an empty world that goes on forever. If I could. . . If I could just. . ."

"Finish what you were going to say."

Eddie stood the puck on end, knocked it flat. A chill wind had come up, carrying snowflurries from Lake Nipigon.

"You sound like my Uncle Cecil: 'Go on, go on.'"

"What are you trying to say?"

"I'm not 'trying' to say anything. I've said it all, over and over. Over and out. You don't really know me any better than anybody else. Leave me alone."

"Bullshit," Robert said.

"You don't."

"Suit yourself."

They silently took turns shooting the puck. Slap—pow, slap—pow. Wishful slapshots from just inside the blue line. Sometimes, in a lull midway through a playoff game, a shot like that could change the course of an entire series.

"It's getting colder," Robert said finally, but Eddie didn't seem to hear him. He was staring across the river.

"Last night," he said, "I watched *Happy Days* with my family, and I counted the number of times the studio audience laughed. In a half-hour they laughed seventy-seven times. In my house, my mother sort of chuckled at the end but nobody laughed out loud even once. I wondered what my father and Uncle Cecil would have thought if I had laughed seventy-seven times in that half-hour. Do you suppose they would have locked me up for good, instead of however long it takes?"

Robert said nothing.

"My father promised I could go back to Presley High next year if I fall into line at St. Vitus. I can't see the bloody line I'm supposed to fall into." He started to laugh. "Do you know where the line is? Could you point it out to me, or give me a hint?"

"You know what he meant," Robert said.

Eddie nodded. "He meant I'm not to be miserable anymore. He meant I'm not to worry him or anyone else anymore. I'm working on it, Rosseter, I swear I am."

Robert picked up the puck, slid over to Eddie and handed it to him. "When I get back I'll give you a call and we'll go shoot the breeze at D'Agostino's, or in the yard at Tupper, like old times. Maybe even throw a football around."

"Yeah," Eddie said. The anger had gone out of his voice, but nothing had replaced it. "You could throw it in the river at this time of year and it would just bounce on the ice instead of floating all the way to Timbuktu."

Robert stepped off the rink and raised his collar against the cold wind.

"Hey Rosseter!"

Robert looked back.

"You've always been my best friend," Eddie called out. "Let's give the world hell together."

Robert waved and hustled down the path to the road as the flurries turned to snow.

. . .

Stepping out of the plane was like walking into a hothouse. The air was ignorant of Arctic flow, even of room temperature. Helen Munsinger squinted up at the sky and laughed out loud. They waited in a shady spot just off the tarmac for the van to their hotel. The sun slid in and out of stately cumulus clouds, but the heat seemed to radiate from the earth upward. Robert breathed deep the mildewy sweetness of flowers and natural rot.

Their hotel, a few minutes south of Bridgetown, was a modern facility, as the brochure had promised. In fact it was so modern that it was not yet fully built. Kathleen, Helen and Robert marvelled at all the workers who leaned on rakes, shovels and pickaxes, sipped beer, shared a joke, ogled the pale North American women in their flimsy swimsuits, and cracked open coconuts with a hammer. Occasionally one of the workers shimmied up a tree and jarred a few more coconuts loose, his grin incandescent in the shade.

That first afternoon, Robert took it all in from the balcony of their room: the westward vista of the emerald Caribbean Sea, the steady breeze filling the colourful sails of small boats and catamarans plying the waters beyond the reef, the sky almost violet against cotton clouds, the hotel staff making the least of a day's work. In his room as in the lobby of the hotel, the lazy music and indecipherable chatter of *Rediffusion Radio* lulled the island through the mad-dog hours of midday.

"Hey!" cried the worker up a tree. Robert peered over at a grove of palms on the other side of the tennis courts.

"You take a picture!"

"Are you talking to me?" Robert called back.

"A picture!" said the workman.

"I don't have a camera!"

"Good picture!"

"My mother has the camera down at the pool!"

"Tell her to come and take a picture!"

The man said something else but Robert couldn't make it out. The workers lounging in the shade at the foot of the tree laughed. "Tell her to come!" the man yelled and waved his hands. Robert waved back and stepped into the room.

The three beds in their efficiency unit doubled as settees in the daytime. He threw himself onto one of them to test the mattress. He wandered into the bathroom. The slatted window looked down on the pool. Beyond stretched the blinding white beach and the endless sun-flecked plain of the sea. He recognized his mother and Helen at poolside, their legs exposed to the afternoon sun, the rest of them comfortably in the shade of a parasol. The manager of the hotel's semi-enclosed restaurant stood in the doorway near the pool, watching a sailboat tack to the northeast. Further down the beach, a young local with long dreadlocks peeled off his shirt and washed it in the shallows before resuming his day-long wanderings.

Robert loved the view from the room and the room itself. He loved the whitewashed walls and the way daylight sought out and captured every cranny. Later in the afternoon, direct sunlight poured into the bathroom. Soon he would shower in soft lukewarm water while the women dressed for a stroll down the Saint Lawrence Gap to a restaurant. If he timed it perfectly he could watch the spent red ball of the sun slip into the sea while he towelled his hair.

Boredom seemed inconceivable under such circumstances. For the first couple of days, Kathleen privately rejoiced every time she and Helen climbed the outside stairs to their third-floor room to find Robert napping like a baby in the shade of the balcony, a paperback propped open on his chest. Someone in the gift shop had told him he could get a perfectly nice tan in the shade.

Robert was reading Philip K. Dick. Even by the middle of his first afternoon on the island he realized the intuitiveness of his choice. Dick's books amounted to an ongoing investigation of the nature of reality. Dick asked fundamental questions about the reliability of the senses within the framework of a hard-boiled fictional narrative. Robert could identify with that. Here— bobbing lazily in and out of slumber to the sweet sounds of unfamiliar birdsong, rustling palm leaves, the surf and the eternal whirr of air-conditioners— here, too, was a passive investigation of reality, a languid inventory of all the components that, together, were emblematic of something called *alive*. What exactly is *alive*, Robert wondered, amazed at how rhetorical the question felt when asked on a hotel balcony in the West Indies. Perhaps, he concluded, life is more Dickian than Kafkaesque.

He heard clogs beat out a familiar rhythm on the wooden walkway outside the room.

"All I know," Helen said, opening the door, "is that the travel brochure told us there was a mini-mart on the premises and the brochure was lying. There's a restaurant on the premises, but there sure as hell isn't any mini-mart."

"The mini-mart is just a couple of minutes down the road," Kathleen said to Robert.

"That's not the point," Helen said. "The point is the brochure quite clearly indicated there was one on the hotel grounds, which turns out to be a crock. Hi, Bob."

"Hi. You caught some sun."

"From the knees down," Kathleen said. "It's a start."

The women draped their towels over the balcony railing. His mother wore a brown one-piece swimsuit. She still had a fine figure; her hair shone the way Robert liked. Helen wore a grey two-piece that made her look more busty than she was.

"I was just telling your mother that the travel brochure said there was a mini-mart right on the hotel property."

"I noticed it when we were coming in," Robert said, nodding.

"Noticed what?"

"The mini-mart. A couple of men were mixing concrete inside it. It probably won't be ready until next year."

"There you have it," Kathleen said. "A mini-mart on the premises. How about an iced tea?"

"Wait a minute," Helen said. "Just because they're working on it doesn't change anything. The fact remains that the brochure clearly said there was a mini-mart right on the—"

"There is," Robert said, stretching his arms and smiling. "It just isn't open yet."

Kathleen laughed from the kitchenette. Helen gazed incredulously at Robert. "Come on, Bobby. You, of all people—"

"You should read this," he said, handing her a Philip K. Dick book called *The Solar Lottery*. "It's all about things that may or may not exist." A whistle from outside diverted their attention. They stepped onto the balcony.

"Hey! You take a picture now!" The worker was back up his tree.

"He was asking me earlier," Robert said.

"Let me handle this," Helen said. She took the camera from her bag, went to the railing and looked at the worker through the lens. "What you do is pretend you're taking a picture, then they don't bother you about it anymore." She feigned clicking the shutter. "There," she said, waving to the worker. She put the camera back in her bag.

A couple of minutes later, Helen was compelled by the good-humoured but persistent cries of the worker to let a couple of American one-dollar bills flutter down to him from the third-floor balcony as payment for the imaginary photograph.

. . .

The week unfolded like an epic dream. They rented a Subaru for three days, picnicked at windswept Farley Hill, visited the caves at North Point where the roiling Atlantic made them dizzy, hiked through Welshman's Gully to ogle the wild monkeys who ogled them back, locked themselves out of their Subaru during an afternoon cloudburst near the lighthouse at Atlantic Shores, strolled through the suburban sprawl of Sunset Crest Village, collected shells on the boulder-strewn beach at Bathsheba, got lost in a jungle of sugarcane somewhere in St. James Parish, purchased flying fish at the market in Oistins, and spent long hours on the beach or by the pool at their hotel.

Kathleen was relieved to see the hint of a spring in her son's step, but it began to annoy her that he spent so much time alone in the room or on the balcony, reading those silly sci-fi novels and doing God knows what else, coming down to the pool once in a blue moon, and usually just to stand at the shallow end and climb out again.

"What's the matter?" Kathleen called out to him from behind sunglasses and a book of Alice Munro stories. "Have a swim, dear. It'll refresh you."

"I feel fresh enough already," Robert said.

"You won't when you're back up in the snow and you wish you'd gone swimming more."

"Maybe."

"Then go on," Kathleen said.

"Why is it so important that I swim in the pool?"

"Because it's there," Helen suggested.

"Does there always have to be a why, Bobby?"

"Maybe," he replied, looking westward to the blinding sea.

"Jesus God."

Beams of light on gentle water. Light itself invisible. Water transparent but heavy. Displacement. Earth orbiting around sun. Also spinning on own axis. Atmosphere moving in great currents. Also the sea. Light ripple in the pool. Chlorine. A child's sandal on tiled bottom. Smell of fruitliquor and suntan oil. *Chick, chick, chick* of a reggae guitar. Standing in shallow end. Now getting out.

"Jesus God."

"You don't have to if you don't want to," Helen said. "This is a vacation."

Like Lake Mead, only sun stronger.

. . .

By some invariable rule of Caribbean logic, their complimentary welcome rum-punch barbecue was held the evening before they were to fly home. All the guests flaunted their tans and a gaudy assortment of local clothing and jewelry. The hotel was buzzing with the news that a woman from Quebec City staying in a hotel a mile down the Gap had given premature birth to a boy that afternoon in Bridgetown. The daughter of a couple from Thornhill insisted Kathleen and Helen see her collection of conch shells, straw figurines and coral trinkets. During the past couple of days, said her mother, the ten-year-old had taken to bartering with the beach hawkers for the sheer sport of it, coaxing ever lower prices out of them, then announcing she was penniless and skipping off to her room, leaving them bemused and exasperated, holding their open briefcase. Her name was Krystyna, "with a K and two Ys. You can come too," she said to Robert, who had been sipping a 7Up on a poolside chair slightly apart from the others. Perhaps out of curiosity, but more probably the involuntary attachment to others that arises when one is about to leave places and faces behind, Robert tagged along.

"Were you surprised not to find a mini-mart on the premises?" Helen inquired of Krystyna's mother as they climbed the stairs to the second-floor room.

"I understand it won't be ready until next year," the woman said, taking the key from her purse.

"That's the story we heard, too. I don't know about you, but our travel folder quite clearly indicated there was a mini-mart right on the property. . ."

Adult voices faded to nothing as Robert fell under the spell of Krystyna's curios and souvenirs. She explained in detail where she acquired each piece, and what the ones she had to buy had cost.

Spread out in such intricate order on the kitchenette counter, Krystyna's shrine reminded him of the icons in Eddie Laverty's home when they were children— something charming but grave. Something that would forever renew a specific moment rather than evoke a simple flawed memory. Had they been alone, he might have warned her she was trifling with powerful forces, that she should hide all her stuff in a closet. She probably would have told him there was nothing she could do about that: The placement of each item was dictated by ancient magic most people forgot long before they spoke their first word. She was the go-between who could take pride only in the fidelity with which she obeyed silent instinctive orders. But what if she lost control of the spell? What was it that made her so fearless?

. . .down now and sample that punch," the girl's mother said, ushering everyone outside.

The chatter at poolside was animated. Kathleen allowed Robert one glass of punch, though he hadn't asked to taste it. He sipped the drink and watched waiters arrange steaks on a large barbecue trolley. Most of the guests seemed oblivious to the last sunset of their holiday; perhaps this was deliberate, to forget their impending departure. Better to toast life with a full punch glass.

Robert wandered onto the beach as the last of the flattened sun dissolved into the sea. Far to the south, a chain of clouds glowed coral pink. Robert watched the clouds for a long time. They stirred a memory with which he couldn't quite connect.

"What does it taste like?"

Krystyna had approached soundlessly. She stood next to him.

"The punch: What does it taste like?"

"It doesn't taste very good."

"Then why are you drinking it?"

"I don't know."

"All the grownups like it, but not for the taste," Krystyna said. "They like it because it makes them act silly. Tomorrow morning I'm going to swim in the ocean and fill a bottle with sand to take home."

Robert nodded. Already the blues of the sky were shifting to more subtle hues. The faroff clouds to the south had drained of colour, their significance lost to him forever. He turned to speak to the little girl but she too was gone— talking now, he noticed, to an old black man by the pool. The evening breeze shot cinders into the sky from the barbecue trolley. Willed jubilation was in the air.

By the time most of the guests had meandered into the restaurant for their steak, the brightest stars were out. Helen, her face flushed, complained loudly to a group at a nearby table about the absence of a mini-mart on the property-- "one that does more than exist," she said, glaring at Robert. Kathleen bantered with Krystyna's parents, who shared their table. The intensity in her eyes reminded Robert of his father at the wheel of the Camaro, eating up the asphalt. The way the punch caused her words to link up, as if she were chanting some interminable ode, reminded him of his grandfather. But as she spoke he sensed that a part of her was trying to hold back, as though in dread of an unknown force, perhaps peculiar to the tropics, that charged every sentiment with a deeper meaning. He and Krystyna ate in silence as the adults laughed and laughed. No one among them had economized on the complimentary punch.

The topic of parenthood came up. Krystyna's mother contributed an anecdote about her daughter's lingering summertime habit of sitting on the edge of the bathtub and soaking her feet in the toilet. The adults laughed. She told a few more stories about Krystyna, at which the other grownups laughed uproariously.

Kathleen picked up her punch glass, gulped a mouthful and set the glass down. The sudden silence at the table was a vortex that sucked words from her mouth.

"Bobby, here," she said, "is a fairly quiet boy by comparison. But if I were to tell you a story or two about what we've been through with him, you wouldn't believe me. Would they, Bobby?"

As though aware that her declaration had tipped a delicate balance, Kathleen continued before he could reply.

"Under that quiet exterior lurks a busy mind. He used to scare me when he was a baby. I had the feeling he knew every thought in my head, every little doubt or twinge of guilt. I'd call my former husband at work and say to him, 'Steven, the baby knows everything. He scares the daylight out of me.'" Krystyna's parents laughed. Helen silently sawed a tough section of her steak. "I'd say to him, 'I swear to God the baby can read my mind.' Now I'm not so sure anymore. He doesn't read my mind the same way, or maybe not at all." She strained to focus on her son's face. "Can you still read my mind?"

"Your steak's getting cold," Robert said and looked away.

Kathleen went on gazing at him.

"Like his father, Giles is a master sidestepper. So was his grandfather. So, for that matter, are all men on earth."

"Eat your steak," said Robert.

"Don't patronize me, Giles."

"Don't call me Giles."

"Giles is the name I gave you when you were born. I'm entitled to call you whatever I bloody-well please. I'll call you Balthazar if it suits me."

"You're making a fool of yourself," Robert said.

Krystyna's mother stifled a nervous guffaw. "I had an uncle by the name of Balthazar. Everybody knew him as Balt."

"Don't you call me a fool. . ."

"He looked like a Balt, if you can imagine that," Krystyna's father said.

Kathleen lapsed into silence. At a nearby table, two young men from Alberta argued with a waiter about whether they had helped themselves to a second steak, for which they would have to pay. The rasp of surf and peep of tree frogs drifted through the open glass doors fronting on the sea. Out by the lighted pool, a tall black woman took her guitar out of its case. The manager arrived and sat down with the two Albertans. Outside, the woman began to strum her guitar. The receding tide worked like an invisible magnet in the dark, drawing out more words.

"You knew," Kathleen said. "You've always known."

Her voice startled him. And her face. A stranger's.

"The grudge you're holding against me is just a habit now. You've always known."

"Known what?"

"Don't try to snow me."

Some of the guests turned to look at Kathleen on their way out of the restaurant. Robert stared mutely at his mother. Helen touched her arm, whispered something. Krystyna's father dabbed his mouth with a napkin and stood up. "That was a super meal; time for some fresh air." His wife and daughter followed him out.

"I don't know what you're talking about," Robert said.

"Bullshit."

"Ma, will you—"

"You know exactly what I'm talking about."

"Can we please save this for when we're in our room? Everybody's staring at you."

"Why should I save it? You've been doing that for years. I say let the whole world know. If that isn't safe enough for you, that's your problem."

"Kath," Helen whispered.

"Does your whole life have to be in code, like your father's? Can't you be different from him this one time? Can't you just blurt out something true about how you feel?"

Robert looked over to where the singer was serenading a clutch of dancers out on the patio. Then he looked back at his mother, who had never seemed more unfamiliar to him than now, yet oddly real— more than his mother.

"I don't have anything in particular on my mind, he said."

"Your father used to say the same thing. It wasn't until after we separated that he told me he was raised mostly by his uncle, that he was juggled back and forth between his uncle and his parents. He didn't have a happy childhood or a real family life at all. You probably didn't know that. You probably just thought his family wasn't close. He never let on, you didn't ask and nobody knows. What kind of relationship do you think that makes?"

Robert said nothing.

"Maybe if your father could have levelled with himself or with me every now and then. . . who knows? Maybe there'd be a family now. Your grandfather thought it was a mistake when I married your dad. You didn't know that, either. Grampa had this notion I could do a lot better for myself than Steven Rosseter. Once a person gets a notion, it never really goes away. It's the worst kind of wisdom in the world. But it was Steven Rosseter I wanted." His name caught in her throat. "Only Steven Rosseter."

Helen leaned toward her friend. "Kath, I think we ought to—"

"Grampa held a grudge against your father for— for marrying me. He never totally accepted him, and he made sure in little ways that your father knew it. It put a barrier between your father and me. It hurt him, more than Grampa realized. They argued and they fought about silly things all the time, but your father looked up to Grampa. I know that. But did he ever come right out and say, 'I love your father', or, 'I wish your father liked me more'? Did he ever say anything even a little bit like that to Grampa's face? No. That was too dangerous. Grampa loved him; he was just bitter about certain things such as the fact that I was never going to make it to U. of T. He had all these great ideas about what his daughter was going to do with her life, like outgrow Presley and conquer the bloody world. He didn't know how to butt out, especially after Mommy died. Mommy would have saved the situation. Your father was bitter about his own life and pretty soon our family was coming apart. Then it did come apart and it made you bitter, and the only thing you seemed to learn from it was to start repeating the same mistakes, saving all the bitterness inside you for a rainy day that never ever comes. Jesus God, Bobby, don't let that happen. Don't. Nobody on this earth owes you a thing. Things happen because they happen. I don't have any guilt left to carry around. It's all too long ago. Grampa thought I was throwing away a lot of dreams when I decided... when I had you. But he changed his mind after you were born. Everybody did. We just never got around to telling each other. I'm not going to make that mistake again. Never. If you think this world is made of shit, you're wrong, because you don't know the first thing about shit. By and large we've all been pretty goddamn good custodians to you. You're luckier than two-thirds of the children in this God-forsaken world. We're far from perfect, we made some terrible mistakes, but we've been pretty goddamn good custodians to you. We've made up for whatever happened in the past. So give it a rest, will you, for once and for fucking all?"

Applause rang out. The singer acknowledged her poolside audience with a smile.

"This room is spinning," Kathleen said.

Helen stood up. "Time to go upstairs." She helped Kathleen out of her chair and motioned for Robert to take the other side. Kathleen put up no resistance as they led her out of the restaurant.

An orange full moon shone through the trees to the southeast. Directly overhead the stars were arrayed in surreal clarity; soon the moon would obliterate all but the brightest stars. Robert sensed something strange about his mother's arm around his shoulder. He realized, seemingly for the first time, that he was taller than she. They slowly ascended the stairs to their room.

Helen put on water for instant coffee and wandered into the bathroom to change. The sound of a band playing outdoors at a nearby hotel wafted into the room. Laughter rose from the remaining group at poolside. Kathleen lay motionless on her bed; the covers had been turned down by the maid.

"Jesus God I feel funny," she murmured.

"A cup of coffee will set you straight," said Helen, weaving slightly on her way back to the kitchenette. Robert took off his shoes and placed them under his bed. He stared at the floor for a time, then went over to his mother and sat on the edge of the bed.

"I don't resent you, Ma. I really don't. I just have trouble making heads or tails of some things."

"Don't try," Kathleen replied, her eyes closed. "It's a waste of time. If you think life stinks, don't smell it so hard. We're all just skin and bones anyway."

"Skin and bones," Helen echoed from the kitchenette. She stirred the coffee, brought a cup to Kathleen, who sat up, took a couple of sips, then lay back down. Helen went to get her own cup from the counter and switched off the kitchenette light.

"Will you listen to the ocean," Helen whispered from her settee. By the sound of it, the group at poolside was breaking up for the night. Robert lay back and felt a powerful calm wash over him. The surf was relentless. The surf was the source of the calm.

". . .Nice part of the world," Kathleen mumbled before she drifted off for good. Soon afterward, Helen was asleep.

Surf pounded the breakwater near the pool. Again. Again. Surf syncopated the breathing of the two sleeping women. Robert let the swirls of stucco ceiling ripple and unravel in concert with the sea. He let all thought slip from his mind until only the natural rhythms governed his awareness, so he was nowhere and everywhere. . . He could have stayed there forever, but something faint and distant nagged. Something needed done.

He tiptoed into the bathroom, gazed out the slatted window. The pool reflected the moon but the restaurant was in darkness. Had he been asleep? He crept back to his bed, put on his shoes and slipped out of the room.

. . .

Further down the beach, a calypso band played something soft for the few remaining dancers on the cool sand. He stopped to watch and listen. He imagined his mother and Helen sitting at one of the candlelit tables, sipping a drink from a tall slender glass, being asked to dance by a pair of personable lawyers from Massachussetts. He imagined his mother, tanned and radiant in her sundress, gliding barefoot in the sand.

No one noticed him watching from the beach. He walked on, until no one was in sight and the only light came from the full moon suspended over the water, outlining the thin low clouds that swept past. He slipped out of his shoes, felt the residual warmth of the sand. Only when the waves broke near the shore did he hear them. They formed not much further out, but in silence and obscurity. At the precise moment they crested, the moonlight captured them, then they broke to shore unseen.

Water washed up to flirt with his bare feet, as if breathing a greeting. Then it subsided. Then it washed up again. Moonlight unimpeded by cloud evolved into bright flecks on the glassy surface of the sea beyond the reef. He watched the flecks multiply until they cut a swath of silver from shore to horizon. As if by reflex, he shed shirt, pants, underwear and waded into the water. Seaweed tugged at his ankles, then he thought of it as a caress. The first warm wave washed past, above his knees. He waded into deeper water. The sea took a deep breath and dragged coral pebbles out from the water's edge. The next wave almost reached his shoulders, then the water subsided again. The world was quieter here. He waded farther out, farther than he dared or understood, yet without a moment's hesitation in the lull between waves. The water rose and dipped, rhythms changed, new forces tugged at the earth under his feet. A wave was heard to break somewhere down the beach, but here all was subdued and almost still. He turned to look at the beach, was astonished by its apparent distance. His white shirt glowed in the moonlight like Eddie's Virgin Mary. Above him, wisps of cloud darted by.

Then silence. Utter silence.

Part of him recognized the silence, told him in advance. But he just had to turn, had to face that impossibly high wall of obscurity rising ahead of him, flowing toward him for that rendezvous with the light of the full moon when it crested, took his life in its hands and delivered it into dark formlessness, devoid of air to breathe—

I failed him long long long ago, before he was born. We didn't know what we wanted but we knew we didn't want a baby. We were ready to do what we had to do. We found a place where we could get it done. Then Mrs.

O'Hagan got worse and Kath couldn't go through with it anymore. We were there, he gave her an anesthetic and everything, but she couldn't go through with it. So I took her home and we never mentioned it again. The next day she told you she was going to have a baby. I never got a chance to make the right decision on my own. I never did. It was already made. She made it, but I would have too. After Bobby was born it scared me to think we came that close. He's alive today because his grandmother died when she did. That's the truth. There's my boy now. There's my little guy. It didn't work out with that moose today but it was just you and me, me and my boy. Where are you taking him? Let him stay. I'm trying to tell you we were just kids back then. We didn't know any better. We were scared. We thought it was the thing to do. I've loved him from the moment he was born. He knows that. We thought it was the thing to do we just thought it was the thing to do

—and released him in a torrent of froth and sand, close to shore.

He collapsed on the warm beach. His eyes and lips stung, his chest burned as his lungs devoured the air. He lay motionless on his back until the scudding clouds made him giddy and the moon was etched on his retina. Then he jumped to his feet and sprinted down the shoreline, naked skin and bones. He ran ferociously with no destination in mind, perhaps in pursuit of the sun, which was still hours away.

* * *

12

> They don't call it a collapsing universe for nothing. Watch your step.
>
> —Theodore Ng

May 1982 brought promises of things to come and reminders of fifteen months past. Overnight storms from the southeast rattled the windows of Robert's room, a convoy of thunder and rain rumbling through the city of Presley. He was awakened by a single thunderclap that actually clanged, as though a massive sheet of metal had been dropped on the street directly in front of his house. He didn't fall back to sleep. Instead he just lay there, immobile as a newborn baby. He remembered when fierce lions and tigers had swooped down over the headboard of his bed as sleep was about to overtake him, when large hairy mammals with sharp tusks and crazed men with long knives lurked in his closet, and the trees outside his window leaned close to the house, their limbs parting the curtains and slithering along the floor to the door they locked to prevent his ever escaping. What a terrifying world had once existed in this house.

Now he just lay still as footsteps sounded on the street below and leaves took shape in the predawn light. Thunder murmured in the distance. The man on the street began to whistle an anonymous melody to the rhythm of his footsteps. A breeze rustled leaves. A car shushed on wet asphalt.

The morning stayed dark, muggy and electric, as if the storms threatened to change direction and pay a return visit. The smell of ozone was everywhere. As Robert dressed for school, the sky darkened further and a distant report of thunder rattled the windowframe. But the disturbance passed, unrelieved. Nearby timberland was no doubt going up in smoke; a new generation of intrepids would be pining for a chance to join the firefighting detachments in the bush and collect material for rich yarns at D'Agostino's.

Robert examined the elm tree, its leaves inverted and heavy with water. His eyes followed the uppermost branches down to the major limbs, and further down the trunk to the dayglo SOLD sticker on the FOR SALE sign at the foot of the tree. The sign's cheery air of accomplishment disrupted the poignancy of the image.

The bareness of rooms and anonymity of cardboard boxes never failed to surprise him when he descended for breakfast. He and his mother had not yet moved, but the soul of the house departed in advance.

"My new boss called last night," Kathleen said during breakfast in the newly barren kitchen. "She told me there would be no problem if we stayed in Presley through to your graduation. My job isn't open until the first of July; they figure it won't take more than a week to train me, so you don't have to worry about that anymore."

"I wasn't worried about it," Robert said.

"You could've fooled me."

Miles away, thunder rumbled.

"What about Dad?"

"What about him?"

"Has his attitude changed?"

Kathleen sighed. "He told me last night it was unforgivable that we were leaving Presley just when things were starting to fall together in his life. I can't imagine what he meant. All they've been doing at the 4P the past six months is laying people off, and the mill closes for good in September. He's going to have to think about moving, too."

"He told me last week if Grampa was alive none of this would be happening. He said Grampa would have talked us out of moving, he would have to us our roots are here."

"Jesus God."

"Maybe he's right. Maybe Grampa would have wanted us to stay."

"There was no recession when Grampa was alive. This whole town is dying, Bobby. There's no way he could have talked me into staying. The move makes sense as far as your future schooling goes, it makes sense as far as the type of work and salary I want goes, and it makes sense because I know it makes sense."

"I'm just saying that what Dad said makes sense, too."

"But does what he feels make sense?"

"Give him a break, Ma."

"I did. I do. I will." She watched rain start to spit on the window. "Your father doesn't remember the past. He doesn't have to, because he lives in it— it's as clear as day to him. I wonder if he ever totally left Sault Ste. Marie. I wonder if he ever totally left this house" *or his mother's womb,* she said to herself. "Not only does he live in the past, he constantly re-imagines it. It's nice to have memories, Bobby, but it seems to me at some point you've got to break with them. I don't know if your father is prepared to do that. He has this idea of an extended family, and things should go on exactly as they are, or as he sees them. I don't want to hurt him but I can't spend my whole life trying to fit into his dreams. I just want to be his friend."

"He's driving me to school this morning."

"I know. He told me last night. What worries me, Bobby, is sometimes I think you feel the same way he does. I think maybe you'd rather stay in Presley even if it is dying. I know there might be a few personal complications for you when we leave, but it's not as if you can't visit every now and—"

"I'm ready to leave, Ma."

"Are you sure?"

"Just say the word."

"And if I don't know the word?"

"Make one up," Robert said with a shrug. His father's noisy Camaro roared into the driveway.

Kathleen let Steven in. "That car of yours probably woke up the whole neighbourhood."

"It doesn't sound like it used to, does it? I kind of like it without a muffler. You can hear the power, the sheer beauty of the engine."

"I just hear a lot of noise," said Kathleen.

"Really?" Steven looked around the empty kitchen. "How can you stand it in here like this?"

"It's only for a couple more weeks. Are you ready to go, Bobby?"

"I've been collecting pieces of antique stained glass and hanging them in my window," Steven said. "You ought to try something like that in your new home. I can give you a couple of mine to get you started. All you need is a decent window with a southern exposure. Do you have an address or anything yet?"

"You asked me that last night, Steven. I don't have an address yet."

"Bob, do you remember where Grampa used to sit in here? He always sat with his back to the window, because he said the glare of the sun bothered his eye. Your mother got mad at him every time he did his crossword puzzle during Sunday dinner. Remember?"

"He was always doing a crossword puzzle," Robert said.

"I remember one time you and. . . you and Eddie hid the newspaper on him and he was on his hands and knees under that table. He thought it slipped off his lap. Where'd you guys put it that time, anyway?"

"I don't remember," Robert said.

"Probably whoever moves in here next will find it. There's always a fair bit of stuff that gets left behind."

Kathleen clapped her hands. "Time to go."

Steven turned to Robert. "Could you go ahead to the car for a minute?"

"Steven, he's going to be late for school."

"Just for a minute."

Robert picked up his books and left.

"I don't see why this can't wait until—"

"I quit the 4P yesterday," Steven said. "I would have told you last night but I wanted to do it in person. I told them they'd have to get someone else to handle the rest of the severance settlements and everything else. I'm through as of Friday."

"So. . .?" Kathleen said.

"So."

"So?"

"So I'm footloose for the first time in ages. I thought I might do like you and check out some possibilities down south."

"Any place in particular?"

"Not yet. Any ideas?"

"No," Kathleen said.

"I thought maybe once you got down to Kitchener or Waterloo or wherever it is you're going, you could keep an eye out for me, if there's anything there for me. Don't get me wrong. I don't want to cramp your style while you're getting established, but I will miss you two. I will miss you."

"We will too," Kathleen said.

"Maybe we've been through too much together not to."

"Maybe."

Steven went to the door. "By the way, I got a job offer from the City of Presley, to work in the welfare office. They're giving me a couple of weeks to think it over. Amazing, isn't it? Should I stay or should I go?"

"I haven't the foggiest," Kathleen said.

After the Camaro had roared off, she sat down at the table and gazed out the window at the budding bastard maple. Eventually she smiled.

In the car, the windshield wipers did double-time while Robert told his father about Caroline Laverty.

. . .

That afternoon, Robert sat in a daze in the collapsible gymanisum bleachers at Presley High. He and a handful of other students watched the cheerleaders flex milkwhite legs and clap small hands together at centre court. *Let's fight let's fight let's. . . really fight*, they chanted.

Caroline Laverty had quietly suffered the derision of her brother Eddie when she signed up for cheerleading in her junior year. Now, three years later, the mantras and incantations came naturally. It was her genuine enthusiasm that drew Robert to her in those dark months before and during his last year of high school. Caroline was timeless down there on the floor, solving the problem of how to make peace with the passage of time by counting it out with her body, celebrating its inevitable flow.

While Caroline and the others leaped and chanted, Robert drifted far away into memory, where the distant and recent past fused. It was as though his life amounted to an epic hypothesis, the fate of both past and future hinging on this moment. Then, without warning, as though clarified by the chants, his mind was made up.

He and Caroline walked silently down the corridor to the main doors. Outside, a steady rain foreshadowed twilight. Caroline sensed he was far away but she said nothing. Her arm was in his. He aqueezed it against him to let her know everything was all right between them. He was still meditating on the mantras back in the gym. *Go, fight, win.* Cars sped noisily past the bus shelter, their headlights reflected on the rain-slick road.

"I was asked to be class valedictorian today," he said.

Cars shushed past. It had grown darker. Echoes of the gymnasium mantra receded, until all that was left was the face of an old friend and an inkling of the things he might want to say. His eyes filled wth hot tears.

"I have to do it, Caroline. I told them I have no choice but to do it."

Caroline respected his tears and the desperation in his voice. Their bus lumbered up to the curb. She helped him onto it, paid their fare and led him to the rear. An old woman stared disapprovingly in the merciless fluorescent glare. The windows were fogged over. The bus lurched into motion, the driver cleared the fare box of change.

. . .

". . .One day, when I was nine years old, Eddie Laverty and I went picking raspberries. It wasn't something we were in the habit of doing, but my mother promised to bake us a pie. Eddie and I walked along the Old Reservoir Road, where everybody said the best wild raspberries grew. When we got there we went our separate ways, Eddie with his collander, me with my big bowl. I hadn't picked more than a dozen raspberries when a fly that had been bothering me for a while flew inside my ear and started to buzz around in there. It didn't take me long to figure out the fly was trapped; it was buzzing so much because it wanted out of my ear. I tried hitting the the side of my head with the heel of my hand, like you do when water gets in your ear. I tried plugging my nose, closing my mouth and blowing out as hard as I could. Nothing worked. When I told Eddie about it he laughed, but he stopped laughing when I started crying. I told him it was a bumblebee in my ear. Eddie said stay calm, the bee will probably die after a few stings. Thanks a lot, I said.

"We decided to head home right away. Reservoir Road was hard and dusty, the way it gets in the summertime when there hasn't been any rain for a couple of weeks. Eddie stopped here and there to study empty cigarette packages. One of the brands was holding a contest of some kind. I staggered along with my head in my hands, caught up in this fantasy about the bee drilling a hole into my brain and settling there— maybe even starting a family in my skull. I wondered what terrible sin I had committed to deserve such a fate.

"There's a bumblebee in my ear, I informed my mother when we got to my house. I guess I was a bit hysterical by then. Eddie said my story was on the level and I'd better be rushed to the hospital for brain surgery before the bee fills my blood system with venom. What venom? my mother said. Bee venom, Eddie said. It can cause seizures. My mother said she'd never heard of bee venom, but she drove us to Doctor Paine's office anyway, where we sat in the waiting room for forty-five minutes. The bee seemed to have exhausted itself in my ear; it buzzed only now and then. I tried to be a man for my mother during those forty-five minutes, but I think I failed.

"When he finally got around to seeing me, Doctor Paine found the whole thing amusing. Doctors have a way of finding many things that don't personally happen to them amusing. He peered into my ear with a penlight and grunted something, then he took this great big needle from a rack of instruments on the wall. I must have started to cry again, because he said don't worry, son, it's only a water syringe and won't hurt at all. He put the syringe into my ear and a jet of warm water flooded in. Most of it poured back into a little plate he was holding under my ear. He peered at the plate, dipped his little finger into the water and brought it up to my eyes. Here's your bumblebee, he said. On the tip of his pinky was the tiniest black fly I'd ever seen. More a gnat than a fly. I guess it had drowned. I didn't know whether to laugh or to cry. I was relieved but I was disappointed, too. That's something I haven't told anybody until this day, not even Eddie: I was disappointed when I saw how small that fly was.

"Eddie would understand what I'm saying. The size of the fly didn't live up to the fear it caused me, because the fear was about what I thought was in my ear rather than with what was actually there. This always seems to be what counts the most in the long run. To see with my own eyes how unrealistic my fear was really threw me. I was just beginning to learn that things aren't what they are and probably the best we can do is estimate. None of our senses gives us a full reading of what's going on, so how can we know anything for sure? I learned that from Eddie. He had no illusions—not the usual ones, anyway. He said to me later that same day: Imagine what that poor little fly went through inside your ear. I hadn't thought of that.

"One time, Eddie stole a drawing I had made of the tree in my front yard. It really bothered him that I used to rip up each drawing after I finished it. It seemed a waste to him. So he took this one drawing home with him, carefully traced it onto another piece of paper, tore mine up and hung his own copy of it on his wall. His mother told me about this the day of his funeral. Up to that day, I had assumed it was my drawing on his bedroom wall. I had always felt secretly flattered by this honour. But Eddie wanted to respect my little picture-ripping habit. The funny thing is, it *was* my picture on his wall: A perfect copy. Things aren't what they are.

"If he were here today, up on this stage, he would probably tell you how much he hates special occasions and all forms of bullshit. His parents and his sister can vouch for the fact that he used to get especially blue around Christmas. If I wake up Christmas morning with a splitting headache, he said to me once, am I supposed to ignore it? To Eddie, real magic was the ordinary day that, because of some combination of atomosphere and togetherness, became extraordinary. That's what he cherished. That's why I only half-prepared this speech. This is supposed to be a significant day, but we're graduating today only because it's a convenient time for everybody. And what the hell is graduation, anyway? The really important changes in our life happen at unforeseen moments, when no one has a prepared speech to read. God forbid that this should be the happiest day of my life, and I don't have a clear idea what the worst one was or will be. The only reason I'm up on this podium today is because the last thing Eddie Laverty told me was to help him give the world hell. He left his tracing of my work on his wall. I have no choice but to leave a tracing of his work in my life.

"Somebody told me— I don't remember who— that Eddie suffered from a disorder that caused recurrent depression, which he managed to hide most of the time but which got worse late in his life. I guess this is meant to clear everyone who knew him of any responsibility for his death. All of us have some experience of a guy who maybe sat next to us in geography class, a quiet type who ups and dies overnight of tuberculosis, or a classmate whose hair falls out from cobalt treatments, or a tough guy who rams his Chevy into a tractor-trailer. We can say we didn't know these people—they were whatchamacallit's friend and the most we ever said to them was hello in the hall. We can say it's really sad what happened to so-and-so, but we never got to know who so-and-so really was. I say everybody whose path we cross— the mailman, some idiot on TV, the little girl in the yard next door, a man who sells vacuum cleaners— leaves an impression of some kind on us. Everyone in the world who touches us, even in the smallest way, changes us. There's no escaping this for as long as we live. That fly in my ear, no matter how tiny it turned out to be, changed me. It made me think of my body as something that could be invaded. Call it the most basic law of being alive: We are susceptible to every other living thing. We're not immune to anything. Very little of what we've learned in this school over the past five years prepares us for that fact. We may think we're unaffected by foreign wars, by famine, by the suffering that's part of the daily life of so many people on this planet, but it eventually catches up with us. Ask my parents, whose generation dreamed of something different but have awoken from that dream with a huge hangover. Ask my fellow graduates, who maybe don't dream enough. Ask Eddie Laverty, whose private nightmares spoke to him about all that had slipped away. Ask me. I was an accident of birth. I wasn't meant to arrive when I did. Because of that, I think I can see the beauty in all the madness and the madness in all the beauty.

"Eddie Laverty was vulnerable; maybe he thought he wasn't supposed to be vulnerable. I don't know. He's someone I loved, so my judgment is clouded. In fact, it's hard for me not to feel guilty even now— to think that maybe if I'd come home from Barbados sooner I could have talked him out of his decision, made him laugh at some stupid joke, given him the will to live one more day, then another, and so on. I'm not obsessed with the memory of Eddie. This is just a duty I'm doing here today. Part of me is still mad at him for letting his anger devour him. Maybe there's no room left for a kid's anger anymore. Part of me is still mad at the world because it gave me all sorts of convenient excuses to clear myself of any responsibility for his death. He was ill. I could even say I didn't really know him. He as much as told me that the last time I saw him. But the truth is a fly in my ear: The truth is we never do everything we can.

"When they write the history of this century, my generation— the disposable generation— probably won't figure in it much. They'll say we were outnumbered and outmanoeuvred by our parents. They'll say we had too few ideals. They'll accuse us of being conservative and materialistic. They probably won't mention all the emotional luggage we inherited from the generation that preceded us. They probably won't mention the cynicism we were born into, the hypocrisy of the generation that brought us up. I say to you parents out there, we're not the ones who gave up all our ideals. You paid lip service to them when you were young and could afford to, then you discarded them when you grew up and opened RRSPs. Your cynicism runs so deep you don't even recognize it anymore. You assume wisdom was your birthright, so now you can walk blindly from one certainty to the next, safe in the knowledge that everyone else has it wrong, when in fact you have it wrong.

"History is nothing more than the institutionalized notions of the majority, and memories are the personal version of that process. The only thing we really have to go on is this moment— right now, here. The rest is doubtful at best. Of course, focusing on right now is the hardest thing to do. That's why Eddie Laverty slipped through everyone's fingers. That's why we have to become better at it.

"Eddie died of indifference, yours and mine. That is a fact. I stand here today as his witness to tell you I have chosen to leave that particular fly in my ear until the time comes that washing it out amounts to something more than just discarding a painful memory.

"In the meantime, I would like to thank the teachers and administrative staff of PH&VS for all the good intentions they have shown us over the years. May all of us graduating today go boldly out into the world and find a job."

. . .

The parents, students and teachers in the auditorium of Presley High & Vocational School that afternoon didn't know what to make of Robert Rosseter's valedictory address. Scattered applause subsided quickly, followed by embarrassed chatter. The editor of the *Gleaner* didn't know what to make of the reporter's account of the speech. Fearing another Boy Samaritan imbroglio, he decided to print only the names of the graduates, with a curt concluding sentence to the effect that G.R. Rosseter spoke on behalf of the students.

Jocelyn Wright, aka the former Mrs. Reilly, was one of the few who sought Robert out in the hallway after his speech. She shook his hand and hugged him. Kathleen stood back and watched.

"You told them, Bobby," the former Mrs. Reilly said. "You really told them."

"What did he tell them?" Kathleen asked.

"Something," the former Mrs. Reilly said with visible pride.

. . .

The city of Presley made peace with the death of Eddie Laverty, as it had with the death of others. Those men and women who raised Eddie's parents' generation will grow old remembering the war years, when everything was so cut and dried, and count the days in sun-bleached living rooms silent but for the passing of time. They will think occasionally of their children and grandchildren, and secretly bless their own fading memory.

Eddie's parents' generation will worry about their careers, worry about whether they are happy enough, fit enough, rich enough, passionate enough. Some of them will pine for the days of the sad harmonies of the protest singers. Others will be relieved that they no longer have to re-invent the world.

As for Robert Rosseter and his class, they will start by going to the prom. Caroline Laverty will condescend to have her hair done in a modified beehive, to be Robert's best possible escort. An orchestra will be hired to play swing-era tunes all evening. Having unaccountably earned a diploma, the Brezinski youth will proceed to get himself and many of his friends as blotto as possible on rye whiskey hidden in the breast pocket of his rented pink tuxedo. Bat Masterson will bring along a provocative escort from outside the board of education's jurisdiction, but will spend the evening flirting with more familiar student bodies. Sue-Ann Reilly will fawn over her ruggedly handsome date for the evening, who will become a bartender and her first husband. Cynthia Thomas will be unable to attend the gala affair because she couldn't get anyone to work her evening shift at Chow's Chow. The memory of Benny Goodman, Glenn Miller, Guy Lombardo, Lawrence Welk and other ghosts of a previous generation's coming of age will be invoked throughout the evening. The theme of the decor in the gym will be Rites Of Passage, an idea suggested to the prom committee by Miss Hornung. The gym will be decorated to look like the deck of the Love Boat, with travel-agency posters of exotic places pasted on the concrete walls and crepe paper suspended willynilly from the rafters. Just prior to midnight, two hundred balloons will float gently down to the dance floor. The Brezinski youth will burst dozens of them by stamping at random with a wild look in his eye as the musicians labour through "Tuxedo Junction". Later, while the combo searches in vain for an appropriate segue into "Mister Sandman", the Brezinski youth's all but empty whiskey bottle will shatter on the hardwood floor. Miss Hornung will rush to him, grab him by the elbow. The Brezinski youth will shake off her grip. "You got no authority over me anymore," he will say. Miss Hornung will take his arm again. "I have the *authority* to *eject* anyone found to be *consuming* alcoholic *beverages* on *school* property." The Brezinski youth will shake off her grip, more violently this time. "Prove it was hard stuff, if you're so smart." Miss Hornung will look around for help, find none. "All right (clap)," she will nevertheless say, "that's enough (clap). You will come with me at once (clap)." The bandleader, unsettled by the commotion, will urge the musicians into a frenzied rendition of "In The Mood". As saxophones reverberate crazily off the concrete walls, a classmate will attempt to restrain the Brezinski youth. They will grapple in a strange parody of dance until they collide with the flowery arbour through which all the graduating students were to have passed at the end of the evening. Pasted in bright velour letters spanning the top of the arbour— yet another pip of an idea from Miss Hornung—will be the word

SHANGRI-LA?

with the question mark intended to connote that the brightest days may well lie ahead, though it's always worth remembering the golden days of adolescence. A male supervisor will manage finally to separate the two boys, but not before the symbolic arbour teeters then topples with a *thwack* on the hardwood floor. The orchestra will have been startled into abrupt silence. As the supervisor leads the Brezinski youth away, the boy will cry out to all his friends and associates, "My name is Karel. Karel Brezinski! Don't anybody forget it. I'm not a youth anymore!" The lone attending custodian will sweep the fragments of whiskey bottle from the floor and the band will launch valiantly into the finale, "Feelings". ". . .Nothing more than *fee*-lings," Bat Masterson will croon devilishly on the dance floor, the palms of both hands kneading the buttocks of his escort. Off in a corner, near a picture of the Jamaican coastline, Robert and Caroline will drift lazily in dance, lost in separate but coincident worlds. Neither of them will have aspired to anything headier than this as, in the eye of the hurricane, SHANGRI-LA beckoning, time and music and the ever-expanding universe will grind to a halt. Overcome by the fragrance of Alberto VO-5, Old Spice, and mutual desire, they will become more than great friends, as though in unconscious obedience of a physical law. In one aspect of the world the music will conclude on an elegant sprinkling of saxophone notes, Miss Hornung will thank each and every one of them and wish them all the best of possible futures. In another aspect of the world, Robert and Caroline will briefly, forever, be one, poised solely in the direction of now. Later, as in various parts of the city the graduates get down to the serious business of destroying brain cells, Robert and Caroline will find a warm place on the banks of his beloved Kekagami, under a halfmoon, where they will lie together, demand nothing of a world fleetingly spontaneous, and afterward watch high cirrus clouds on their long night journey across the moon to the sea. This, too, is a physical law.

But let's conclude by celebrating exceptions; for were we to follow the winding course of the Kekagami into the Great Lakes and, far beyond, the Gulf of St. Lawrence, and orient ourselves by the same moon across the vast Atlantic to where day has arrived, we might watch an inflated football complete its five-year odyssey by washing up on a Moroccan shore, where a boy discovers it and runs off to tell his friends of his great fortune.